THE SOCIETY

BOOK 1, THE SOCIETY SERIES

KAREN GUYLER

To Jasmine Walt

With heartfelt thanks that, when you reached backwards to help those behind you, you took my hand

1

T he lipsticked smile of the queen of British morning TV shouted at Eva Janssen, you're supposed to answer my questions.

What she wanted to hear pressed itself into Eva's mouth, but she held it in, wrapping it up with the other things she couldn't say. Couldn't, wouldn't, they'd all been on the restricted list yet here Nadia was spilling the suggestion of them into the five million plus homes who started their day watching 'Your Good Morning'.

Eva grabbed at the failing interview. "Our new campaign, Every Drop because every life matters, kicks off tomorrow night with a charity ball—"

"You're a bit of an anomaly, Eva, for a CEO." Nadia swooped in again. "Setting up a charity isn't on the agenda of most twenty-five-year-olds and, if it was, I'm sure they'd shout about it. But your profile for the last seven years, since you founded Every Drop, in fact, has been, shall we say, quiet?" She wouldn't dare go there, would she, on live TV? "Before then, it's non-existent. So tell us about your life before."

She went there. 'Your Good Morning' must have an excellent legal team.

Eva probably only had another five minutes of this torture left, she needed to talk faster. "Every Drop's focus needs to be on the work, not on me nor any of the amazing team I'm lucky to work with. We're trying to put right the crime that millions don't have access to safe water."

Her gaze flicked to one of the cameras, don't do that one of the production people had said. If the millions on the other end of that lens gave a small donation, Every Drop could complete all of its installation plans. What a difference to the world that would make. "Do you have the phone number for the pledge line?"

"You founded the company in honour of your father, that's quite a memorial."

Eva followed Nadia's gaze as it swivelled to her left. The Tower Bridge backdrop pixellated away. Eva's heart rapped so hard on the inside of her ribcage that her lapel mic must be picking it up. It couldn't be the photo. They'd signed to say they wouldn't use it.

And yet, as Eva watched, the image reformed from the white edges inwards. Her hand strayed to her jacket. Don't touch the mic, another of the many warnings they'd given her.

The white edged into wisps of light hair blown by a long ago breeze against a distant blue sky. Her father's smiling face leant into the top of her head where he held her five-year-old self, her back against his chest, her long blonde hair teased into a tangle with his.

Not the photo.

Eva breathed. Her hand dropped back into her lap.

Their twinned ice-blue eyes and their mirrored grins of pure delight at being together made her smile. But the tenderness in his gaze as he'd looked at her that day, and often, in the fleeting time they'd had before he was gone, prickled at the back of her eyes.

She swallowed.

Not the photo.

"For the benefit of our viewers, your father was Mathias Janssen, an investigative journalist, killed on assignment in the Middle East. You were obviously very close, are you like him?"

That part of her life wasn't subject to the Official Secrets Act, Eva could have answered, but that was between her and her father.

"He's big shoes to fill, isn't he? All that he achieved."

Eva didn't need Nadia to remind her, particularly not this week. Get the conversation back where it should be. "He'd be proud of Every Drop's work."

Nadia leant closer. "Given what you said about safe water being a human right, how do you reconcile the statement released by Stuart Worthington yesterday. He's your Chairman of the Board, isn't he?"

"Which statement is that? Stuart's in the news a lot." Part of the reason Charles was right that he was a good fit for the Board.

Eva and her father morphed into blue pixels overwritten with white letters spelling out a disastrous message: "On an overpopulated planet of limited resources, access to water cannot be an inalienable right."

Eva took a breath. She had to remember where she was. "I can't speak to the context of Stuart's remarks. We have a donation campaign run—"

"If your own Chairman doesn't believe it is, how can you sustain your position?"

"Our position? We're stopping people dying, shouldn't

that be everyone's position? What would you, your viewers, what would they do to ensure the safety of their loved ones? It's easy for us, we turn on a tap and know we can trust what comes out of it but for too many of the world's population, if they even get access to water, they're risking sickness, or worse, if they drink it."

Eva caught herself, not so emotional, dial it down. She tried again.

"Climate change means water is on everyone's agenda. Take our ingenious distribution method," she looked at the poisonous words between her and Nadia. "Do you have a picture of that?"

Movement in front of them distracted her, the production assistant waving at Nadia, flicking her hand across her neck in a cut, cut, cut gesture. Was it going that badly?

"I'm afraid we're out of time." Nadia responded. "Eva Janssen, CEO of Every Drop, thank you very much."

Filling Eva's unused minutes, Nadia announced part two of their special feature right after the news headlines, dismissing Eva with most of her message unsaid. She'd blown it. The production assistant beckoned her, come on, come on. Eva fought the urge to lunge in front of Nadia and shout out the donation number.

A wave of noisy busyness reached for them as they left the TV studio behind, welcoming them from that sterile vacuum back to real life. The production assistant marched along as though they only paid her for the minutes she spent by the cameras.

A flick of a glance to her right stopped Eva. She took a step towards the glass wall that separated the open plan office from the corridor. The world disappeared. Except for the computer screen that displayed the photo no child should ever see. The last one taken of her father.

Eva's heart rammed a whirling churning through her. She closed her eyes against the hammer blow of his loss. But the image had been inscribed on her mind, the betrayal in that moment when he—

A banging on the glass shocked her back to the present, the production assistant gesturing furiously at the desktop user. The photo winked to a minimised icon.

"Sorry about that. They're waiting for you, hurry up. Must be serious if they've tracked you down here."

Eva followed on not quite steady legs. "Can I—"

"No time, in here." The production assistant flicked a sliding sign so the door proclaimed the room was occupied. She pushed it open and Eva saw that it was, by a man looking at a complicated coffee machine and a woman sitting at the table writing in a small notebook. "Right, I'll leave you to it." She slammed the door.

"Eva Janssen?" The woman's dressed for anything dark suit gave no hints about what must be serious.

Eva nodded, trying to catch up. The woman pulled something out of the inside pocket of the parka drying on the back of the chair next to her.

"DC April Truman." Her warrant card.

"DI Elliott Smith." The man held up what was presumably an identical ID, though Eva couldn't read it from where she was. "We need a word."

2

Police at the TV studios to talk to her? Eva grabbed at the back of the closest chair. "My family? What's happened? Lily and Charles, are they okay?"

"We're not here about them." DC Truman gestured at the chair opposite her. "We'd like to talk about your relationship with Eric Hill."

"Eric Hill?" Eva parroted, as if she didn't know who he was.

"Please sit." DC Truman waited.

"Do I need a lawyer?"

"Do you?" With grey eyes and light brown skin, DI Smith was arresting to look at. A quip like that, Eva should have been seeing BBC comedy. He watched her as though he could read her stupid thought. She felt herself flushing, not the time. Hopefully, he wasn't as hard as his shaved head claimed. A man used to getting results that much she recognised from being married to one.

"It's your right, we'd be happy to meet them at the station. That makes it more formal then." DC Truman stood up, making Eva decide what she wanted. "Right now we just have a couple of questions."

Eva took her time pulling the chair out, sitting. Why were the police asking about Eric? The back leant too far backwards; she fidgeted upright, perched on the edge of the cold wooden seat.

DC Truman sat down, pen poised. "What's your relationship with Mr Hill?"

"We don't have one."

"Yet you saw him yesterday."

"Yes, I did, I mean before then I hadn't seen him for years."

"Why would he note your appearance here in his calendar then?" It wasn't so much her question that side-swiped Eva, or even that Eric had noted this—had he wanted to ask her again, persuade her to change her mind? —but how had the police got access to it? And why?

DC Truman might seem young—dark hair caught up in a probably more messy than regulation bun, no make-up, fresh-faced, serious brown eyes—but her gaze was sharp, hard to not squirm beneath.

"I have no idea." Eva's brain was still playing catch-up, the sense she was searching for lost beneath the glimpse of that photo. "Maybe he wanted to watch me make a fool of myself on national TV?"

"You have that kind of relationship?" DC Truman's pen was busy.

"We used to work together. Apart from yesterday, I haven't seen him for years."

"You said that already." DI Smith threw the remark over his shoulder, as though he was only interested in the huge pink and blue neon scribble sign on the end wall he was now examining. "Why yesterday?"

"Has something happened?"

He turned around to watch her reaction. "Mr Hill died last night."

"Died? But he, we were, he was good." Eric dead, how was that possible? "How?"

"Did you get on?"

"Yes, we did. What—"

"Why did you stop working with him?"

"I left to set up my charity. What happened?"

"What did you talk about?" DI Smith continued his rapid-fire questions, strolling around the room as though the answers were inconsequential. He had to be aware of who Eric worked for, but Eva couldn't confirm it.

She fished for something to convince, but she only had what she couldn't say. "It's not, it's so hard to take in. He was only in his forties." Which left a disturbing truth. "Was it an accident?"

"What did you do when you worked together?" DI Smith pressed.

"Nothing special, we analysed data, wrote reports." Eva caught herself glancing away. Look him in the eye, own the lie.

"Had his family situation changed?"

Eva shrugged. "I don't think so, we—"

Should she say they hadn't done small talk like normal people? Wouldn't that lead to more questions she couldn't answer? The detectives waited.

Eric dead on British soil. Gordon could tell her what she couldn't ask the police.

"You were the last person to see him alive." DC Truman fixed her with that uncomfortable gaze again. DI Smith was training her well.

"Apart from the people in the street when we left—"

"You were the last person to see him alive who knew him. Why do you think that is?"

"We what?" DI Smith had reached her side in his slow checking out of the meeting room. "You said 'I don't think so, we', we what?"

Sorry, Eric, but they'll find out anyway. "Eric's an incurable philanderer. He dates, dated, he dated more than one woman at the same time."

"Did you try to cure him?"

"I'm sorry?"

"You said he was an incurable philanderer. Suggests you tried to mend his ways."

"No, I'm happily married. I meant he had no intention of changing. He's, he was, a one-off, charming, which is perhaps why so many would share him."

DI Smith walked behind her, resuming his stroll around the room. "Do you know their names?"

"Not current ones." Saucy Sue, what doesn't she do? She remembered he'd been with her for a long time. Eric, did you hurt someone you shouldn't?

"Why would you want him dead?" DC Truman's expression didn't change, even though she was asking the worst question.

"What? I don't, I didn't."

"Last person to see him alive though."

"That doesn't mean anything."

"I think you'll find it does."

"Nothing sinister." Eva was losing her second interview of the morning. "How did Eric die?"

"You met where?" DI Smith arrived back at the neon scribble.

"Coffee Espresso on Russell Street. We had one coffee each, he had cake."

"What time was this?"

"I got there at five fifteen, he was already there. I'm sure the staff can verify that, Eric would have tipped well."

"Is money important to you?"

Eva frowned at his unexpected question. "I run a charity, I'm used to trying to wring as much as I can out of our budgets, the donations. The good use I can put it to is important to me. How did he die?"

Again he ignored the most important question. "Any of his ex-mistresses have it in for him?"

"I'd be surprised, Eric always looked after them."

"That's it for here." DI Smith's comment had DC Truman closing her notebook.

That was it? Eva tried to tame the hurricane in her mind. Had she said anything she shouldn't? She wasn't sure of the protocol for this situation—

"Ms Janssen?" He was holding the door open for her.

"Thank you." She looked up and down the corridor. Where was the green room that housed the locker with her things in it?

"I believe we can get out this way." DC Truman gestured that Eva should precede them to the left.

Past the open plan office with that computer in it. She needed a minute. "After you."

DI Smith shook his head. "You're coming with us, I'm sniffing obstruction in your answers. At the station you might feel more inclined to be truthful."

3

"You're popular."

Sitting directly behind him in the detectives' car, Eva couldn't see DI Smith's face, but he didn't sound thrilled at her receiving yet another call. She messaged Dario, 'what's up?'

'Are you still at the BBC? We need you here now.' Not what she expected, being unflappable was one of the reasons he was her deputy.

'A friend of mine' Eva deleted the words. 'I'm with the police.' Her thumbs paused on 'helping them with their enquiries', trite words she'd heard on the news a hundred times that made her shiver now she was on the wrong side of them.

Never suppose, her father had said it often enough, one of the many life instructions he'd drilled her with.

She deleted the words, tried again. 'Anything to do with donors, you deal with, everything else delegate to Vaishali. I'll be there as soon as I can.'

She put her phone on silent, dropped it in her handbag, stared out of the window. What happened to you, Eric?

Her ring tone filling the car confused her until she heard DI Smith answer his phone. "We're in the middle of something. . .No, but—statement. . ." His voice sounded tighter with every syllable. "Yes. . .I will. Understood, DI Smith, DC Truman responding." He disconnected, "pull over," turned round to Eva. "There's a major incident," held a business card out to her. "Report within five days to give your statement."

Eva reached for it, but he held onto it. "Don't make me come and find you."

"You won't have to."

DC Truman roared away, lights flashing, sirens blaring. By the time Eva got back to Every Drop, Breaking News confirmed the incident was on the tube network. Lily, at school and Charles in his lab, they were safe. Eva felt her tension level dropping. For her, at least, the most important thing was going right today.

"What happened?" Dario stopped Eva passing his office. "You've been ages, 'Your Good Morning'," he added at her blank look.

The interview, how could she have forgotten that disaster? "I said you should have done it."

"It wasn't as bad as you think."

She leant against his door frame. "Except for me not getting out anything I went there to say."

"Except that. But we didn't lose—"

"Except for what Stuart apparently said. Did he really?"

Dario gestured at his desk. "Haven't had a chance to look. Logistics for the next supply wait for no one."

"What's going badly?"

"How—?" He caught himself running his hand through his straying into grey dark hair for what must have been the hundredth time. "Ah." Always a hundred percent, a smile for him, sparkling his brown eyes, showing off neat teeth, extra white against his olive skin. His Italian heritage embraced emotion.

"Hair like a bird's nest, it's your poker tell. What's the problem?"

"Nothing specific, the whole thing's a bloody nightmare."

She'd known it would be, but to get the new installation operational before Time Magazine announced their company of the year was so important to her. "Is it the schedule?"

He shrugged, nodded.

"You need me to help?"

He gestured at the wall between their offices. "You've a stack of messages."

"Catch up later then, with coffee?"

"If you're offering, sure." His grin made her smile back, something normal.

Her office welcomed her in, but she felt more conscious than usual of her father watching from behind the framed cover on the wall when he'd been Time Magazine's Person of the Year, serious in army fatigues and a microphoned headset on his helmet, and again from behind his framed photo on her desk. He smiled at her from that one, his hand raised against the glare of a strong sun that highlighted the colours around him: sand, sky, washed out khaki clothing, the corner of a red daubed building, the perfect composition.

"Daddy." Always whispered, not so much because she'd never progressed to the more grown up 'Dad', more that she didn't want people to know she talked to him. Their special bond, my daddy, my Evie. The 'my father' she talked about to others had a remove, a distance to it that had never been between them, until he'd made his fateful decision.

Eva touched the glass, asked him the question she always did. The echo of him remained stubbornly silent, as always. She still didn't understand.

The urgent firefighting for the ball took until late afternoon before she could snatch the minute she needed to dial a number she hadn't in seven years.

"The number has not been recognised. Please check and try again."

She did as the automated voice ordered even though she knew she hadn't got it wrong; memorising things like that saved lives.

Gordon could have retired. That most unlikely scenario could be an explanation. More likely he'd moved departments, changed responsibilities, his number might have been compromised. Could have, might have been, always worse, the imagining.

"SIS, how may I direct your call?" Bad enough that MI6 could be found through Google, but it had been Americanised? He'd hate that.

"Gordon Stamford, please."

"One moment."

The number rang, once, twice—

"Yes." Hearing his voice catapulted Eva back to when she was a different person. She opened her mouth to reply as Charles burst into her office, her present smashing into her past. She slammed the phone down.

"Your friend didn't come through." His accent was stronger in his agitation, more Royal Family than his namesake.

"Friend?"

"Per Larsson, not much of a friend." She bit back that

her godfather and his wife were the only family that counted to her, apart from him and Lily. "I didn't get it."

Oh, no. Eva's dart of disappointment for him made her wince. He must be devastated.

"He can't sway the judgement of the committee, you know that." She said it gently, trying to be on both sides at the same time.

"Chairman of the Committee, that's exactly what he could do."

It was Charles' upset lashing out; she knew he would only want to win on merit.

"I'm so sorry you're disappointed." She put her arms around him, her head on his shoulder, and waited for the few seconds before she felt him relax against her, hug her back.

"Don't say it."

"I wasn't going to." But not getting it this year didn't mean forever. He was only forty, plenty of time to try again. She squeezed him tighter.

"This changes everything," he murmured into her hair.

"It doesn't change what's important."

"It's a disaster."

He released her. Beneath her smile, his frown softened but she'd never seen him so crushed. Closed about his work usually, he'd invested all his hope in this, his ultimate recognition. That would be what hurt, that he believed his peers had found his work and, by consequence, him lacking. Setbacks wounded, even if your dream wasn't as grandiose as a Nobel prize. She still had to reality check herself at Every Drop that she was sitting amongst hers.

"No for now doesn't mean forever." She couldn't help saying it.

"You planning on being late home?"

"I never plan it, but it'll probably happen. Can you be there for Lily? I promised her pizza tonight. Things'll calm down after the ball. Did you get a tux yet?"

He shook his head. She stroked his stubble, more silver than brown these days, but she loved they were growing older together. Eva ignored the pressing weight of the ticking clock—he needed her for that moment.

"I can escape to help you choose one, but only if you promise you'll trim this. Go for less of the academic I never remember to shave, more of the designer stubble." His still mostly brown hair had grown into tighter curls, he'd get away without getting it cut.

"I could manage that." He tried for a smile back.

The cold air snatched their breath, the temperature agreeing with the forecasters that early snow was on the way, but the rain-slicked pavements wouldn't hold on to it for long.

"We can walk up to the City, there's a couple of suit hire places."

"At City prices?"

"Probably, but we can try TK Maxx first." Where she'd got her dress.

London Bridge was ordinarily busy, the major incident couldn't be near there. Buses and heavy traffic rumbled over the choppy Thames beneath them. Charles let her precede him through the pedestrian filtering bollards that marked each end. Barriers ran the length of the pavements, keeping pedestrians safe from terrorist drivers. Eva could remember when walking over a bridge in London wasn't anything, when no one would have tried to mow people down to make a point. The times in which they lived.

"What is it?"

Charles had stopped, was looking behind them. "Nothing. Come on, before it rains again." He grabbed her hand.

Eva smiled, that was nice. When they'd first met they always held hands, but when they'd got back together seven years ago, it had slipped out of the pattern of being them. Not so easy to do that and wrangle a four year-old.

"You can slow down, they won't sell out before we get there."

But he glanced behind again, sped up further. Eva pulled her hand away from him, but he gripped her tighter. "Charles, I'm wearing heels."

They were north of the Thames now, on the City side of the bridge. The green man telling pedestrians it was safe to cross faded ahead of the traffic lights changing from red.

Eva slowed to wait but, as the traffic restarted, Charles ran straight into its path, pulling her with him.

4

———

"Charles, move." Eva pushed against him but he held her, rooted between the left hand and middle lanes of London Bridge, a fragile human island in a sea of cars and vans, racing to beat the traffic lights.

"Stop it, we're safer here."

"No, we're not."

A double-decker hurtled towards them, its driver beeping the warning there wasn't enough space. Eva wrenched out of Charles' grip and charged back the way they'd come.

She lunged for the safety of the pavement, but a weight smacked into her just before she reached it. Eva crashed onto the dropped kerb. Her knee popped loudly, pain reverberated down her leg. She'd broken it, no, no, she couldn't have, she'd just get up and—

"Don't move," a woman with spectacularly plaited hair held her hand out. "You're safe there, you might have internal injuries. I'm calling an ambulance."

"Eva," wide-eyed with concern, Charles squatted beside her. "What were you thinking?"

"Me? What were you thinking?" The dimpled pavement was digging into her side.

"A cyclist hit you." The woman clarified. "Courier probably, couldn't get out of here fast enough. I can't get an ambulance." She looked at her phone in disgust.

Major incident, Eva heard it in DI Smith's voice.

"Don't move." Charles looked through the forest of legs crowding them as some pedestrians slowed for the drama, some stopped to help.

"I'm fine." She shifted her weight to get up off the wet, cold, hard, hurting ground. "It's just my leg."

"Eva, please, you're bleeding."

"You recording this?" The woman with the fabulous hair slapped the phone of the teenager beside her. It fell on to the pavement. He yelled at her, scrabbling to pick it up. "You need some respect. What's the matter with you? Get out of here."

"Yeah," A couple of the other crowd members backed her up.

The teenager snatched up his phone, held it up as though he was going to take the lady's photo. She squared up to him. "Go on then and I'll do a proper job of trashing it this time."

He mumbled something and walked off.

Rain fell on Eva's face. The kind lady held an umbrella over her.

"Thank you." Eva murmured.

"Don't mention it."

No good deed. If Eva had done what she was supposed to be doing, she'd be safe at her desk right now. Those damn pools of liquid chocolate could always make her do whatever their owner wanted. Charles' eyes now darkened almost to black, as he looked from her, up at the ring of fast disappearing people around them, nothing exciting enough to keep them there in the renewed rain.

Only a cyclist. It wasn't like it had been the bus. Eva had to speak to Gordon, probably had another pile of messages stacking up on her desk. She wiggled her toes, nothing hurt more, she was fine. She sat up.

"Eva—"

"I'm okay."

"You're not."

She wiped the raindrop rolling down the side of her face, held her hand out for him to help her up. He gestured at her fingertips. Red, oh. She wiped them down her coat. Dry clean only. She wouldn't be wearing that tomorrow.

"Honey, I don't think—"

"Honestly, I'm fine." Eva smiled at the umbrella-holding lady. "Thank you so much for stopping. Charles."

He helped get her vertical, her weight on her right leg, hop-stepping her away from the road. "We can get to hospital by taxi."

"There's a major incident, I'm only walking wounded, I have zero chance of being seen before the ball tomorrow. Dario's pretty handy with a first aid kit," one perk of having an ex-paramedic on the staff. "Get me back to Every Drop."

She'd padded at her face with an increasingly red tissue three times before Charles gave up with the taxi apps on her mobile. With an arm round him, she was able to put more weight on her left leg with every step until they reached her building.

"I've got it from here, you need to get a tux."

"That's not important right now."

"Yes, it is, one less thing for me to stress about. And you need to get home for Lily."

He pulled her into a hug, only reinforcing where she was busy bruising. "Thank God you're okay. I'm sorry I panicked. I would never mean for you to get hurt."

He pulled out his handkerchief, pristine from where she'd washed it.

"Don't get it—"

He patted gently at her forehead, held it against her cut. "Don't work too late." He kissed her on the top of her head and left.

"What happened to you?" The shocked refrain followed her up the building, echoed last by Dario as she limped into his office.

"Disagreement with a bike courier."

"Shouldn't you be in A & E?"

"Definitely not."

"You want help?" he gestured at her face.

"I was hoping you'd ask."

"Sit, I'll be right back."

The tea he handed her was welcome, even with its surprising sweetness. He peered at her face, appraising for longer than Eva was comfortable with.

"That bad?"

"And you're certain you didn't black out?"

She nodded.

"If you get it stitched, it'll be less of a scar."

"Let's go with steri-strips for now."

"Your knee sounds like ACL damage, the ligament, you'll need a scan," longer in A & E, "if you're lucky it might just be a sprain but you could have torn it." He cleaned her wound, making her gasp, and dressed it gently. "There you go. It probably won't hold, but it'll do for now. You really need—"

"I know, thanks, Dario. You're a lifesaver."

He kept her supplied with tea and snacks, coffee and takeaway until the 22:30 alarm on Eva's phone cut through her last fruitless try of Gordon's number. Go to bed, it ordered.

The Google tab she'd opened to search for up-to-the-minute stories on the impact the Seitu installation had on the local population for her keynote speech had changed. She hit refresh, but the date on the bad news stayed the same. Today.

"Dario, have you seen this?" She called him into her office where he read over her shoulder.

'Reports are coming in from Seitu township, where a couple of hundred people have fallen ill. A viral epidemic is not believed to be responsible and, with the population density so high here, the authorities can only hope not. Living conditions in this shanty town may be to blame, but the charities adopting innovative ways to get clean running water to the residents have justified their intrusion by claiming such outbreaks would be a thing of the past.'

Eva scrolled past the photo in the middle of the article. The spiderweb of Every Drop's raised water pipe network looked stunning against the African sky, an award-winning architecture in its own right, beyond how it had saved lives.

'With no available ground space through which to run pipes, this method was thought to provide a better, safer way of getting water to the people.'

It was a better, safer way, it was the only way. Eva knew everyone who now didn't have to trek miles to collect dirty water were grateful for it.

Think about it like the analyst she used to be. Logically,

a couple of hundred cases wasn't anything to get panicky about; the slum housed people in the high thousands. It might not even be the water. But any infection could spread like Ebola in the time between cooking dinner and sleeping.

"Do we have anyone close?" Eva asked. Close could be two days of travel away on the African continent, but she knew the answer. "We're all in on India, aren't we?"

Dario nodded.

It had been such a coup bringing the raised installation through all of its logistical challenges in Africa she'd expected them to carry on rolling it out there. But the Board had other ideas which made sense, given that Chennai and Hyderabad were in the top five most water-stressed megacities. It had been unanimous that Every Drop's infrastructure would help the most people the fastest there. No point wishing it could be different now.

"Never thought I'd say this but let's hope it's a virus or food poisoning," things people would recover from, "even better if it's just the media being lazy, connecting the closest dots because it gives them a quick story." She sighed. "All we can do is monitor it." She closed her laptop, disconnected it from the dock. "Home now, that's an order."

"You're on your way to hospital, aren't you?" Dario asked.

Eva padded a whisper touch at her dressing, wet through now. "It'll be fine."

"I can probably call in a favour to get you through quicker, so I'm taking you. That's an order."

5

Eva's neck ached. Her laptop was dead, slipped half off her lap when she'd finally fallen asleep. She rolled her shoulders, winced. She wouldn't do that. Connecting her charger, she pressed the on button until her laptop booted up. Nothing more on the Seitu situation. Could it be what she hoped, a food contamination that could be easily contained, with no one else sick or worse?

The bathroom mirror showed her that walking up the stairs like an old lady had less to do with spending the night on the sofa, more to do with the state of her. The bright white of the dressing over her stitches just drew attention to the spectacular bruise that had blossomed outwards from underneath it round her eye, curving down onto her cheek like a question mark—what happened to you?

It was going to make a statement, shame it was the wrong one.

She looked like the bus had hit her and she was shuffling around as if she was older than her mother. She pulled herself upright. She should have taken the extra strong painkillers the hospital had offered.

Should have, she should have stayed in the office.

Tonight was so important for Every Drop, Eva wanted to scream. She'd chosen her dress with great care, shimmering blue, subtly reinforcing her message about water, and now all anyone would see, would want to know about, was the mess of her face.

Her left knee was the most worrying. As she walked down the stairs into the kitchen diner, it felt more swollen than it was. Did it matter? She hadn't planned on dancing tonight anyway, she only had time to schmooze and loosen bank accounts.

"I made coffee. . ." Charles' face was an apology. He stepped into her to hold her but his arms fell back to his sides. "Anywhere not hurt?"

"Eyelashes, fingernails, my toes are okay."

"God, I'm sorry. I didn't mean—"

"I know, it was just a stupid accident. Coffee will help."

He handed her a mug.

Eva blew the drink. "What did you mean we were safer in the road?"

He gestured at her. "Safer not running at buses and bikes."

"Safer staying on the pavement." She ran a hand down his arm, an apology for her wisecrack. "How are we doing here?" She gestured at Lily, sitting at the table, half-hidden beneath her long brown hair, her cereal spoon paused mid-way to her mouth, her attention entirely on her phone.

Charles shrugged.

"Lily, eat, you're going to be late." If Eva's every morning nag popped up on Lily's phone screen, she might take some notice of it. "Lily," Eva raised her voice. "Earth to Lily."

Lily did something on her phone and looked up. Golden

brown eyes widened and her mouth formed an actual 'o'. "You look awful."

"Thanks. Lesson for you, make sure you only cross the road when the green man is showing." Eva concentrated on not looking at Charles while she put bread in the toaster. "You're going to miss your bus."

"It's good." And Eva had lost her.

"Do you want me to take your tux? I'm going straight to the hotel from work. Charles?" He turned back from the window when Eva repeated her question. He looked like Lily when she hadn't done her homework. "I thought you were getting it yesterday. Tonight's important."

He nodded. "I know, don't worry, I'll meet you there, all decked out."

She resisted reminding him about his beard, focussed on Lily instead. "Have you packed your bag for Anya's?"

"Yeah, it's by the front door."

"You've got everything you need?"

Lily pushed herself up from the table, tossed her long hair behind her shoulders and fussed with her school bag's contents. "Mum, relax yourself, I'm not five."

"Got your phone charger, toothbrush?"

"If I've forgotten anything, I can borrow it. It's only one night."

"Here," Eva held her arms out, giving Lily an 'I'm so proud of you' hug. So together, so confident, at only eleven. "Call me later."

"You'll be busy." Lily reminded her.

"Not too busy I can't talk to you but maybe make it before seven." Eva gave her a tighter squeeze and released her to get the butter dish.

"What do you have there?" Something beneath Charles' tone made Eva look up, made Lily freeze, one hand in her bag. Eva's toast popped up in the perfect silence bounded by Charles' demand and Lily's guilt.

"My school bag, what else?"

"Show me."

"You can't go down my bag."

"As I pay for it and everything in it, I think you'll find I can." Eva bit back her 'what are you doing?' It was hard sometimes to not contradict each other over Lily's care.

"I've got rights, you know."

"Give it to me." Charles held his hand out.

"Mum." A long drawn out wheedling do something.

"Charles, what do you think Lily's got that she shouldn't have?" Surely she was too young to be trying drugs or sex. But weren't parents the last to know? Eva was certain she'd have told her mother everything if she thought she would listen. Doubtless making up for that, she'd told Lily countless times she'd always be there for her, no matter what, so she hoped Lily would confide in her when the time came.

Charles looked so uncomfortable at the sanitary pads he pulled out of the first side pocket he unzipped, Eva expected him to drop the bag.

"You want to take those off me, Dad?" Lily now in full teenager strop.

A selection of folders, a pencil case, hairbrush spilled onto the worktop. Charles rifled through screwed-up hand-written notes, a half-eaten tube of sweets, and a couple of crumpled tissues.

"Empty your pockets." Something in his eyes reduced Lily's protests to a huff.

"This will have to wait, Charles. Lily's going to be late. Can we do this—"

"Now."

Lily smacked her travel pass and house keys on the

breakfast bar, her purse flew off the edge. The note its zip made as it smacked onto the floor was far too jolly a sound for whatever this was.

"Happy now?" Her sulky outrage was turning, Eva could hear the threat of tears edging it but Charles seemed oblivious.

Eva began repacking Lily's bag. "Charles, this needs to wait."

"That pocket. I can see it's in there, give it back." he insisted.

"I haven't got anything of yours." Lily yelled. "Want to search me?"

"Show me."

"For God's sake, you're such a Hitler." Lily yanked off her blazer and threw it at him.

He dug into her pockets. "What's this?" He held up a silver chain, peering at the pendant on it.

"None of your business."

He slammed it down on the worktop. "Have you been in the loft?"

"Are you mad?"

"It's a simple enough question."

"Up there with all the spiders? What do you think?" Lily snatched her blazer back. "I'll miss my bus now so I'll be late home every day this week with detention, thanks a lot. Hope you enjoy your father of the year award you're never getting."

She yanked her coat off the stand, swept up her overnight backpack and slammed the front door behind her in the best soap opera style.

"What was that about?"

But Charles ignored Eva's question, his feet snapping at

the tiles on the hallway floor in Lily's wake. Eva followed him. "Did you have to be so hard on her?"

Charles snatched up his own coat and slammed the door too, with Eva's reasonableness on the inside in the stained air, his and Lily's anger on the outside in the frigid October day.

Today, really? She could bang their heads together.

Her turn to yank the door open, but her shout for Charles to remember a tux rebounded back to her from where it smacked into DI Smith and DC Truman standing on her doorstep.

6

"We usually have to knock." DC Truman's smile froze. "What happened to you?"

It took Eva a couple of seconds to realise what she was asking about. "Run-in with a cyclist. That's why I haven't been in to give my statement, I spent most of the night in A and E."

"We have a couple more questions for you. Can we come in?"

Eva looked beyond them, but there was no sign of Lily or Charles in the street. She let the detectives in, waited for them to begin.

"You might want to sit." DC Truman's assertion made Eva's heart jump. What now?

She led them into the kitchen, leant against the units.

"That looks nasty." The woman detective gestured at Eva's face.

"It doesn't feel so great from this side either."

"How did it happen?"

"Mistimed crossing the road."

"We saw your husband leaving, he seemed to be in a bit

of a temper." And there it was. DC Truman let her accusation sit there.

"It was nothing, family stuff." It sounded weak, an excuse, but she didn't know what it was. Eva picked up Lily's bowl and scraped the abandoned mush into the food recycling bin. Bending to put the bowl in the dishwasher made her gasp.

"Are you okay?" the detective persisted.

"I'm fine. What did you want to ask me? I have to get to work."

DI Smith propped himself against the kitchen door frame. "Eric Hill, did he eat anything at the coffee shop?"

"A piece of chocolate cake, I thought I told you."

"Did you have any?"

Eva shook her head. "I don't like cake." She half-expected the usual jokey outrage that followed that admission, but this wasn't that type of conversation.

"You eat anything there?"

"No, why?"

"We believe Mr Hill was poisoned."

Poisoned, but that meant—Eva dropped onto the nearest chair. Keep it together, she couldn't panic in front of the police. It was only the tiniest chance, the most unlikely of explanations. "Poisoned, are you sure? Was anyone else taken ill?"

"Why d'you ask?" Was DI Smith testing her?

She grasped at the distraction of the coffee maker, making them drinks to give her time to think.

Its rumbling and the shrillness of grinding beans filled the kitchen. She let the machine blast the water, steam the milk, growl through the process again to make a cup for DI Smith, hoping they didn't notice her shaking hands fumbling with the portafilter, mistiming locking it into the housing. Trusting they thought the screeching warning of no water in the reservoir where she forgot to check its level was a normal thing. Her insides knotted themselves tighter, tighter. She made herself an unwanted cup.

DI Smith sipped his drink. "Good coffee. Why d'you ask if anyone else was taken ill?"

Careful. Eva spoke slowly, weighing up each word before she said it.

"Because that would imply a random attack, like the one yesterday, everyday terrorism or a disgruntled employee at the bakery or the coffee shop."

"And if not?"

Eric, I'm so sorry.

"It was targeted." Eva let the words swirl around them.

"Who would want to hurt him?" DI Smith peered at the notices on the fridge as though he might find the answer in Lily's half-term arrangements or on their favourite pizza place's pre-Halloween takeaway offer. "Any of his ladies not so keen on sharing?"

Eva swallowed, grateful her breakfast was still in the toaster. More so that they were looking at this through the prism of poison usually being a woman's weapon.

"I don't know who's in his life right now."

"You didn't say why he wanted to meet. Not seen each other in years and then yesterday, coffee and cake."

Eva's mind was a blank. She should have made her statement last night, then they might have left her alone.

"He wanted to pick my brains, he wanted a second opinion on something he was working on." That much she could give them. "I told him I couldn't spare the time right now." Eva gabbled past the lie, warming to her imagined memory. She concentrated on keeping her face blank, nothing to see there, no secrets being kept.

"Does he have a temper?" DC Truman asked.

"Not that I ever saw."

"Your husband, does he have a temper?"

"No more than anyone else. His background is academia, they can seem eccentric, out of sync with the rest of us, a law unto themselves almost." She gave the usual spiel to explain Charles' sometimes odd behaviour without thinking. DC Truman called her on it.

"But not above the law."

"Charles didn't hurt me, a cyclist did. Is there anything else, I really must get to work."

"We can drop you." DI Smith said, "after you've made your statement."

A statement he didn't appear to believe, even though he made her go over it four times. Each time under his questioning it became more difficult to keep it as contained as what she'd said yesterday.

When she got to Every Drop, there was thankfully no worse news from Seitu township, and Dario and Vaishali had mopped up most of the hiccups. After dealing with the 'take notice of me' messages, Eva made the call she needed to.

Today was the worst day possible to be ducking out, but she had no choice now.

7

A couple of centuries ago the side street down which Eva limped must have been a powerhouse of activity. That it looked like it hadn't been in use since then was probably why it had been chosen.

A white van overtook her, its brake lights tapping out a Morse code: this building, no, that one?

Her instructions had been very clear, so no use wishing she could have got the taxi to drop her closer as she dodged puddles in the pitted pavement. Forgetting her umbrella was on her. Keeping her head down was all she could do to keep her dressing dry.

Clunking from inside the back of the van disturbed the graveyard quiet. Black numbers showed her she'd reached her destination.

But the delivery driver.

Past number thirty-seven, she slowed, slower again, to not reach the dead end before he left. He re-appeared out of the back of his van. Nothing in his hands, striding in her direction.

Maybe he was picking something up. There was one

building until the end of the street. Eva crossed over. He cut diagonally to her. Younger, stronger, fitter.

"You have signal?"

She shook her head. "It's a black spot here, next road over, you can get signal there."

"You show me."

"I have no signal. Out of here, take the first right, it works there." She realised her mistake.

So did he.

He reached for her. She sidestepped backwards, her knee reminding her not to do that. She shuffled awkwardly away from him, her heart pounding.

Mistake number two.

He grabbed hold of her coat.

"Let go." She grasped his arm.

He didn't even look old enough to be driving. But Eric. Was this guy the perfect disguise?

"Please, I have more deliveries. I no find fifty-one, I have no time to not find it. The numbers run out. Please." His accent thickened as his voice wobbled. "You nice lady, you help me."

Eva summoned up the foreign syllables she hadn't used for so long. "Leave me alone."

Her Russian worked. He dropped her coat as if it might poison him. His face changed and he gabbled his explanation at her so quickly she lost its meaning every few words.

"Slow." She gestured at him. He nodded, so eager to please.

A simple mistake to make turning into St George's Grove when he wanted St George's Place. He looked so grateful when she gave him directions; she thought he might hug her, but he leapt into his van, crunching the gears in his haste to get back on his deliveries rat race.

Eva blew out a breath into the silence. Five minutes of peripheral exposure and already she was reading too much into things. And that was before she did this. After they knew, things would change but she had to tell them.

Time had been a hammer there. From the top left corner of the largest building in the street, thirty-seven's façade was partway through a metamorphosis. Starburst growths of black mould pocked the white render. The windows were grimy but dark beyond not being cleaned, covered by a counter-surveillance film.

Eva rang the bell and looked at the underside of the portico, knowing that from beyond the peeling paint someone watched her. The door looked like it would be grateful for the sniff of paint fumes, but it was solid in its frame, metal cold to the touch. She was in the right place.

When it opened, she stepped inside and pushed it closed behind her. The lock engaged with a decisive clunk: no way out unless she had permission. There was no denying where she was now. She stood in an airlock, beneath another camera, the glass door in front of her firmly closed. In the current climate, it wasn't surprising they had so much security, even in this outpost.

A woman with salon-perfect big blonde hair bowled towards her. Grinning like Eva was her favourite person, Nora slapped a hand, still favouring a bright red manicure at the unlock button, and the interior door swished open.

"Eva!" Her name accosted her before Nora did, enfolding her in a protocol be damned hug. "Times like this we need our people around us." Eva winced beneath her enthusiasm.

Nora released her, frowned. "You've been in the wars."

"It's nothing. How are you? Your daughters and grand-children?"

"Eight little monkeys now keeping me busy. How's your little lady? Let me see, picture please."

Eva flicked through a few photos of Lily while Nora cooed and clucked like the mother hen she was.

"Muuuuum," Lily hadn't wanted Eva to film her that day, poking her tongue out, until she laughed, tossing her hair, fluttering her eyelashes, golden-brown eyes wide as she pulled exaggerated catwalk poses.

"Look at her, she's so grown-up."

Eva smiled. "Eleven going on fifteen."

"It's a fun age. Come on then, I know Gordon's chomping to see you. We can catch up afterwards."

Eva followed her down the dark corridor towards a utilitarian staircase at the back of the building.

"I'm happy Gordon has his own unit."

"Despite himself, you might say. What do you think of our prestigious office space?"

"This is some place." Eva allowed. "Hiding in plain sight?"

"Something like that," Nora puffed up the second flight of stairs. "Got to get my 10,000 steps in."

"I wondered if you might have retired by now."

"I thought about it, but what would I do? Bake cakes, there's only so many of those I should eat. Coffee mornings? I'd go mad in five minutes. I've got a few years before they put me out to pasture."

"They'd hate to lose you for sure."

"There you go," Nora rapped her knuckles on the first closed door on the top floor before presenting a swipe card to the panel beside it. When it beeped permission, she pushed the door open so Eva could step inside the office and seven years into the past.

"Eva, it's good to see you. Would that it were in happier

circumstances. We don't lose one of our own often but when it happens, it hurts." Gordon Stamford gestured at the chairs in front of his desk, shunting over to one side so he could see her around the enormous monitor that took up most of its surface area.

"I know." Eva shook his hand. "Thanks for seeing me. There must be something in the water here, you and Nora look almost the same as you did the last time I saw you."

"Though a few too many lunches, too much whisky," he patted his rounded stomach. Still a full head of unruly hair, though it had worked its way from sandy brown to light grey and keen blue eyes behind his rimless glasses. Gordon didn't miss much.

"How are you? How is everyone?"

"You know how it is. Right now we're all shocked, then will come anger, the need to avenge him if foul play is suspected. That'll be harder to manage. He stayed in Vauxhall Cross when we moved here, but he had strong ties to people in this unit." He peered at Eva's face. "You don't look like you're taking good care of yourself."

She stopped herself from shrugging. "A disagreement with a cyclist. Congratulations on your unit chief position. It's well deserved."

Gordon laughed. "Sometimes I think they put me over here to get me out of the way. So why the visit now?"

"The police have questioned me twice about Eric, they just told me they think someone poisoned him. Do you know what it was?"

"I know nothing yet. So far it's being treated as a civilian case." He frowned, his face settling into well-practiced furrows. "Why are they interested in you?"

"Because Eric and I met the day he died. He told me he needed help on something but—"

"Official Secrets Act still covers you."

"I know but I'm so far out of the loop, I'm barely in the same country, I have no clue what's current, who the major players are, might be. Things have changed so much since I was here, they have agendas now I couldn't have dreamt about then."

Gordon's desk phone rang. He held up one finger and hoiked the handset to his ear, listened.

It was like a time warp, his office. The cracked leather-bound books in the case behind him were probably still in the same order they'd been over in Vauxhall Cross, everything transported over here and reassembled exactly. She'd never seen him need to refer to them, his extraordinary memory was the stuff of legend. Apart from that one time.

He finished his call. "What is it?"

It was hard to smile there, then. "I was just remembering when you and Eric were testing each other, him on Google and you with your books."

"And a lot of fine whisky."

"He only just beat you."

"Because I was topping everybody up." Gordon smiled too. "It's a good memory, Eva, thank you." His voice changed, all business now. "I only have a few minutes, I'm needed." He checked his watch, he still favoured expensive timepieces, this one showing the interior workings in gold.

"Yesterday's incident?"

He nodded. "You'll hear it on the news. The powder was inert, nothing dangerous, the 'victims' psychosomatic."

"Who's claimed it?"

"That's the strange part, no one. We're pooling resources, see if we can figure it out. Could be anything, could be nothing." He sighed. "Terrorism has the easier hand, they can lock down any part of the country, terrify a population with a hoax phone call. We're labelling this a win for the intelligence services and police. An extra drill, expertly carried out. Why did you come?"

"Because I know something I didn't tell the police." She forced the words out. "I might have been the target."

8

Gordon didn't miss a beat, apparently shelving his summons elsewhere. "A blow by blow account of your meeting with Eric then."

Eva closed her eyes, shredding the unfamiliarity that had wrapped itself around what had been an integral part of her time in MI6. Pulling it together in her mind, she described a re-enactment of what happened through the enhanced memory of her senses.

"Eric asked if I had half an hour to meet, said he had something he needed my advice on. I suggested Coffee Espresso, it's where I always go."

Gordon nodded at the significance.

She could see the table by the window. "When I arrived, he already had his coffee, and he got me one from the barista at the counter. He told me he'd been Head of the Russian desk for five years, that he was investigating something he wanted my opinion on to see if I would reach the same conclusion as him. Because what he thought didn't make any sense."

Eva could hear the vanilla chill-out music being played

over speakers in the corners at ceiling height. See the brown walls displaying paintings for sale, striped paper on the back wall.

"It was busy, noisy, so we weren't in danger of being over-heard, but we kept the conversation cryptic, obviously. After about ten minutes a barista, probably at uni, a tall thin girl with a long blonde plait and a blue starburst tattoo on the top of her right wrist came over with a slice of chocolate fudge cake. She said the man at the counter sent it over for me, but she couldn't see him when I asked about him. A mother and daughter probably were waiting to be served, a young Indian guy, head down, scrolling his phone, behind them. Not him, the barista said, he was white, average everything. I thanked her, left the cake where she'd put it on the table."

"You still don't like it, or you were being cautious?"

"Still don't like it."

The crucial part. Eva let the remembered sounds wash around her, holding that moment in her memory as vividly as she could. The dampness escaping from winter coats and soggy woollen scarves into the coffee tinged-warmth, the smell of hot chocolate, strongly sweet. "Eric joked it was probably from the barista, that we should meet more often, picked up the fork and demolished it. If it was poisoned, it wasn't fast acting. We were in there probably another twenty minutes while we finished our drinks and he tried to persuade me to say yes."

She should have. Things might have played out differ-ently if she'd been there to help him when he felt ill.

"He said nothing about strange feelings in his stomach or throat. He didn't complain about pain, feeling sick. Didn't mention anything off about the taste." She let the memory dissipate as the warmth from the coffee shop had when they stepped out into the cold early evening and opened her eyes. "We said goodbye outside, a quick hug," she pushed through the memory, the sadness of his death catching at her throat. "I went back to the office. He didn't say where he was going."

"People around you?"

Eva focussed. "No one close, a couple behind me, Eric kept an eye but didn't show any concern about them. Lone student working at the nearest table to us. Headphones on, head down, studying a laptop the whole time."

She waited, Gordon's silence reminding her how he worked.

"You need to keep a low profile." he finally said.

She nodded. "I do, mostly."

"Can you work from home?"

"I'm safe at Every Drop, we have building security."

Gordon's frown deepened, but he agreed. "Home and work only until we're sure."

"After tonight, absolutely." She filled in her excuse at his questioning look. "I have a charity ball to host."

"You can't go."

"I can't not." Eva took a beat, Gordon didn't respond to histrionics. "It's the biggest event in Every Drop's history, it's the donations to fund our next programme. Our new installation depends on the ball being a success."

"Look at the evidence, Eva." He leant forward across his desk. "Someone gave you poisoned cake, that wasn't an accident."

"It hasn't been substantiated that the cake was the culprit, and anyone who knows the first thing about me, knows I wouldn't eat it."

"Poisoning though, whose weapon of choice is that?"

"Exactly and Eric was Head of the Russian desk, they knew I'd give him the murder weapon."

Gordon steepled his fingers, tapped them against his lips. "That presupposes a level of finesse that probably isn't there, our friends the Russians have always been a blunt instrument. Eric kept an experimental antidote at home, something we've issued to everyone attached to that part of the world. We need to check, of course, but if he took it, it not working suggests they used something exotic."

"Or that the police are wrong."

"We both know that's unlikely, they wouldn't have mentioned it to you unless they were sure. You wouldn't be here unless you thought it mattered."

The nauseating unease that had been grating her insides stepped up. Eva took a deep breath. She was fine.

"Any idea who might want to harm you now?" Gordon voiced the question she'd been asking herself since DI Smith first mentioned poison.

She shook her head.

In her time at MI6, she rode a desk, anonymous to anyone outside the Russian unit. And all of that was eight years ago, distant past in the intelligence world. And now? She was a mum and ran a charity, why would anyone target her? There was nothing to gain, no message to send, no leverage to achieve by killing her. She clung to the logic.

"It makes little sense for me to have been the target, it must have been Eric."

Gordon laughed, a short sharp bark at humour. "Since when does anything we deal with make sense? You shouldn't put your head above the parapet, for now."

"I have to go tonight." She tried another tack, but wasn't sure who she was reassuring. "I know everyone who'll be there. I know enough to be careful."

"If you're the target, they won't miss again. Being killed isn't the part of his legacy your father would want you to repeat."

"This mission is so important, it will save millions of lives." And Every Drop being deemed worthy by Time Magazine would be the best salute to her father she could think of, a way to cement his legacy that would have mattered to him. She could imagine the Every Drop celebration cover framed next to his own on her office wall as clearly as if it already hung there.

"What about your family, Eva? You want your childhood for your daughter?" Gordon really knew where to hit.

"It's not the same thing."

"Isn't it? You want her to be that angry with you?"

Anger was underrated. Eva used it to drive her and her vision for Every Drop. Anger at the injustice of a world where power and money meant more to those who chased it than the lives of others was a force for good. She tapped into it often.

And the other, the monstrous presence of her personal fury, she thought she kept that hidden. She knew she fed it too often, the rage at her father for leaving her, for taking away his haphazard constant in her life, for leaving her to scream and cry in her empty bedroom, in the silent tomb her childhood home became, for leaving her alone.

She sat straighter. "I can't delegate my obligation, the donors will be more generous for me because I know how to press their buttons."

"Hit that guilt trip, eh?"

"Always, but with a smile."

He picked up a pen from his desk, held it between the fingertips of both hands, looking at it as though it was something priceless, dangerous.

His door burst open, and Nora was a whirlwind over to his desk. "Look at the news."

"Which site?"

"Any of them."

Something big. Gordon turned his giant monitor sideways so they could all see the footage. Sirens wailed through the speaker.

It was hard to tell where it was from the street scene of nondescript buildings. A woman in a fur-edged coat addressed the camera. "There is no official word of anyone claiming responsibility. Authorities will release a statement in due course, but this will have a far-reaching impact on diplomatic relations between the US and Russia."

The feed returned to the studio where the presenter looked suitably serious. "We will bring you more on that story when we get it. To recap, the American Ambassador, Hunter Malone, and two aides have been killed in Moscow by a suspected car bomb. A statement from The White House has condemned the incident. The newly appointed ambassador was a friend of President Jed Carson."

"We know anything else?" Gordon asked.

Nora shook her head. "Not beyond he got into his official car with his aides to attend a long-standing engagement set up for his predecessor when it blew."

"What are the White House doing?"

"No red flags yet. We'll keep on it." Nora left them to it.

"Assassinating the Ambassador? What were they thinking? And a car bomb?" Eva asked. "That never used to be the Russians' style. I'm out of touch, but I'd stake money it wouldn't be now. Unless they're dissembling, shifting the blame onto someone else. Would they want a war?"

Gordon muted the news feed, let the silence stretch around the room.

"You're right. This is a deviation, not in line with current behaviours. I'd like for you to come back as a consultant on this. I can protect you then, if you are being targeted."

"You're into protection now?"

His hands on his desk switched position, right over left. "Let's just say one of the biggest advantages of having my own unit is that I can deploy resources as I see fit. It's in my interests to keep my people safe."

The reminder on Eva's phone silenced her maybe, her tell me more, the wondering how she could make that work with everything else.

"It's impossible."

"You underestimate what you're capable of, but you have to do what you have to do."

"I'll be in public tonight, lots of witnesses."

"As was the ambassador, as was Eric."

She couldn't argue with that. "Take care, Gordon. It's nice to see you."

"Good luck with tonight. Put me down for five hundred."

"Thanks, I really appreciate that."

He stopped her at the door. "Be cautious, not just tonight. If you think something's suspect, it will be."

9

Eva's ringtone intruded into her checking the streets as the cab took her to the hotel hosting the charity ball. She grabbed it out of her clutch bag, but it wasn't Charles calling her.

"How's my god-daughter today?" Friendly, warm, the voice on the other end, just what she needed.

"Per, can't you find the hotel?"

He sighed. "I'm still in Stockholm, marshalling a spat between two public figures who ought to know better, but the outcome matters. I'm sorry to let you down."

Eva tempered her disappointment. After Charles' behaviour that morning, Per's absence would be better for him, but it had been too long since she'd last seen her god-father. "That's a shame."

"Listen, why don't you come here for Christmas? I bet I can convince Lily Santa Claus is real."

"That I'd love to see. Let me talk to Charles, see if we can co-ordinate some time off."

"Tell him I'll get a whisky in that'll blow him away. How's he doing?"

"Disappointed." What else could she say? She hadn't understood his reaction at all. Her logical, clear-thinking husband being almost superstitious in his expectation and predictions of disaster.

"If his work had made it through the preliminary round, I'd have stepped aside to let the consideration be without bias, based on what he's achieved."

Oh, Charles, out in the first round, that would hurt.

"You shouldn't tell him," Per went on, "but it might help you guide him going forward with this work. It is cutting edge, it would have won, but we had intelligence that it wasn't original."

"Charles would never cheat."

"The information's source is impeccable."

"A rival?"

"Not even in the same arena. Someone we couldn't discount, I'm sorry."

Eva sighed, she couldn't tell Charles. "You have nothing to apologise for. When do you start the madness again? I'm not asking for Charles. I'm just checking you're having enough of a break in between."

"I'm not leading the selection process next time. I've done my share."

"You're retiring?"

"I'm effecting a gradual stepping away in the buzz speak. Then I'll be free to see my god-daughter whenever I want. You'll do Mathias proud tonight, Eva."

She blinked hard; she hoped so.

"You getting out, love?" The cabbie's question told Eva she was taking too long scoping out the front of the hotel. Poisonous cake, if that was what had killed Eric, was subtler than an assassin's bullet. She was probably safe to march right up the middle of Kensington High Street, but getting out of the cab and inside the hotel foyer was hard enough.

"Eva, Eva Janssen!"

She looked for who shouted for her before she thought not to. The woman didn't look like a threat, but the cake hadn't either.

"Amelia Moore," shorter even than Eva, young, a messenger bag slung across her body. She jabbed a phone between them, its red recording button a warning. "What's going on at the Every Drop sites?" Sites? "What happened to you?"

The phone waved a circle in front of Eva's face.

"What do you mean 'what's going on'?"

"People are falling sick. I thought your water was going to be their salvation."

"I don't have the scientific data—"

"You don't need scientific data to see that you're poisoning them."

"We're not poisoning anyone, but I won't comment beyond that until I know the full picture."

"If you're giving me a 'no comment', I'll just print that you don't care."

Amelia Moore had a lot to learn about interviewing if she thought going low right away would get her what she wanted. 'You get more flies with honey', Eva's father's words flickered through her mind. It was almost funny. The night affirming his legacy and here she was being roasted by a young reporter.

"Research me, it'll take you less than a minute to see how much I care. That's why I won't comment until I know the truth. Speculation and innuendo might sell articles, but the truth is what matters." Eva made for the lift, dogged by Amelia. "The event I'm going to is ticket only."

"That's okay, I'll wait until you come out."

Making the guests feel scrutinised and uncomfortable wasn't the way to get them to open their wallets.

"Why don't you come to my office tomorrow morning and I'll give you your comment then."

"An exclusive?" Amelia looked as though Eva had offered her a promotion.

"Until I know what I'm dealing with, I can't promise that, but I will give you first shot at this, if it's even a story."

No time for Eva to wonder if she'd sold her soul, just enough after going through the reassuringly tight security, to fail to reach Charles again. If he was angry she hadn't backed him up that morning, now was the time for him to let that go. She needed him here, smiling, talking the science.

Everything in the ballroom looked perfect. Eva toasted her staff her thanks just as the guests began to arrive and they dispersed to be perfect hosts. The security process nicely staggered the arrivals into the pre-function room so she had time to mentally cross reference every face she greeted.

"Eva."

She turned around. From the Chairman of Every Drop's Board's expression, she could have been forgiven for thinking she'd walked into the room, but her dress had stayed outside.

"Hello, Stuart. Pleased to meet you, Felicity. I'm Eva." Stuart's new wife shook Eva's hand as though her injuries were contagious. She reminded Eva of a wren, tiny, unobtrusive, unnoticeable even, on the periphery. Stuart was more like a hawk. His grey curly hair was still thick, but age had not been kind to his nose, which now dominated his face, ruddy with the pay-out from long-term drinking. Much taller than both women, he looked down at Eva, staring at her face longer than the doctor who'd stitched her up. "What on Earth happened?"

"Nothing serious. Did you see my interview on 'Your Good Morning'?"

Perhaps not the best time to question him on his alleged quote, but at least here, in front of this crowd, he'd have to answer her something. She gestured to the enormous bar behind them, wanting to help that along. "What would you like?"

"Someone else to do the keynote. You can't do it looking like that." Stuart's hand wafted between them.

"It's about what I say, not what I look like."

"There's an image commensurate with Every Drop." He smoothed the lapel of his tuxedo, tailored well enough to make it less obvious he'd put on more weight. "The right one makes the donors feel more at ease. You have to know how to court them."

Clearly she did, they couldn't turn around without hitting a peer, celebrity or captain of industry. Lord and Lady Butler meandering behind her were an ideal foil.

"Lord and Lady Butler." Eva said as though surprised they were there. "How lovely to see you."

"Oh, my goodness. What happened to you?" Lady Butler asked.

"I had a disagreement with the pavement. It's fine, it looks worse than it is."

"You're very brave to go out looking like that." Her hand flew to her carefully maintained jawline. Her face might have been as aghast as Stuart's if it had still been able to form any emotional expression.

"So tell me, Lady Butler, which lots do you have your eye on?"

"Well, I am rather partial to the 'have your portrait painted'. I have just the spot for it in our drawing room, don't I?"

"Yes indeed, it would look splendid in the drawing room." Her husband replied.

"Did you notice the opportunity to be featured in a spread in the House Beautiful Yearbook? It would be rather lovely to have your portrait in one of those photos." Eva said it innocently.

"Yes, it would." Lady Butler's face tried to light up. "I want that one too."

Eva's work there was done. "It's been lovely to chat but please forgive me, I must mingle." She beamed at them both, trying not to wince at the cracking of her grazes.

Stuart followed her away from the Butlers. "I realise this is disappointing, but I have to insist."

"Is it true you said water isn't an inalienable right?"

He drained his champagne, holding his glass out to his wife, who took it and walked away in search of a full one. "We all know it, I'm the only person courageous enough to say it. Water is the scarcest resource we have. It's fair that everyone pays for it."

"It's hardly the same for people in crisis."

"This is the way of the world, you can't be an idealist forever. Now, where's that Indian girl? She can do it."

"The one born in Whitechapel?" Stuart didn't appear to get Eva's sarcasm.

"She ticks more diversity boxes than you, she should have been doing it anyway."

"Apart from her not having the experience, knowledge or passion, and the guests not knowing who she is—"

"I've made up my mind." Stuart's attention snagged behind Eva. Jonathan Trainer and his wife had arrived, the best potential donor there amongst a lot of heavy hitters. Stuart walked over to greet the new arrivals as though they were long-lost family and it had been his idea to invite them.

Eva would rather meet him away from Stuart's fake camaraderie. She found Vaishali at the bar to give her the heads up to ignore whatever Stuart said. Eva's electric blue sequined dress felt as though it was trying too hard next to Vaishali's exquisite embroidered turquoise sari.

"Thirsty?" Eva gestured at the two shots lined up in front of her.

Vaishali picked up one, Eva grabbed the other and coughed as the fire after downing it spread through her chest. "Aren't you supposed to have lemon with that?"

Vaishali shrugged, signalled the bartender. Eva shook her head at him and he turned away from them in mid-stride.

"You okay?" Eva asked.

"Another couple and I will be."

"Anything you want to talk about?"

"Don't you need to mingle or something?" Vaishali gestured at the bartender again.

"Would you rather go home?"

In Vaishali's eyes Eva could see a shadow beyond the tequila. "If you're not okay, go home, we've got this covered." Vaishali looked more miserable. "Get a taxi on our account, reception can arrange it for you."

"I just, I," Vaishali shook herself. "I'm fine."

"Two more, please." Eva ordered. "Let's do this the right way. Thanks, again, for all your help, couldn't have done it without you."

"I only do social media."

"Nothing is anything without it." They clinked the tiny

glasses and drank. "Want to help me round this lot up for dinner?"

Gordon's warning whispered through Eva's mind as the waiter offered the vegetarians on her table their meal choice. She took the meat option as though she could eat the exquisitely presented lamb. She picked at the vegetables and potato, trying to not be obviously wiping the gravy off them, pushing the meat to one side.

"Shame about the no show, Charles Buchanan." The man beside her read the silver calligraphy on Charles' placeholder.

Eva tried to smile. What in his work had become more important this time? He never spoke about it, in fairness she wouldn't have understood it if he had. But she told him about her setbacks and triumphs at Every Drop. It was that sharing she wanted; to feel a connection to that part of his life. She didn't even know what of his work he'd put before the Nobel Committee.

While coffee was being poured, Eva pre-empted the celebrity MC's announcement of the keynote speaker, limping up to the lectern before he could announce Vaishali.

"Good evening, ladies and gentlemen." She moved the mic closer to her mouth. "I hope you're having a good time. I'm sure you're wondering what happened here," she waved a hand in front of her face, "why I look like an extra from Casualty."

It was then, looking around at the smiles in her audience, that Eva noticed him. The man who didn't belong.

10

---

va hadn't seen him before, she would have remembered.

A whispered ripple pulled her attention to the fact she was standing in front of over a hundred people, all expecting her to say something. It had almost been a flippant comment to Gordon that she'd be in public, lots of witnesses, like Eric and Hunter Malone. She pulled her gaze from the man, licked her lips. Focus.

"In shanty towns and slums around the world, water is a currency." But the facts and figures she was going to tell them had evaporated like liquid on sand.

The stranger smiled at her. Around her age, brown hair perfectly styled. With the chiselled looks James Bond casting directors loved, the way he wore his tux would have won him the role instantly.

Eva gripped the lectern. "It's, I. . ." The whisper was rising.

He couldn't hurt her from there, shooting her would be too obvious, he'd be stopped before he could make his getaway. She had to get it together.

"Women and girls mostly, walk miles to access water we wouldn't wash our clothes in." Eva picked up her glass as though emphasising her point to her audience. It looked safe, it should be, it had been beside her since the waiter poured it from a half-empty jug. She scanned the room. No one was bending over, rushing out. She replaced the glass in its sunken spot on the lectern. "Too many end up looking like me, simply fighting for the right to hold on to what they've managed to carry. Cartels of criminals supply grey or brown water at exorbitant rates. Or worse for those with no means to pay."

No whispering now, she could have been the only one in the room. The weight of the stares on her was heavy as the truth made her audience uncomfortable, but none as much as that from the man on her right. She patted at her forehead, checked her fingertips. Not red-coated, she was just sweating from the lights, the heat, her break-neck heart rate. That was all. Please, not a poison.

"It's so easy for us to not even think of how it must feel to not be able to trust what you're putting into your body." Don't poison me, I haven't done anything to you. "What choice is that? If I don't drink, I will die but the dirty water in the jar I've collected, what is in it that might kill me? Will it make my child sick? My mother, my husband?"

Eva resisted the call from her dry mouth.

"In our auction this evening, we have an amazing array of lots that money can't buy. If you're wondering how much is enough to pledge, think of my injuries on a seven-year-old girl beaten for the water she trekked five miles to get for her family."

Eva lifted her glass, the man was doing the same. "Sip your water, hold it in your mouths, taste it, this miracle that supports life on our beautiful planet. You have the power to give that gift to others, to save their lives. To safe water for everyone."

The audience rumbled the toast back to her and silence held for that moment while they did what she asked. She hoped they were thinking about what she'd said, really thinking about it.

"Now I'll hand you over to our fabulous auctioneer," Eva grasped the lectern and leant towards her audience. "Please, be generous."

Gordon's warning propelled her downstairs to hotel security, where she asked to see their registration list for her event. She took her time studying the list of guests they'd checked in. What the uniformed security guard represented felt oddly comforting, even though she was certain the stranger upstairs would best him if it came to it. They had admitted no one unexpected; the hotel prided themselves on giving their clients exactly what they requested they explained to her twice.

An icy worry trailed down her back when she checked her phone. Radio silence from Charles still? Surely he wouldn't let himself be so distracted that he'd miss the biggest night of her career? He knew what this meant to her. Had something happened?

She was staring at her phone screen as if she could conjure up an answer when the door to the disabled toilet clicked open and a couple practically fell out of it into her.

In that snapshot second she looked up at Jonathan Trainer, Head of the Transit Group. Not Mrs Trainer stumbling with him but one of the other guests, Annabel Grayson, apparently having forgotten about her Prince Charming fiancé.

In a blur of red designer exquisiteness, probably real diamonds and an animalistic, most unladylike roar,

Annabel launched herself. She collided with Eva in a scream of "No, you don't!" knocking Eva's phone onto the marble tiled floor. The possibilities of broken glass made her wince more than the slapping, scratching onslaught.

Jonathan Trainer was sidestepping away, disappearing in the opposite direction of the running footsteps of the concierge.

"Ladies, please."

Everywhere Eva looked, tried to move away, she met slaps and scratching, hair pulling, squealing, yelling.

"Stop it." Eva tried to push Annabel Grayson off with one hand, defending her stitches with the other.

More running feet, a crowd gathering.

One last shriek from her attacker, followed by the horrendous ripping of a dress not designed for a catfight. Hands on Eva, not pinching or scratching, but unwelcome all the same.

The man she didn't recognise was right there, too close, lifting the tattered remnant of the front of her dress to cover her bare breasts.

11

Eva snatched the torn fabric of her dress from the hands of the man she didn't recognise. His hazel eyes held her gaze as he took his jacket off. She looked right back at him, hoping somehow that would cut off his peripheral vision so he couldn't see anything he shouldn't be seeing.

He held his jacket out to her. "It'll detract."

Annabel Grayson was yelling something about selling pictures, but at least now it was at the hotel staff, busy trying to calm her down and move the indiscreet guests filming this disaster away. Jonathan Trainer was nowhere. Eva hoped they'd got him sneaking off.

Who was she kidding? She'd be the one all over YouTube, not to mention probably back on 'Your Good Morning' on the 'what's in the papers today' feature under some innuendo, 'CEO of Every Drop drops everything for charity auction'. Breaking one of her cardinal rules.

Realising she didn't have enough hands, the stranger stepped behind her and laid his jacket over her shoulders. She looked at him, his face close to hers.

"It's okay."

Eva shivered into his borrowed warmth, slipping her arms into the sleeves, buttoning his jacket while trying to hold the front of her dress up underneath it.

Reinforcements of hotel staff had arrived to restore the five star order the guests paid for.

"You'll be hearing from my lawyer, I'm suing your arse." Annabel Grayson had a lot to learn about being ladylike. "Don't even think about touching me."

She slapped the manager trying to cajole, placate. He stepped backwards, letting his colleague try, turning to Eva.

"Madam, how can I be of assistance?"

"Can you get me a taxi, please?" Home to change and hopefully back before the auction finished, before anyone questioned where she was. Time enough after tonight to weather how this would undermine Every Drop's reputation, that image Stuart was so concerned about. If he thought a couple of bruises would destroy it, he'd be apoplectic about this.

"Of course." The manager strode away.

In the now emptying space, she could see it. "Oh, no."

"I've got it." The stranger collected as many of the smashed remains of her phone as he could, although, really, what was the point? There was no putting that back together. But such an extension of a person, the way we interact with the world through those tiny rectangles, it felt like she was leaving a glimpse into her soul over the marble floor. "Is this yours too?"

He held out her clutch bag. She wrestled both lapels into the grip of one hand to take it.

"Who are you?"

"Luke Fox."

"You're not on the guest list."

"I'm here on behalf of Addison Clarke. He was supposed to tell you." He hefted the remains of her phone. "This is pretty irredeemable. You want me to take out the SIM?"

"Please."

"Shall I?" he gestured at her clutch.

"Thanks." He stepped towards her to take it from her. "Do you mind if I borrow your jacket, while I get changed?"

"Not at all, my driver can take you."

"No need, the taxi's probably already here. Thanks."

In the cab, Eva stared at the shimmery beauty of the skirt of her dress. This disaster hadn't featured anywhere in her planning for all eventualities. Surely, once she sobered up, Annabel Grayson would make the rational decision to keep her prospective in-laws' press office away from YouTube by staying silent about the whole thing. Her minor royal fiancé might not have a title or as much of a fortune as Jonathan Trainer, but he was still a Windsor, the catch every 'it' girl desired.

Eva unlocked her front door. No deadlock on? How ironic, rushing out with the police meant she hadn't locked up properly. Had that only been this morning? She slid her key into the top lock and pushed the door open.

Except it didn't.

She pushed harder. Something was behind it. Oh, come on, she didn't have time for this.

"Is everything okay?" Eva jumped at the unexpected.

Not a passing neighbour standing at the bottom of her short garden path, but Luke Fox, just a few steps away from her

12

"Did you follow me?" Eva's question was stupid, Luke Fox clearly had. "Why are you here?"

She looked up and down the street, as quiet as it usually was at this time. Would Hugo next door hear through his closed front door if she screamed?

"I just wanted to check that you're okay."

"You don't know me, why the interest in my well-being?"

Luke had his mobile out. "Look, can I show you?"

He held his phone up for her to see, open on the contact for Addison Clarke, mobile, a number that Addison kept very private. After all the times she'd spoken to him, she didn't have it.

He pressed dial.

"Addison, Luke Fox. Can you say a quick hello to Eva Janssen, convince her of my bona fides? . . .of course, here," Luke held it out to her.

"Hello?"

"Eva, I'm sorry we couldn't be there this evening but I hope Luke is doing a good job as our proxy." Addison's voice filled her ear, no sound of stress, coercion, the usual confidence, at ease with himself, the world all his. She was reading too much into this.

Sometimes a delivery driver was just a delivery driver, sometimes a good Samaritan was just that.

Luke shivered beside her.

"He's going above and beyond the call of duty."

"That's what I like to hear."

"Sorry to have disturbed you."

"Not at all, it's always sensible to check the unexpected. Good luck with the fundraising."

Eva handed Luke his phone. "Thanks, sorry." I thought you might be a killer.

"Let me help." Luke pushed on her front door so she could squeeze inside to pick up the coat stand that must have fallen over in her rush out that morning.

But then she saw the open drawers of the hallway cupboard, spare batteries, blank birthday cards, the washing machine manual, gift bags and two screwdrivers strewn over the floor. What were they doing there? She looked into the lounge. Why were the sofa cushions, covers stripped off, thrown around like six-year-old Lily was building a den? Eva's feet crunched on something, shards of broken glass, a smashed photo frame.

Poking out from beneath the rumpled rug was her memory box. She snatched it up, holding it against her front, the wood cold on her bare skin, gripping it so it dug into her.

They'd been here. In her house. They'd come for her, the people who'd failed to kill her with the poisoned cake. Eva's thoughts rammed into each other, crashing, colliding with the violence from which she'd apparently escaped again by pure luck.

But she didn't have nine lives. She didn't know how to

outrun professional—what were they? A hitman? Assassin? Sitting behind a desk in the Security Services had equipped her with precisely nothing—

Luke's questioning touch on her arm grounded her. "Wait here." he whispered.

She snatched up the fireside poker.

"You're going to skewer the intruder?"

"If I have to."

"You're injured, he could blow you over. Let me." He took the poker and she listened to him moving around the house, the creak just down from the top stair, the floorboards that no number of handymen had been able to fix on the landing. The opening, closing of bedroom doors.

The landline handset wasn't in its cradle, but Eva found it on the carpet. She listened for no ring tone, but her movie expectations weren't reality.

"Is the intruder still there?" The 999 operator asked.

The stairs signalled Luke was coming back down, less stealthily than on his way up.

"The police need to know if anyone's still here."

He shook his head. She relayed his no.

"No one's hurt?" The operator asked.

"The house was empty." But what if Eva had given in to Lily's demands that she and Anya could spend the night there, that they didn't need to have a babysitter? Eva dropped onto the sofa base.

"We'll get CSI out, but they won't be there until tomorrow at the earliest. Is the house secure?"

"Yes."

"Is there somewhere else you can stay tonight?"

"Yes, thank you." Eva's lie sounded definite enough. The curse of her and Charles being only children, the excuse of being too driven in their careers for time to socialise, two lonely lives entwined.

"Can I take a contact number for you?" The operator asked. Not now her mobile was in pieces. She gave Charles' even though he still didn't have it switched on. "Here's your crime reference number," Eva mimed writing at Luke and he tapped it into his phone as she repeated it.

The dressing on her forehead, brighter than her hair, was reflected to her from the black mirror of the TV screen. Still there, the TV, the Sky box, the silver and black gizmos Charles had installed that made the tech work together. All untouched, centred on their black glass shelves. The mantelpiece was curiously normal, mementos and photos in their places.

Amidst the chaos, she replaced the handset where it belonged. "The police are sending CSI over tomorrow. They actually call them that, the forensic people. I'll just get changed, I need to get back."

Rising slowly up the stairs the temperature dropped. The loft hatch was open, the coldness in the roof space sucking the warmth out of the upstairs. They'd even gone up there?

A jigsaw had rained its 2,000 pieces everywhere in its tumble to the landing. Eva moved the box to one side and pushed the hatch closed with the walking stick they used to pull down the loft ladder, discarded by the burglars.

The lamp on its timer switch in their bedroom lay on its side, illuminating the carpet. Her bedside table was away from the wall, one drawer lying on the floor, the other left open, a firework of notes, photos, bookmarks, a now unfolded silk pillowcase exploded over the floor. Coloured piles of clothes pooled in front of the open doors of the wardrobes, her shoes flung out of the boxes in which she kept them. The doors on Charles' side were closed.

Eva laid her memory box on their bed. The lid was askew, off kilter, a bit like her. One of the small brass hinges pushed against her when she opened it, creaking alarmingly as though she was trying to force it open by crowbar. Inside, the jumble of things her father had brought back from his assignments, because he'd known his Evie would love them. Her fingertip inventory checked the precious mementoes off: sand from the Sahara, a piece of a dry stone wall which had taken bullets for him in Iraq, an exotic pressed flower from the Philippines, a worry doll from Guatemala. She paused on the bright pink and orange bracelet he'd brought her back from somewhere she didn't remember made by a little girl just like you, he'd said, selling them to get pennies to go to school. Eva had tried to copy it but the knots in the turquoise ones she'd made, one for him, one for her, were clumpy and uneven. She picked both bracelets out from her treasures and slipped them onto her wrist.

None of this made sense. If the people who'd killed Eric were after her, why show her they'd been there? Because they could. A chill that had nothing to do with the air temperature shuddered through her. They were toying with her. We can get you anywhere.

Dropping the useless blue dress in a shimmer of dying gorgeousness onto the carpet, she changed into her other option, a purple halter neck which could just about pass as a ballgown. Shaking loose her shoulder-length hair, she pulled her falling down style out, no time to repair it.

The landline rang making her jump. She charged into the tiny boxroom they used as a study and grabbed up the upstairs handset from where it lay on the desk, knocked out of its cradle.

"Charles?"

"Stuart Worthington, why aren't you here?"

Caught by her phone, she couldn't lie. "My house has been burgled. I'm on my way back. Is there a problem?"

"It's your job to be here."

"I'm fully aware."

"I've got a big donor who wants to meet with you. You'll need to charm the literal pants off him for making him wait."

"Have a drink—"

"We've all had enough champagne."

"So give him a cocktail menu, all the shots, the best whisky, dance on the bar, whatever it takes. I'll be twenty minutes."

"I think I prefer you in that." Luke looked at her hands, carrying only his jacket and her clutch. "No overnight bag? I'm guessing CSI would rather you didn't stay here. I can get you a room at the hotel."

She didn't doubt that he could, even if they were allegedly full. But the decidedly un-CEO-like wage she took from Every Drop wouldn't stretch to their nightly rate. Most months the Travelodge was out of their reach. And she had to get back to redeem herself in Stuart's eyes. No time to pack anything, she'd figure it out after the ball. She shook her head and picked up a photo frame lying face down on the tiled hallway floor.

"Fine looking family." Luke looked over her shoulder at the smiling Lily, Charles and her.

Eva touched Lily's face. "Thank God she wasn't here."

"Good thing none of you were, put the photo back where you found it for CSI."

Eva put the photo back on the floor. "Thanks so much for your help, you're an excellent knight in shining armour."

"In Alexander McQueen, at least," he smiled.

In the car on the way back to the hotel, Luke asked the question she didn't want to answer. "Your husband didn't attend tonight?"

Excuses poured out, well-rehearsed, the variations different each time she used them. "He's a kind of academic, they don't work on the same timetable as the rest of the world, he's at a crucial stage in some research." Probably.

"What's his field?"

"Chemical engineering, but it's no good asking me anything else about it because it's beyond me."

"You're a very understanding wife."

"Our careers are important to us, we support each other."

"Find me in the bar after your meeting," Luke held the ballroom door open for her. "You can buy me a drink."

She tried to join in with his easy smile. Saved by a hotel member of staff, "Ms Janssen, you have a phone call."

Eva picked up the phone to which the young woman steered her.

"This is Eva Janssen."

"It's me."

"You're okay, where are you? I've been calling all day."

"I need you to come home."

Eva closed her eyes. "I've seen it, dealt with it. The ball's not over yet. I'll be back about two."

"Come home now." Charles' voice was tight. "If you come back then, I'll be gone."

Nothing he was saying made any sense. "What're—"

"Come home now otherwise you won't see me again."

13

The barman served a scotch for Luke and a double gin and tonic with two slices of lime for Eva while Luke watched her standing at the end of the bar. Her fingers rested on the phone handset as if she expected it might jump up and hit her if she didn't hold it down.

A man tall enough to hide the fact that he was obese, said something that flustered her. Eva limped to the exit, but he followed, Luke a few seconds behind. He heard their voices, the low tightness of an argument in a public place before he caught sight of them on the switchback of the grand staircase.

"You know me better than that." Eva limped down the next flight of stairs, gripping the marble banister.

Luke stayed beyond their eyeline on the first floor landing.

"I'm not in the habit of having people walk away from me."

"I'm not walking away from you, Stuart. I'm walking into an emergency. If you can't secure their donation, Dario's as good as me."

"The donor wants you. I have to insist."

Luke heard Eva's awkward stepping down pause, the man's shoes clipped to a stop.

"You know what Every Drop means to me so I don't need to tell you I wouldn't be doing this unless it was life or death." She sounded lost, wounded.

"If you're walking away from your responsibilities here I can't be responsible for what happens." The man snapped at her, ignorant or uncaring of the breaking in her voice.

"Seems we all have to do what we have to do." Eva reached the bottom step before the man's shoes rapped his annoyance back up the stairs, past Luke as he went after Eva.

Outside the hotel entrance, she shivered, rubbing a hand over her non-bruised arm. He imagined he could smell her perfume from where his jacket had laid on her skin. A black cab drew up and Eva got into it.

Luke showed the concierge the ID that always shattered the data protection defence and he told him where she was going. Curious.

The drinks he'd abandoned waited for him. From his trouser pocket he took a tiny vial and, subtle beyond notice, he passed it over the gin. He sipped at the scotch. Very good. Thanks, Addison, for your charge account.

He picked up both glasses and wove his way into the main function room where the diamond encrusted audience was still congratulating itself on such generosity. Passionate about her cause, Eva's speech hit all the right notes. He'd have donated himself, if he were who he was playing.

Easy to spot, her bright red, too short, too tight, too low, just out of place, dress a beacon. Luke held the gin glass out to Annabel Grayson. "You strike me like you might be an," anything in a glass, "gin and tonic girl, am I right?" He smiled his best at her.

She giggled. "Am I so easy to read?" Enough compensatory champagnes had passed between the incident downstairs that she didn't appear to recognise him.

"It's quite some night, isn't it? Cheers." He touched his glass to the base of hers and they drank. "That's Jonathan Trainer?" He nodded in Trainer's direction where he was holding court with a wife resplendent in a silvery dress that caught the light when she moved. "Is it true he's the richest person here?"

"I wouldn't know." She took a step away from him.

"You're not going to drink with me?"

"You're too James Bond for me."

Luke burst out laughing. "How can anyone be too James Bond? You don't like bad boys?"

"I'm engaged."

Not for much longer after her performance earlier, but her bare finger explained it.

"Does that mean you can't share a drink, chat with someone new? I flew in from Monte Carlo this morning." Annabel looked him up and down. More so when he carried on spouting his bullshit. "Reckon I'd give Trainer a run for that title."

He smiled and wet his lips with the whisky, watching her mirror him with a gulp of the gin. So predictable, so boring. Her reaction to him was nothing to do with the drug in her drink, everything to do with pound signs.

He leant closer. "What do people do around here for fun?"

"That depends what kind of fun you have in mind." She took a baby step sideways. It was working.

"Let's take a seat." Luke took her elbow and steered her to one of the empty tables at the back of the room.

When she dropped onto the chair, her gin slopped over her braceleted wrist. "Oops." She giggled like a schoolgirl on her first glass of wine, ran her tongue over the cheap jewellery, watching his reaction. It wasn't the hardest smile he'd ever had to hold.

"Is that from your fiancé, it looks like it could be from the Royal collection?"

"You know him?"

"We go back a long way. So what's the deal with you and Jonathan Trainer earlier?"

Her baby doll face crumpled into a frown, the drug told him what she wouldn't have said otherwise. "I didn't use anyone for anything, we're all adults here."

Whichever way she had to justify it, she must be on the way out to risk it all so publicly.

He went with his hunch. "Who told you to compromise Eva Janssen?"

"Whadyoumean?"

Luke leant forward, his forearms on his knees, making her duck to hear him, enhancing the drug's effects, making her feel off balance, unsettled.

"The media threats, even though you wouldn't want your fiancé to see that you'd been getting jiggy with anyone else. You have way more to lose than Trainer does, it's just money to him. You're risking your marriage?"

"It's not," she covered her bare ring finger on her left hand with her thumb. "What happened with her. . ." She half-shrugged, a brief touch on her stomach telegraphed her plan. You sad sod, Trainer. This evening would cost him a lot more than whatever donation he'd made. How would

Mrs Trainer take that? Not delighted for there to suddenly be an heir to the fortune, with nothing to do with her.

"Was your first plan to set Eva Janssen up better than what happened? I bet it was, wasn't it?" She matched his nodding. "Your partner will be pleased though, right?" He followed her gaze, a glance, involuntary under the drug's influence. Which of the group of people standing by the stage was it?

"He will." Annabel slurred.

Ignoring the two women in the group, Luke took out his phone. "Let's have a photo." Annabel preened at the camera, well-practised, but she wasn't in any of the shots he took.

"So I'm staying here." Trying to walk her fingertips up Luke's thigh, Annabel had to grab his leg to stop herself falling off the chair. "You wanna join me?"

He helped her get vertical and steered her towards the lift. "Which floor?"

"Six, as in 69." She tried to press herself against him, but he sidestepped her. The doors opened and Luke helped her in, propped her against the side. "Don't be a spoilsport."

Luke pressed six, "I don't do money traps."

The reception area was busy, late check-ins, people leaving the ball, assistants steering, cajoling. He chose one of the large leather chairs facing the entrance, and, back to the wall, checked no one was paying him any attention before he logged on to the encrypted server.

His message could only be read by his intended recipient, but he kept it cryptic, this mission being what it was. 'Staged burglary at the house, possible other player showing their hand.'

He uploaded the photos he'd taken of the three men Annabel had pointed out. His money was on the one Eva had called Stuart, but he knew hunches had to be proven.

The screen remained static while the person at the other end deliberated.

'Too soon to move in, call it a night, new orders tomorrow.'

The response Luke had expected.

In Addison's car, he looked at the seat Eva had taken. But orders were orders.

14

Eva's front door opened easily this time. "Charles?"

In the lounge, he nursed a whisky, staring at the TV frozen on the image of the US President's press conference where he had vowed he would hunt down those who had murdered his friend, Hunter Malone. As though this was a normal evening.

Charles didn't hide his surprise at how she looked.

"What's all this about? I'm in so much trouble for walking out of the ball. How could you have threatened to leave me? How could you hold our marriage hostage?"

"I'm trying to keep you safe."

"By strong-arming me?"

He tried for a smile. "I know how stubborn you can be."

"You don't get to do that, make this about me. Explain or I'm going back, see if I can salvage anything of my reputation."

"This isn't going to make sense but I need your phone."

"It's in pieces. We can't be here, the police said—"

"The police?"

"I had to come home earlier, I reported the burglary."

"We haven't been burgled."

"Are you blind?"

He sat so heavily on the edge of the sofa, the contact with the wooden frame jarred him. He got up and threw the coverless cushion on it, sat more carefully. "I was looking for something."

Eva opened her mouth, closed it again, searching for the right words, but her shriek that came out wasn't. "You trashed our house? You did this?"

"Tell the police it's a mistake, we can't have them turning up here."

She pinched the bridge of her nose, closed her eyes. What the hell was he talking about?

"I need you to trust me. Tell the police it was a mistake."

"We promised when we got back together there would be no secrets, we'd be a team. No non-communication."

"I know."

"So what is this?" It hurt to admit it. "I'm not calling the police until you tell me what's going on."

"It's not safe for us to be here."

"If you did this," she gestured at the carnage of their things, "how can it not be?"

He looked at the TV. "You trust me, don't you?"

"You're my husband, of course I do."

"We need to leave, we're in danger here."

"What about Lily?"

"She's best off where she is."

But if he trashed their house, it meant whoever had poisoned her cake hadn't been there.

"I'm not going anywhere until you talk to me. Where were you this evening? You know how important the ball is and now you've made me leave it and for what?"

"There's no time." Charles walked to the lounge door. "If you won't come, I can't make you, but I can't stay here."

He went out into the hallway. She heard scuffling. He'd picked up their family photo and replaced it on the cupboard.

"You're holding us to ransom again?"

He put his hand on the front door handle, "I wouldn't call it that." Turned it.

"Wait, look at me." Eva gestured at her dress. "Let me get changed."

Charles looked out into the street, closed the door. "Two minutes."

15

"Have I got this straight?" Limping up a hill behind Charles, Eva was getting out of breath. "Someone is after us, but you can't tell me who for reasons you can't tell me. You've lost something vital, but you can't tell me what. But it's so important, not having it puts our lives in danger and running around London all night will keep us safe? Did I miss anything?"

"No, that's quite succinct."

A laugh burst out of her, but nothing about tonight was funny.

"Down there." He ignored her sarcasm, gestured at the side street on their left.

"No, Charles."

He pulled up short. "What do you mean, no?"

"No, niet, non, nein, take your pick. No. I'm not wandering around the streets. My knee's killing me, I got hardly any sleep last night and today has been, well, least said about that. I'm not going anywhere until you tell me what the hell is going on." Eva's demand echoed around the quiet street. "No one's following us."

But the only place they would be safe was somewhere she couldn't take him. He didn't have clearance to go in Gordon's building and she couldn't get in anywhere else until the morning at least.

"They're after us, we just can't see them."

"Who?"

He looked around as if he expected whoever it was to leap out of a building or from behind a parked car. "We won't know them, they're just there with orders to kill."

"Why?" Did he know that what happened to Eric was meant to happen to her?

"I can't tell you."

Why was he putting up this wall between them? "Then we'll go to a police station, we'll be safe enough there."

"No, we won't. These people, you don't understand."

"Tell me then, so I do."

But he was off again, loping down the street.

She limped after him, stopped after a few steps. Enough. "Charles."

He came right back at her call. "Ssh, no names."

Eva grabbed his hands. "Let's go to your lab. You have decent security there."

"Absolutely not, no." He broke away from her, was halfway across the road.

He'd been behaving so weirdly since he'd lost the Nobel nomination. Maybe he was having a breakdown or something. She knew nothing important about his long dead parents, his family medical history.

"Are you okay?"

"What kind of question is that? Come on."

She gestured at her knee. "I can't run."

In the streetlight something flitted over his face, but

from the distance she couldn't tell if he was upset or angry at her or himself.

He came up to her again, whispering, "We can perhaps get a train out of London—"

"I'm not leaving Lily."

"It's only—"

"Not doing it."

The headlights of a car had Charles ducking into the front garden of a mock Tudor house. "Eva, here." The bush didn't quite conceal them both, a toddler would see past their flimsy camouflage. Eva's knee protested.

The car passed by.

"Enough." She limped back to the pavement. "We're grown-ups, Charles, not actors in a spy spoof. Are you going to tell me what's going on?

He looked up the dead street, down. "It's safer if you don't know."

Maybe it was Charles' odd behaviour, maybe how ridiculous the night had been finally hitting her, it didn't matter what or why. Hysteria nudged at her, she was close to screaming, crying, laughing, probably all three. "I'm not spending the night out here. Up to you if you come with me."

16

"Late night or early start?" Eva didn't recognise the security guard at the entrance to the building where Every Drop had its offices. But even she didn't normally come to work at this time.

"I've been wondering that myself." She pretended he wasn't inspecting her face, the dressing on her forehead, concentrating instead on signing Charles into the building with a scrawl no one would be able to read.

"Lock it." Charles said when they reached her office.

"We're behind two card swipes in an access controlled building with a security guard and a direct response alarm company, that's why you agreed to come here. I don't need to lock this door too. Now explain."

He checked the blinds she'd closed against the darkness before the ball, then at the all-glass door and the floor to ceiling windows that looked into the corridor. The blinds she never closed rattled against the glass, bucking into place when he released them.

"Now you talk to me." she said.

He nodded, pacing around while his brain wrestled with

whatever this was. Was it so hard to share? Eva dropped onto her chair, smoothed her jeans, pressed her lips together. She wanted to give him the time he needed, pretended to ignore the hurt that he had something he couldn't bring himself to say to her.

The sudden ringing on her laptop made her start. Too cheerful, the Skype incoming call tone.

"That's probably urgent."

At that time of night he was right.

She woke up her laptop, scrabbling to click the right places when she realised who it was.

"Milo, where are you?"

His profile picture was an echo of every borrowed memory she had for her father when he'd spoken to her through patchy comms, the shots that made the evening news, a shorthand to the viewer something awful was coming: a tumbledown building, everything flat yellow, bleached by a harsh sun, unforgiving heat and blinding light by suggestion.

Milo appeared on her screen, his image a little fuzzy. "What happened to you? I'm the one supposed to be in the danger zone."

Eva should have disabled her video. "Are you?"

"I'm not sure. There's more sickness at Seitu, cause still unknown. I was sorting travel there but people are falling sick in Tirupudur."

That's what Amelia Moore was talking about when she'd said sites. "Is it the same?"

Milo looked to his left, back at his camera. "It's hard to say with no one on the ground in Africa. What do you want me to do?"

Seitu, smaller than Tirupudur, was logistically more of a challenge, but any sickness would spread in Tirupudur faster. Africa losing out again to another part of the world, but she had to follow the logic.

"Do we know it's the water? Could it be an outbreak of disease?"

"I'm talking to people, nowhere near enough yet to establish anything beyond doubt, but so far the common denominator is the water."

Eva pushed her hair back, brushed her bruised cheek. Shouldn't do that. "Stay in Tirupudur, can you get labs run? Once we've identified what we're dealing with, we'll have a better idea how to treat it, and that'll give us a benchmark for Seitu. Any of the other agencies have anything yet?"

Milo shrugged. "On the ground it's taken us by surprise, hundreds sick already."

Hundreds? How could they get ahead of that, a sickness spreading that fast would be impossible to contain. "Have there been any fatalities?" Eva discounted the conclusions her brain was lining up. They didn't know enough yet, but what were the chances of a pathogen leaping from Africa to India so directly?

He shook his head.

"What are you doing to stay safe?"

Milo's face froze, his voice had stuttered to silence.

"Milo, can you hear me?"

She disconnected, pressed recall, letting a minute tick by, two, giving him the chance to call her back, tried again, again, half a dozen more times. The line stayed stubbornly silent, India not co-operating. Eva closed her eyes, she could have slept right there sitting upright in her chair.

She typed a message to Milo, then one to her staff outlining the situation. She tasked the logistics team with hunting down water purification options, Dario to co-ordinate with medical agencies on the ground while they worked on identifying any common elements that might explain what was happening.

Beyond that, she needed to sleep. Just a few hours, enough to reboot. Massaging her temples, she blinked a few times. She was actually seeing double.

In the staffroom Charles had curled up on the smaller sofa, his legs flopped over the end. He'd left her the three seater, even though he was taller. In spite of the day, the everything, she smiled at him, zonked out, like Lily able to sleep anywhere.

Painkillers, then sleep for her too. She took the cushions from the staffroom sofa and laid them on her office floor, closing the doors between her and Charles so at least he could sleep uninterrupted if Milo called back.

The sound of her name made Eva claw her way back from her welcome oblivion.

"I've heard of taking your work home with you, but this is new." Stuart was standing over her.

Dream-addled, her brain took its time to catch up. Sleeping in her office, not an ideal way to be found by anyone, and definitely not the Chairman. She rolled up and off the sofa cushions that had parted company during her short night. Still sore from her pavement tumble, she stretched out the kinks in her back while she checked her laptop. No missed calls.

"Sorry, Stuart, I don't have time to chat but Charles is in the staffroom, he'll be happy to have coffee with you."

"Right now I've got damage control to deal with."

"I'm waiting for a call about Seitu, but a similar thing is happening in Tirupudur. Milo's been trying to call me, he's on the ground—"

"Not Africa or India, I'm talking about here, with you."

"That's not important when we're looking at people

falling sick." She checked her laptop screen again, hit refresh.

"I wish I had your confidence. Annabel Grayson is beyond reason, she's threatening to blacklist us."

"For what? You know what happened, don't you? I wasn't filming her, I was waiting for a call. I don't make it my business to film people having sex in toilets. I don't care what they were doing. I'm the one who should sue her for attacking me and smashing my phone."

"It's in the media so it's truth for the public and our donors." His voice softened. "You must see how damaging this is to Every Drop's image. Annabel Grayson has dynamite contacts we can't afford to alienate. And then there's the matter of not capitalising on a whale donor. I'm afraid we have no choice."

He held out a sealed envelope.

"Sorry I'm late." The journalist who'd accosted Eva at the hotel walked into her office as though she worked there. "Stuart Worthington, Chairman of the Board." She stuck her hand out at him alongside Eva's own, reaching for the envelope that he withdrew. "Amelia Moore, I'm here to interview Eva, I can do you too, Stuart, two for the price of one, excellent."

Eva didn't have time for this today. "I'm sorry you've had a wasted trip, Ms Moore, I still haven't heard anything."

Amelia's gaze sharpened. "The sickness spread so much?"

Eva aimed for dismissively calm. "It's Africa, communications take longer, break down all the time. As I've already told you, it would be irresponsible of me to speculate on anything. I'm afraid you'll have to come back." If she and Stuart would both go, she could get on with her job.

"This is me coming back."

"Did you cover that the Every Drop infrastructure hasn't made anyone ill?" Eva looked at Stuart, it hadn't? "It's the other suppliers who have the problem. Every Drop is honouring its promise to provide clean, safe water for all."

Since when had he taken a PR pill?

"How does that reconcile with your comment that no one has an inalienable right to water?" Amelia snapped back.

"Taking remarks out of context, I'm sure you can do better than that." Stuart fixed her with his steely gaze. "You must excuse us, that's all we have time for."

"How did your fundraiser go?"

She'd seen? Eva felt a flush rising up her face. Of course she had. Along with far too many other people. "It's too early to say, but we're hoping to reach a significant milestone with the donations."

"What happened—"

Eva cut her off. "As I said yesterday, you'll be the first I call once I know anything. Sorry you've had a wasted trip."

"Oh, nothing's ever wasted."

That was what Eva was afraid of.

"I'll show you to the lift." Stuart handed his envelope to Eva as he fussed the journalist out.

The contents were something she'd never expected to see, something she'd never have predicted pushing her from calm to raging quicker than Lily, when she'd been the tantrum queen of two-year-olds. Eva's wild gaze around her office snagged on the black-and-white photos Stuart should have paid attention to: moments of Every Drop's successes measured in the smiles of children around a standpipe, relief on the faces of pregnant women, a high five almost like a prayer, one hand black, one white, an angled shot of the expanding labyrinth of their ground-breaking aerial network of pipes.

"I imagine you'll need a couple of minutes." Stuart looked in her door.

"You can't do this." She jabbed the paper at him.

"It's legal, all the Board members signed it last night."

"It might be legal, but it's wrong."

"What's all the shouting? Stuart, hello." Charles shook his hand like everything was normal. "Good to see you."

Eva brandished the letter. "They're putting me on sabbatical."

"There was an incident last night between Eva and one of the guests. It has the potential to bring Every Drop into disrepute with some key donors. We're only asking her to step back for a time—"

"How long?" She interrupted. The letter's open-ended 'until further notice' made her nervous.

Stuart held his hands out as though he were placating a small child. "As long as is necessary to repair the damage, soothe some offended egos."

Charles was nodding. "That makes sense. It'll be good for you, Eva, to take a rest. You've been working too hard."

"A rest? Now? Right when we're facing a crisis?"

"You're not the only person who can deal with it. Your number two seems capable." Stuart waved his hand at the corridor beyond Eva's office.

"He is, but. . ." Dario hadn't used his inheritance from his father's far too premature death to set Every Drop up, its mission wasn't in even his heart as deeply as it was in hers. "When Every Drop needs me the most?" The hurt in her voice cut through the anger in the room. "I can't just walk away."

"You recognised the statutes we're invoking?"

What difference did that make? Kicking her out was kicking her out.

"It's the ones you insisted on, Eva, to keep Every Drop beyond reproach."

How could he use that against her? She'd had them written into the regulations to stop others from jeopardising Every Drop, she never would.

"Without you involved in the new campaign, there won't be any need to dredge up videos from last night. Look at it as a holiday. If I were you, I'd want to be out before everyone arrives, it'll make things more pleasant. I'll stay here to brief them."

It might be more pleasant for him, but she didn't work that way. "I'll tell them myself."

"It's not a choice, Eva. You are to leave now. As per the terms of the clause activated by that letter," he nodded at the crumpled mess in her hand, "you're trespassing. We'll call the police in five minutes."

The police, again, for the third time in two days, wouldn't that be awkward?

He produced another envelope from the inside of his suit jacket. "If you don't leave of your own volition, I have the power to supersede that letter with this one. I'm sure I don't need to tell you what's—"

"You can't take Every Drop away from me."

"You know very well no one is above the Board, you set it up that way as a safeguard. This means you are to do nothing related to or for Every Drop until such time as the Board reappoints you.

"But the crisis—"

"Will be handled."

Her father's face smiled out at her from his photo. Tread softly, she could almost hear him saying it. Would you though, Daddy, for something that meant everything to you?

Her gaze traced every two-dimensional contour on his face as her child's fingertips had his skin, the lines that gathered at the edges of his smiling eyes, the strength and surety of him. All gone to dust now.

"What's it to be?" Stuart persisted.

Eva closed her eyes.

Tread softly? Like hell.

18

___

"You ain't gonna get no answer, even knocking so the dead can hear ya." The old man peered out of the front door next to the one Luke was banging on. "S'not funny though, is it, seeing as 'ow he's an actual goner. No family, who's gonna do the necessary for 'im?"

The neighbour didn't know about the brother? Interesting.

"Do you have a key?" Luke asked. "I'm from the funeral home, I need to get something suitable to bury Mr Banks in."

"You're a bit pronto, ain't ya? They only took 'im yesterday."

"I was in the neighbourhood, it'll save us time later."

The man shook his head, his jowls wobbling. "Nah, didn't trust no one, that one. Quiet like, anti-social. Not like the old days, used to be everyone looked out for everyone 'ere."

He gestured at the Victorian terraced houses on both sides of the road, busy with parked cars even in the middle of the day, then dipped his head.

"Gawd rest his soul. Found him halfway out the 'ouse I did, lying right there, nose on the path. Already too late, but I called the old bill anyway, no point tying up an ambulance. Not 'ow you expect your day to go, is it?"

For the average person, maybe not, but for the man ordering a hit on the President of the United States, maybe certainly.

"Anyway," the neighbour went on, "he used to 'ave one out the back, a key. All secretive, like, but he never fort we was watching. You want to jump me fence?"

A glance at the front of Banks' house, no flashing light on the alarm box - dummy or just not activated? Luke would soon find out.

He followed the old man into his narrow hallway, through a lounge where the sun was trying to get through the French doors. Down two steps to a clapped-out kitchen that smelt of smoked fish, where he struggled with the shoot bolt at the top of the back door. "Me daughter's put it on again. What's the point in that, I can't reach it no more."

"Would you like me to?" Luke gestured at it and waited for the man's nod.

"You wanna cuppa, got to be a rotten job, what you do, ain't it?"

"It's a hell of a way to make a living. Thanks for your help."

"Don't mention it, mate. Go down the garden, fence is easiest there."

Past the six-foot panels, round the skeleton of a tall fruit tree the man had probably planted in his youth, the fence thinned to greyed out spindles, weathered almost to drift-wood, strung together on wire. Using the concrete support of the proper panel and a foot against the tree trunk, Luke got over it easily. Not as obvious as under a plant pot, Banks had taped his key to the side of the concrete step beneath the French doors.

The silence and stillness of an empty house greeted Luke. Through the kitchen, dining room, front room, up the stairs, Banks had been show-house neat and minimalist. Until Luke reached the master bedroom doorway. A chair, on which Banks had placed trousers and a shirt, lay on its back, the snake of a pink tie coiled beside it. The duvet looked as though someone had tried to throw it on the bed from the other end of the landing. A crack splintered one of the mirrored wardrobe doors, fragments of a smashed up mobile had been ground into the red carpet.

Banks hadn't died a natural death, Luke would bet money on it.

Had the killer left anything behind? Fast but methodically, Luke rifled through the things Antonio Castillo—Tony Banks as he'd been known in London—had thought worth keeping. Nothing in his master bedroom, or the bare two others to offer a clue why he wanted President Jed Carson killed. Nothing to suggest he could get anywhere close to the figure Luke had given him to carry out the job. Mortgaging this house ten times over wouldn't be enough. Even less to suggest who had killed him.

"What's your story, Tony?" Luke asked the silence. "You couldn't do this on your own, so who's paying the rest of the fee?"

From Luke's visit to Banks' brother state-side, he knew he couldn't stump up more than a few hundred dollars. Different names, different continents, he probably didn't know about Banks' demise. Luke would have to call him. The brother, digging out the number he'd been paid to call if anyone came looking for Banks, had retrieved it from inside a boot at the bottom of a pile of well-worn footwear. Was that a family thing?

Luke looked in the cupboard under the stairs, accessed from Banks' kitchen. At the back he found a pair of wellington boots, cracked mud smeared on them. He tipped them upside down, knocked them on the floor. An old-fashioned mousetrap fell out of one, snapping its jaws together as it hit the lino.

"What're you hiding?"

Grabbing a wooden spoon from the cutlery drawer, Luke poked around inside the boot. No other nasty surprises. He risked his hand once he'd checked with his phone torch that the only thing he could see looked innocuous enough. Fingertips tentatively probing, he retrieved the something wedged in the toe.

A crinkled covered little black book.

What would this tell him its owner now couldn't? Banks hadn't been sociable, only a handful of names in it. He flicked the pages backwards. Under 'W' Rory and a handful of American phone numbers, in Washington DC if he'd remembered the area code right. Under 'S' Nancy, 'O' Aleksandr, under 'L' Duncan, 'M' Hunter. Hunter Malone, had to be. And then under 'B' more paydirt - Ted and Charles. Charles Buchanan? If Luke had learned anything, doing what he did, it was that coincidences were rare.

He pocketed it and, for the sake of the neighbour, took one of Banks' suits as he let himself out of the front door, pulling it closed behind him. For the sake of his mission, he took the back door key. Always good to be prepared.

One more step to confirm what he suspected.

19

Eva and Charles blew into the Tate Modern along with a sudden squall of sleet. She hadn't expected today to take her there.

A succession of similar paintings greeted them featuring a purple square in different positions which interrupted parallel lines of arrows marching from top to bottom. Every arrow that touched a square stole away a drop of purple that slid down the shaft until it dripped into a jagged pool at the bottom. She felt exactly like the squares.

Charles nodded his satisfaction at his idea. "We should be safe here for a while. I need the gents, why don't you go order something. You have cash?" Charles fumbled a couple of notes into her hand.

"What do you want?"

"I'll decide in a moment."

Eva limped through the busy café on the ground floor, ignoring the self-service bar with treats to tempt. She didn't want anything other than a rewind to when she'd sat down opposite Eric, but that wasn't on offer beside the crème patisserie strawberry tarts and roast vegetable rye bread sandwiches. A waft of coffee wormed its way into her, the welcome leached out of it. If she stayed there, she'd be sick. She turned around too quickly, twinging her knee, limping back to the toilets where she'd left Charles.

Stuart had told her to treat this like a holiday. Fine, she would. She'd take a long bath, watch a mindless movie, fall asleep in her bed, she could even try to pretend that sounded perfect.

Charles was taking a while. She wandered to the entrance doors, looking out at the tourists rushing away from and towards the dry and warmth of the art gallery. Was that? Eva stared harder. No mistaking it, a sober navy blue wool coat amongst the brightly coloured snow and cold-repelling down and ski jackets of the tourists. Charles walking away from the Tate.

Out into the freezing world, she limped after him. He'd reached the footbridge, heading away from her.

"Charles, wait." Eva dodged round a group of tourists arranging themselves for a photo. "Charles!"

Why was he leaving?

He walked too fast for her limp, widening the gap between them so he was partway along the Millennium Bridge before she got onto it. He flicked a glance behind him, sped up again. Had he seen one of the people he'd been so worried about last night?

She scanned the not dangerous families and the non-threatening tourists lining the edges of the bridge, taking selfies and group shots of the view up and down the Thames. Could she discount the business men? The lone woman on her phone?

There were too many solo figures between Eva and Charles. Which one had spooked him? Was it whoever had tried to poison her? She felt a rush of warmth towards him walking away, bowed bare head, shrugged into his coat, poor protection against the day, leading someone away from her. But this was her fight.

Her limping-running made her remarkable, exactly as she wanted. Look at me, not him.

Only half a dozen between her and Charles now, five as a man in a long camel coat overtook him. A woman in jeans and a too recognisable fur-trimmed parka, probably not her. Nor the one wearing such bright white trainers they begged to be looked at as welcome relief from the greyness of the sky and the water, the steel and concrete of the bridge.

There, Eva had him, the one Charles was drawing away from her. Dark trousers, forgettable black coat, so non-descript any of the field agents she'd worked with would have picked him up immediately, without the proof of him slowing his pace to keep the same distance between him and Charles.

It's me you want, leave my husband alone.

St Pauls Cathedral loomed large in front of her, a sanctuary for many in its long history but a trap for them today. Charles was off the bridge, striding up the road away from it.

Eva dashed towards the man as they followed her husband in convoy. "Stop. . .thief, hey. . .that man, there. . .you. . .stop him." He ignored her as much as the other pedestrians did.

She pushed herself harder to catch up. She wouldn't let him hurt Charles. As they got off the bridge, she grabbed for his coat but he arched out of her grip, shoved her sideways and she crashed down onto another cold wet pavement.

Eva got to her feet, testing her leg, holding her knee. Nothing broken, her panicked explanation as she'd tumbled to the ground. Not even the 'it might give way' the Accident and Emergency nurse had warned her about. She was mostly obeying his 'don't stress it' instruction. It was okay.

Charles. Out of her sight now, no warning could reach him.

It took too long for a black cab to stop, too many traffic lights on red while she got him to crawl the area in an expanding circle searching for Charles or his pursuer. No sign of him meant nothing awful, he could have found his own cab, got on the tube, taken a bus.

Fingertips pressed against the window, she scanned the streets a second time. No sign of anything terrible having happened, no blue lights, or sirens, no running away of people to suggest a stabbing. She'd cling to that for now.

Nothing more to do there, she directed the cabbie to Lily's school.

The world was calm, quiet, everything as it should be on a weekday there. Buzzed through the main door to reception, none of Eva's lies why she had to collect Lily right then would work.

Because none were needed.

"I'm sorry?" Eva's mind couldn't process what the receptionist was telling her.

The receptionist sighed, said it louder. "Lily Janssen has already been picked up."

20

—————

Luke knocked on the door of the morgue and went in.

A woman in her late twenties with bright auburn hair pulled back into a ponytail was leaning close over a body on her post-mortem table. The unfortunate person was missing both legs below the knees.

Luke walked around the other side of the table and waved in front of her. Last time he'd interrupted her with a tap on the shoulder, her punch had only just missed him. He was a quick learner. And he tried not to hit friends.

Georgia tapped one of her AirPods, then took it out. "Here about this one?"

"No, but I could give you a clue what killed him."

She waved a gloved hand over the missing limbs. "You think that? Ha, you'd be totally wrong. How many times? Supposition is not our friend."

"Looking for Tony Banks, he here?"

"Yeah, but not urgent, query heart attack."

"Can I look at him?"

"Knock yourself out." She waved in the general direction

of the bank of doors behind which the dead waited to spill the secrets of what put them there. Replacing her AirPod, she peered into the cadaver's mouth.

The card in the metal frame on the front of lucky door number five had Tony Banks written in Georgia's swirling writing. She would have needed two if he'd been using his actual name when he died, she'd have embellished all those looping letters in Antonio Castillo. What had prompted his name change was one question on Luke's growing list.

Even being the older brother didn't explain how Tony Banks had aged so much quicker than his sibling. The younger Castillo's head of slick black hair had faded on Tony to a thin comb-over that probably had fooled nobody. Luke thumbed the light on his phone and used a magnifier to inspect Tony Banks far closer than either of them would have been comfortable with if he were still breathing.

Nothing around, no swelling inside his mouth. Nothing in the nail bed, nor between each of his fingers. Luke moved to his feet. Nothing there either. He looked more closely at Banks' chest, at a mole, larger than the two beside it, almost joined by the tiniest of discolorations. He zoomed in. The killer trying to be clever, but in the struggle, the injection had gone just wide enough that it had left the tiniest trace.

Luke repeated the ritual to get Georgia's attention. She took her AirPod out as if she were a mother dealing with a demanding toddler. "You're interrupting my flow."

"You should push Banks up your list. Here," he showed her the photo he'd taken of the injection site. "He struggled, might have some post mortem bruising developing. Can you let me know what the tox screen shows?"

"Could have been an empty syringe, using an air bubble to kill him. I'm about done here so I'll get on it next." She looked around the room. "You seen him in here? My assistant? Sneaky bugger keeps disappearing. What's your interest in Mr Banks, then?" She shook her head, "I know, you can't tell me. I'll shout you if I find anything."

"Thanks, I owe you."

"You do, it's about time I cashed in these favours. You can take me to dinner somewhere very posh."

"Just name your time and place, I'll be there."

"Except this week?"

Luke laughed. She knew him well. "Except this week, I'm on assignment. When it's over, I'm all yours."

"That's what you always say."

"We'll do it, bring your girlfriend."

"Hoping to convert us?" Georgia was nothing if not direct.

"Looking forward to more of your stories about this place, you should write a book."

She burst out laughing. "Yours would be better." She waved her AirPod at him. "It's a non-date."

Luke checked his watch on his way out of the morgue, sidestepping to give a mum space to manoeuvre her baby's pushchair between him and the crowd of a group. Breakfast time in the brother's state, but he probably wasn't an early riser. Luke would let him sleep longer before delivering his news.

A quick cab ride and outside a glass office block, his next call was answered straight away, as it always was. "Josiah Johnson."

"Hey, Mr President." Luke's joke on first meeting Josiah had developed into a codename between them.

Josiah laughed his loud guffaw. "You should talk to the big boss, tell him I deserve a raise for my important sounding name."

"Question for you, why would your tribe bump off a middle-aged expat?"

The slightest of pauses. "We did?"

"Query heart attack until I found an injection site."

"I can't confirm or deny—"

"I'm outside, only need a minute."

Josiah burst out of the building and strode around the corner, Luke gave him a few seconds then followed.

Josiah looked Luke's suit and shirt up and down as he approached. "Man, you look rough, off the peg today?"

Luke gestured at Josiah's large checked trousers. "If I ever wear a pattern like that, I'll agree with you."

Josiah patted his afro. "You don't have the style."

"Absolutely, I don't. The name Antonio Castillo mean anything to you?"

"Your corpse?" Luke nodded. "One of ours?"

"US citizen, moved to London, changed his name to Tony Banks. Something not quite right about his situation. His brother, still State-side, had a number if anyone came looking for him. When I did, I'm guessing he called."

Luke held back what Tony Banks had instructed The Society to do, Josiah was a true patriot, and he'd call in everyone he could on this if he had a ghost of an inkling. Luke didn't need all those investigating bodies muddying everything. The trail was already hard enough to follow.

"I'll check it out."

"Appreciate that."

Josiah shook Luke's hand. "Cheers."

"Cheers? You've gone native."

Josiah adopted a shockingly bad Cockney accent, "Gotta blend in, mate."

"Best change those trousers then."

While Josiah got to work, Luke let himself into Eva's

house. The new cameras he was trialling were easy to install —four in place in less than ten minutes—leaving him time to check what had piqued his interest in his walk around last night, even before he'd understood he wasn't looking at a burglary, but at a search gone badly.

He used the walking stick on the upstairs landing to pop open the loft hatch and pull down the ladder. The suitcases and boxes, stacked with an engineer's precision, had been discounted in the frantic search that had tornado-ed through the downstairs. So why go up there and not look through anything? Luke stepped around the stacks. On the joists up against the neighbours' wall was his answer. A safe, door left open. Luke brushed aside the spilled chess pieces and board to pull out the only paper inside it.

The folded sheet showed a copy of an old photo, pre-digital. At one end of the row of smiling people, he recognised a much younger version of Eva's husband. In the centre, was that? Could be, but the fold had worn away some detail, he'd need to check. It could be a lead.

Time to make that call.

He folded the photocopy into his inside jacket pocket, put back everything he'd disturbed, and let himself out of Eva's house before he rang the number.

"Yo, yo, yo." Castillo had been watching too much Breaking Bad, Luke almost hung up.

"It's your English friend."

"You shouldn't be calling here."

"What did I tell you about not using that phone number?" His silence confirmed Luke's hunch. "You didn't remember your promise to me."

"You were pointing a gun at me, I'd have promised you anything you wanted, stop you pulling the trigger."

"Why did you give up your brother's location?"

Castillo huffed. "Aw, shit, it's no big deal. It was Antonio's idea, tell 'em I got his location, get them to give me the big pay-out."

"Why now?"

"It's important he said, to take care of business."

To pay Luke's fee for carrying out the hit Banks ordered? He was all in on this.

"Did you get it?" Luke asked.

"No man, any day now."

"Yet you gave up your brother's location."

"I ain't dumb, I only told them London, they don't get more till they pay up."

They were more organised and had weight beyond that suggested by the burner phone number Castillo had used, dead as soon as Banks was.

"When I said don't call the number, I meant don't call the number. You trying to rip off big hitters, it comes with consequences. Your brother died."

"You're lying."

"I've got nothing to gain by lying, Westminster morgue in London can confirm." Luke hung up.

21

Every parents' nightmare didn't have to be Eva's.

Lily. Eva forced her face to relax. "My husband managed to get here? He wasn't sure he could."

The receptionist delivered her bad news with a smile. "I'm afraid I can't say, data protection."

Eva switched her weight to her good leg, wincing at the tightening of her damaged tendon, the stiffness she could feel puffing out the surrounding tissue. "I'll need confirmation from you it was my husband, Charles Buchanan. If you've let Lily go with her biological father, I'll have to get the police involved because she's the subject of a court order."

Eva's biggest lie got her a hurried call to the Head of Pastoral Care, a large lady who fussed and worried at the boundaries of protocol until Eva asked to use her phone to advise the court that the school was in contempt.

"I can put your mind at rest, Mrs Buchanan." Eva let the mistake slide. "It was Lily's uncle who picked her up."

Lily's non-existent uncle.

Eva clamped her mouth shut on her scream.

Using Lily to get to her was far more controlled than handing her poisoned cake. But using a child, her child. Eva swayed, gripped the counter.

"Which one?" Her question squeaked out. "Can I see the footage?" She nodded at the camera above her.

More boundaries intervened, but the head must have felt something for her distress. She swung the visitors' book around, pointed at the penultimate entry. "Bernard Stel. . .Shrel, he has terrible penmanship."

It was all in the 'B', winking at her, the B of Buchanan. Eva hung onto the counter, anchoring herself beneath the surge of relief. Charles had got away and made sure Lily was safe.

She hobbled out into the darkening daylight and the uncertainty of how to find her family. Charles would have his and Lily's phones off, with Lily's GPS tracking disabled. How, how? And then she had it, one chance, a teeny tiny possibility.

Eva held her breath while the PC in the internet café searched. No matter how she wriggled on the hard seat, she felt she was twisting her knee. She logged into the email address she and Charles had used when they got married. The password—Iloveyou4ever—always used to make her smile. Today everything was harder.

Surprisingly few junk emails had accumulated in the inbox, nothing received today. Eva clicked into the spam folder, into drafts. The last one had been her asking if he wanted to invite anyone else two months before their wedding.

He hadn't remembered.

Never suppose, her father's voice instructed her. She knew that. Charles was apparently good at this, whatever this was. Maybe he watched spy thrillers when she worked late, the false name, his paranoia over smartphones and their microphones, their GPS tracking. Maybe he just hadn't got onto a PC yet. She left the tab open and clicked into her personal email.

Nothing there from him.

One from Per, worrying about not being able to reach her, congratulating her on the success of the ball. He apparently didn't watch YouTube.

'You're just like Mathias, Eva, making the impossible, crazy dream happen, how proud of you he'd be. I'm so proud of you.'

Per, wish you were closer. Would it be so crazy to go there now? He'd invited them, they'd simply be a few weeks early. The break would do them all good.

Eva sipped her peppermint tea, willing the zingy mint to ground her, stop her charging out of the café because where could she go? This was her best, only, shot at finding them.

No family, no home, no Every Drop, everything she cared about stripped away. But not one by the other, that tiny nagging she shushed whenever it raised its voice to be heard over the shouting of her to-do lists, it hadn't been a prophecy. Her work hadn't taken her from Lily and Charles like her father's had taken him from her.

Daddy, what would you do now?

Her fingers were typing his name, the entries loading almost before she realised. Mathias Janssen. Could Google resurrect him enough to guide her? Eva clicked straight into the first entry, which loaded so fast it didn't give her the necessary warning.

It was there, filling the screen, filling her world as it had for the first few years he was gone, but never enough to fill the Daddy-shaped hole in her heart, her life. Her shaking fingers touched his image on the monitor. The photo of his last moment that had won a Pulitzer and every other award on the planet. Her hero, her daddy, scooping up a terrified child, holding her close as if she were his daughter, turning his back on the maelstrom of shrapnel an exploding building whirled around them, taking the force of man's brutality to man. Choosing to save the life of a stranger instead of coming home to her.

Daddy. The photo blurred as it always did, as if Eva had never cried herself dry over and over for the rest of primary school and at secondary school at night alone in her room. She swallowed, reached for the mouse.

Then saw it.

She double tapped the cursor over his hand where he clutched the little girl to zoom in over his four fingers. A turquoise band, sun-faded and grubby but unmistakable. She fingered her own brighter, newer-looking bracelet, a time link between them.

In that moment, he'd been thinking of her.

Eva closed her eyes.

"Mummy, that lady's sad."

Be polite, don't talk about people in front of them, the little girl's mother's shush was loaded. Eva wiped at her face and smiled at the girl sitting on her mum's lap a couple of terminals down.

He was still teaching her, her father. She remembered he'd stopped in his rucksack packing and drawn her into a hug when she'd asked once why he had to do his job, why couldn't someone else? Just for a little while so he could watch her in the nativity play at school.

"Because, my little Evie, everyone else is running away from the bullets. I'm the only one running towards them."

"You shouldn't run towards bullets, they'll hurt you."

"That's true, but the bullets I run towards are words,

photos, recordings of phone calls. Nothing that can hurt me."

"Promise?"

He'd squeezed her tighter. "Love you, lilla gumman. Want to fight this zip with me, help me close it?"

Eva had laughed, "Silly, Daddy, I'm not an old lady."

She closed the browser down. Running towards the bullets, Daddy, I can do that.

And she knew where to start.

22

———

The non-descript building that stole her husband away nearly every day didn't look more dangerous to Eva than it had any other time she'd been there. No one around that shouldn't be, so far as she could tell.

The entry keypad was the same as she remembered; she entered his code. The panel bleeped green.

She let herself into Charles' hallowed space. The story doesn't start when you become aware of it, you need to go backwards for the origin, her father's words that had wrapped themselves around her all the way there dissipated now like so much smoke wafting away.

This was point zero; his office and adjoining lab had to be Charles' origin. So where would she find something to explain why he believed they were in danger?

She used his desk phone to call first his mobile, switched off and voicemail deactivated, then Lily's, waiting for her to pick up. "Hey, sweetheart, it's Mum. Can you and Dad come and meet me? He'll know where I am from this number. I'm waiting for you. Love you."

It could be a while before Charles turned on Lily's

phone and then they had to get there. Eva had all the time she'd need. She started her search with his desk and the stacks of journals, but nothing didn't belong in his neat, orderly organisation.

"Where, Charles? Where would you hide anything?" Her look around his office stopped on the door to his lab. No, that was sacrosanct. He would only allow himself and his precious science in there.

Which left the bookcases. Shaking out each book and returning it just so should have been calming, therapeutic almost, but it didn't get close to chipping away at the knot in Eva's insides. She rolled her shoulders, the stretch of tendons and muscles tightening, screwing up on themselves. No relaxing until she held Lily again.

Surprise waited at the end of the second shelf of trying, wedged at the back hidden within the pages of an A4 notebook, a mobile. Eva turned it over in her hand. A basic phone, like his regular one, but grey instead of black. She switched it on, looking at the office door: its entry keypad had let her in with the code she remembered from years ago. He was a creature of habit. She tapped in the pin he'd always used for his phone and it opened its secrets to her.

She redialled his most recent call, 'Tony Office'.

"Hello." The woman's voice was tiny, apologising almost for answering.

"I'm trying to reach Tony, can you put me through, please?"

"No, I can't."

"When can I call back?"

"No, you can't, he died, Tony died." The woman's voice choked.

Maybe Charles wasn't so paranoid after all. "What happened?"

"He had a heart attack at home, he was—You can speak to one of the other partners."

"I'm sorry for your loss." Eva disconnected and redialled, mimicking Charles' RP pronunciation.

"Hello, I'm the PA of Charles Buchanan." She paused, giving the woman time to acknowledge him, recognise his name, anything. Nothing. The silence stretched. "We're all sorry to hear about Tony. I wondered if you knew anything about the funeral arrangements yet."

"No, no, it's all too soon."

"I'll call back another time. Again, deepest condolences."

Eva hung up and studied the calls list. Two calls to Tony over the last two days. Nothing before then.

She thumbed through the sparse list of contacts. Nancy with two London landline numbers and a mobile, one London number for an Aleksandr, the Russian spelling, Duncan, Hunter—Hunter? That was an unusual name, could it be Hunter Malone?—Rory, Ted, none of the names meant anything to her, who were they to Charles?

She pressed the call button for Nancy but, before it connected, she heard the sound she'd been hoping for. She turned the phone off and slipped it back in its hiding place, limping to the window looking for the cab that had pulled up. But the car outside wasn't a black cab, didn't have any taxi signs on it.

The driver and passenger got out, one car door clunking closed, followed by the other. No need for stealth; the neighbouring units, an advertisement agency and a photographers, had closed for the night. The men looked around, one heading in her direction, one the opposite way round the building.

It's not safe there, Charles' exclamation in a quiet street

mocked her now. She scrabbled at the keypad into his lab ante-room. Please don't have changed this one either. Bleep, bleep, bleep, bleep. Eva pressed enter.

Green light. Shoving the door open, she threw herself inside and forced it closed.

The office door burst open.

The lab ante-room door clicked shut.

Eva charged past the bunny suits of protective clothing. A slam behind her as the man crashed into the door, hammering on the safety glass.

She heaved the lab door open, rushed inside, letting it close on its automatic closer. She winced as the man shot out the entry pad to the ante-room door, thumping on it, then shooting at the safety glass, when it wouldn't open. Didn't matter how much shooting he did, her opening the lab door had activated the airlock, he'd have to wait thirty seconds for the system to reset.

Thirty seconds.

The guy fired into it enough times she hoped he'd emptied his magazine while she hurried to the bottom end of Charles' kingdom. She slapped at the green button on the wall to release the fire exit door. Then she saw the driver, turning, realising he was looking in the wrong place for Charles' lab, sprinting towards her.

Outside Eva would have had a chance, always go for the getaway, she'd heard it bandied around MI6 enough times. But right then she couldn't run anywhere, couldn't reliably walk even.

She had more chance in the lab, if the door shut in time to keep the running towards her driver on the outside.

The fire exit closed over a laugh coming from behind her. The lab door had released.

"Now we get to play Jurassic Park, I'm the velociraptor and you're the kid."

The lab where Charles cooked his chemical formulations, made individual substances bend to his will in concoctions that behaved like magic, was like a kitchen. He had his hi-tech housed in chrome and white, with the lab benches set out in long rows. She understood the guy's reference. A tiny thanks to Charles for opting for such a big lab for just him and his occasional assistant, the space gave Eva half a chance.

The man's slow footsteps teased down the row of lab benches in front of Eva. "Except I'm way smarter than an extinct dinosaur. Plus I have a little twenty-first century help."

If she could get up to the top and reach the lab door before he realised her plan, she'd have another thirty seconds to put some distance between them.

"Let's play a better game." He was enjoying this.

A crash of breaking glass from where she wanted to get to made her freeze. Eva crab-scrabbled up her row, stealth abandoned now as another crash got closer to her.

"Having fun yet?" He shouted, his voice muffled now. She shot a look at him advancing on her, the other side of the first row of lab benches. The respirator he wore signalled his intentions. "Let's see how good a chemist I am." He lobbed a glass flask towards her that fell short but hissed and fizzed on the white floor. He pitched another, the liquid inside puddled amongst the broken glass. "That's boring."

He emptied the cabinet closest to him of flasks, pitching them onto the floor, at the walls in Eva's general direction.

The driver was banging on the fire exit door but his partner was all caught up in his boasting how long it would take him to hit upon chlorine gas, see how he'd have some real fun when he knocked her out. Beneath the bench beside Eva stood a padlocked cabinet. She changed the combination to the same code as the door and pulled.

Not right.

Eva tugged the padlock. Another crash. The air was tainted with the sharp unpleasant tang of chemicals making her cough.

He'd better be thinking like a normal man there, Charles, or she was in trouble. No mathematical sequences for the combination, please. His birthdate? No. Lily's? The padlock snapped open. Eva scrabbled out a flask in each hand.

"I can play this too." She stood up as the man spun round towards the sound of her voice and threw them both at him.

Speed of light fast, the chemicals ignited when the glass broke, one on the floor, the other on his chest. Faster than she could comprehend, the man was a fireball.

His blood-curdling screams, unmuffled now, chilled her even over the sudden blare of the alarm. It was a terrible way to die. The automatic response from the fire brigade would take too long. She dithered in front of the fire extinguisher array. What was it Charles always said about the hazardous stuff? Flammable on contact with air and/or water, she grabbed up the CO_2 extinguisher and fired it at the man writhing on the floor.

Eva squeezed the trigger until the extinguisher was empty, long past when his screams stopped. Gasping for air, she realised her mistake. She almost collapsed against the fire exit where the driver leant against the outside of the door, shaking his head at her.

She dragged herself away. The other door then, but it was so far. Her lungs screamed as she scraped in a breath that had nothing in it, the oxygen gobbled by the CO_2 she'd sprayed everywhere. A lurching stagger past the burned man and she could pull in a scrap of a breath. Dizziness made her crash into the bench, drop to the floor. Come on, get up.

She pulled herself onto her feet, gripping the bench like a crutch. The lab wavered, mirage-like. Eva pulled herself along it, half a breath. Another step, thank Charles again for the size of the lab. But it was his space, and all that that meant was disastrous.

A warning siren split the fire-alarm into a whisper. A sun-bright light strobed Eva's vision.

Another step.

"Warning." The computer generated voice sounded like every sci-fi disaster movie she'd ever watched. "Air purge in ten seconds."

23

L uke selected the feed option from the last of the five cameras he'd placed that day. Not as choppy as lapel cameras tended to be. Had to love the twenty-first century, the tech got better every time he used it.

The wearer of the jacket to which the tiny device was attached lowered himself into a seat, sighing out his inconvenience, but there were worse places to wait. The light was too muted, but what Luke hoped to see wouldn't play out there in the dark wood-panelled corridor but, with everything going to plan, in the office beyond the self-important door opposite.

He scrolled through his other feeds while he waited. Still no one at Eva's house. He'd apparently dropped the ball on that one.

The office door opened and the camera feed picked up a back-lit woman Luke knew was Anna Bailey, wrapped up in a dark coat. Maybe it was the plush carpet's thickness, the reason she wobbled on her high heels, rather than the surprise of seeing an ambush.

"Gordon, you're waiting to see me?" She looked around

as though someone else might have materialised who could be used as an excuse to put him off.

Gordon Stamford heaved himself to his feet and fetched up a dilapidated briefcase. "I am, Anna, a word?"

"I didn't miss an appointment."

"I didn't have one."

"My assistant didn't tell me you were waiting otherwise I'd have seen you earlier."

Otherwise she wouldn't have seen him at all, but her bluff was believable.

"It won't take long, one whisky."

"A whisky discussion?" her voice rose. "You'd better come in."

The light was more Luke's ally in there, he could see her and her surroundings clearly. Richer and grander than the workaday spaces, leaded-light windows behind her desk reached up towards the high ceiling in stone arches that had seen the comings and goings of men plotting and scheming through the centuries. The secrets those walls could share. What must they have thought when a woman took the office?

Bailey slipped her coat off and poured a generous measure into two crystal tumblers, sauntering to where Gordon had settled himself into one of two easy chairs facing each other. More in control of her heels in there. A flatter carpet or she believed she was driving this.

Luke waited for her to discover his tech, but she held out Gordon's drink and sat opposite. No handheld scanner, Director General? You trust too much in the gatekeepers at the entrance of Thames House, outdated already as it had let the lapel camera through. He wanted to know if would have picked it up had she used a scanner.

"Your good health."

"And yours."

"Why not an official visit?" she asked.

The camera studied the face of the woman opposite it. Blonde hair, carefully dyed and styled, dark eyes made darker by her make-up, bright red lips, a brave choice for an ex-smoker, but no sunshine rays of colour gave her away. Her face moved freely, no fillers interfering with her reactions, masking her years of intelligence training.

Luke watched Gordon place his glass on the table beside them and withdraw a folder from his briefcase.

"Bit early for that. Still laying the foundations. I wanted to run something past you."

"Our remits don't coincide, Gordon. You should go through your—"

"Our remits are perfectly aligned, we all have the security of the country at the heart of what we do." He laid two photos on the table, turning them around so she could see the faces. "These people mean anything to you?"

"Ambassador Hunter Malone, of course. But killed on foreign soil, that's nothing to do with MI5 and, being an American national, nothing to do with Six."

Gordon leant forward to retrieve his whisky and the camera's line of sight showed the other photo, Tony Banks.

"He's deceased too, here in the UK."

"People die here all the time, it's not a matter for the security services."

Gordon's index finger tapped the man's photo, "induced heart attack. Then there's this man," another photo joined those of Banks and Malone, "a Duncan Leadbetter, who hasn't been seen since last month. There are links between them and her," he laid down another photo, "him, him, all of them." He filled the table between them with seven photos.

The Director General of MI5's gaze slid over them, dismissive. "And this concerns me or the service how?"

"The links are strong enough to suggest these aren't accidents."

"You want to share your intel." It wasn't a question.

"Is there a hit for hire organisation operating on British soil?"

Luke leant closer to the screen in front of him.

Gordon filled the silence while Bailey sipped her drink. "We don't need to insult each other's intelligence by pretending they don't exist, that we don't know about them."

Bailey raised an eyebrow. "You've been watching too many spy movies."

"You must have eyes on the most troublesome." Again Bailey thought she'd out-stubborned her guest. He addressed his whisky. "Me seeing you like this, off the record, gives you plausible deniability," He raised his glass to her, took a sip, "I'm covering your arse for you. If I went through official channels, well, we know how messy that would get with all the oversight."

"If such a thing were happening, anything on British soil would be MI5's remit, not yours." She enunciated her words a little too roundly. "Is there any proof these aren't just random deaths?"

"That's why I'm asking." Gordon leant forward, "We need your help to investigate this. While we believe its roots are abroad, it's playing out here on our home stage."

Luke peered at the camera feed. There it was. Her eyes tightened, just slightly. Very accomplished, Ms Bailey. Had her guest seen it?

"Do you have assets that could monitor these others?" Gordon was saying. "They're all British, on home territory."

She looked at the photos again, back at Gordon. "I'd

need some credible intel that their lives are in danger before I could consider deploying anything, we're all stretched."

Gordon finished his whisky, took his time putting his glass down, collecting up his photos. "Let's hope none of the others are taken out. Malone could be explained away, maybe Leadbetter needed a break away somewhere and he'll pop up some time." He tapped Banks' photo as he put it on his pile, "This one, this is the one I'm interested in."

"Why? Anyone with an interest in crime drama knows how to induce a heart attack."

"Knowing and doing are two different things."

When Gordon's lapel camera had filmed him leaving Bailey's office, Luke terminated the recording and leant back in his chair.

His phone bLeeped, Josiah's investigations complete. 'Banks' not our work, so far as I can tell, loose word is it's some group calling themselves The Society.'

Except Luke knew it wasn't.

In the shifting sands of this mission, he didn't need new orders to tell him his priorities had changed. Most urgent now was to figure out who thought they could get away with impersonating The Society.

Then show them they couldn't.

24

In the phone box, Charles replaced the handset. Tony, dead. Charles should have gone into hiding yesterday, at the least he needed to accelerate his plans.

He pushed open the door where Lily ambushed him from where she'd been playing imaginary hopscotch to keep warm.

"How much longer?"

It felt like only two minutes since she'd last asked.

"Not far now." At least this time it was true. "It's just down here."

Charles led her down the turning to the industrial estate that housed his lab and office, put his hand on her shoulder. "Wait." He could hear an alarm. "You wait here."

"By myself? You're going to leave me, a girl, on my own in this deserted place without my phone? Seriously? Do you ever watch the news?"

What was he thinking? She was right, that wasn't a solution. "Stay close."

Lily huffed. "I'm trying to."

She walked beside him over the grassy corners to the

entrance and while he led her to the back quarter of the site. The alarm got louder with every step. They must have triggered the burglar alarm getting in. No automatic response—he didn't want anyone looking at what he was doing—but the thought there might be may have chased them away.

Charles knew his lab was under surveillance, as if he'd installed the cameras himself. The man who watched was only too aware of the hold it had over him. Partly why he gave him unlimited funds to pursue whatever piqued his intellectual curiosity, whatever could turn a good profit for both of them. Every scientist's lottery win Charles thought he'd already paid the price for.

Until now he'd thought it of no real consequence but with Duncan's disappearance, with Hunter's assassination? That meant only one thing, attacks coming at him from both sides. Tony's death gave him no clues where it would come from, only the deepening certitude that he was next. Charles looked behind him again, staring into the darkness, almost willing an apparition in black into being. At least then, in a physical form, he'd know what he was dealing with, who it was after him.

"This is where you work?"

"Ssh."

He couldn't see in the lamppost-lit darkness, but Lily would be rolling her eyes. Steering her to the perimeter hedge, they approached the building from the rear. Charles grabbed her shoulder, leaning towards her to hush her.

"What?" she whispered. "The man?"

"Yes." He breathed.

The bulk of the figure in black silhouetted against the lit-up lab fire exit door was nothing good. Had Eva been followed?

"Let's try the other entrance." Charles led her to the office end of the building.

The fire alarm box set above the open door was flashing, the entry keypad was in pieces. No smoke, a possible ruse on Eva's part. Hackneyed, but effective. He led Lily up onto the grass bank on the window side of the lab.

"Can you wait here, I'll get Mum."

"Go, I'm fine here, I know where you are."

He left her there, Eva would be cross about that.

The clamouring alarm in his office was deafening, making it hard to understand the strident countdown.

"Three, two, one. Purge."

Purge?

What had happened there?

He kicked the bullets and casings stacked up in front of the ante-room door out of the way and peered in between the opaque indentations in the safety glass. He'd been right to be stringent over his lab security. That would have saved Eva.

The automated system let him through the ante-room but locked him out of his lab until the reset was complete. Nothing untoward, but there, broken glass on the floor. Whatever had been in that flask could have triggered the purge, but—Eva! Charles banged on the door, twisting from side to side, but he couldn't see more of her than a snatch of bright blonde hair and a red down coat encased arm flopped on the floor. He shoved the door, even though he knew the system would hold it closed while the safety purge sucked the contaminated air out of the lab and replaced it with clean.

Eva didn't have that long.

He charged back in to his office, waking up his PC.

Come on, come on. He logged in, hit enter harder each time until he reached the purge over-ride.

Purge activated, the welcome message told him. Yes, yes, he knew that. He clicked on release lab doors. Enter password, the machine replied. That would release the fire exit, let the man outside in. He'd be armed. But perhaps they were only there to take her hostage, use her to strong arm him into paying what he couldn't.

To survive anything, Eva needed oxygen. He entered his password.

Incorrect, the system admonished.

The alarm shrilled against the inside of his skull. He tried again.

The programme welcomed him in with all the options. He clicked on open doors.

How long had it been?

He raced into the lab, barging through the door before it was fully open.

The smell hit him first, the sharpness of chemicals in the air caught at his throat, made his eyes run, made him gasp, but the air was so thin he couldn't pull it into his lungs. What had been spilled to have triggered the alarm? Over everything, the thick, cloying stench of something burned.

A gasping, then oxygen, thick, welcome, cold. He pulled in the breath he was searching for.

Eva, coughing, gasping, held Lily to her.

"It's okay, Mum," Lily soothed, "you're okay now, we're here."

"How. . .?" Charles' gaze took in their daughter in the lab, the broken window she'd climbed through, the, "Is that a bin?"

"Sorry about your window." Lily's voice was muffled in Eva's hug.

"It doesn't matter. Eva, are you okay?"

"Lily saved me." She jerked her head behind her and Charles understood why she was holding Lily so closely. No child should see the burned husk of the man lying on his lab floor.

"We need to go," Even over the fire alarm, he heard the rising sound of sirens.

"Doesn't Mum need to be seen by the ambulance?" Lily asked.

Charles positioned himself in the way of Lily's view of the dead body. "Lily, can you go over there and hold that door open while I help Mum up? Keep an eye out for the firemen coming in through the office door." Lily nodded and did as he asked.

He brushed Eva's hair off her face. "Are you okay to go? You probably want to tell the police what happened here," he lowered his voice, "but you don't know these people, Eva. They will have already covered their tracks, the police won't find any answers to their questions at his end, which will make them more suspicious. We must go."

25

———

A lady with two white fluffy dogs that yapped at everything was the only person Eva, Charles and Lily had passed for the last few minutes. A taxi pulled up in front of them and a man in a suit jumped out and disappeared into the adjacent house. The taxi waited at the kerb, perhaps hoping they'd get in. Eva gripped Lily's hand tighter.

Charles stopped, Eva and Lily copying until the driver realised they weren't interested. While they waited for him to roar off in search of an actual fare, Eva murmured at Charles, "I need to talk to you about the men at your lab."

She couldn't put it off anymore, she had to tell him about Eric being killed. If the men had chased her to Charles' lab, they weren't safe anywhere, even on this mystery tour Charles was dragging them on.

"I've been thinking about it too, you need to know so you can be wary." She had to lean closer still to hear him, "I thought it was just me they were after, but it's not. They're called The Society, they're a group of assassins."

"A what? Why would they be after us? Who would want to kill you, Charles?"

"It's not safe for us to be out here."

He hurried away from her and Lily.

Eva held Lily to her, pulling her close, rubbing her back to make her warmer. It took about ten strides before Charles stopped, hesitated, then returned to them. "Eva, you don't understand—"

"Damn straight I don't because you won't talk to me. An explanation right now otherwise we're going home."

"I told you it's not—"

Eva stepped closer to him. "That man just tried to kill me and it wasn't the first time." He looked shocked, but she silenced him. "You owe me an explanation. If you're so worried about who's after us, we can fly to Sweden, Per's invited us." Charles shook his head. Of course he wouldn't want to see Per now, after his failed nomination. "We can go to India, I can check on the installation at Tirupudur—"

"No, we can't."

"I've got our passports with me, why not?" Eva hugged Lily closer, small comfort while her parents hissed their argument at each other. How damaging was that for her, knowing they were in danger, that men, faceless, nameless, were after them?

"They'll have flagged our names at airports, ports. Our passports are useless. We're going to see CJ, a contact of mine. He can help. He's our only way out. The longer you stand there, the closer these men get."

"Does this have anything to do with why you trashed our house?"

"I was looking for something, I thought Lily had it. Turns out I was right."

"You should have told me they were important." Lily

said, proving she'd been listening all along. "I'm not psychic."

"Locked away, Lily, in a hidden safe, I shouldn't have had to tell you not to break into it."

Eva looked from Charles, "We have a hidden safe?" to Lily, "You broke into a safe?"

"It's not that big of a deal."

"You're eleven, how did you know—"

"Does that matter?" Lily sighed. My parents, the Gestapo, her current favourite insult. "I just recorded the bleeps when Dad was opening it once. I've got an app that tells me what keys are the likely ones. Can we go now, it's cold."

"You have a safe-cracking app?" Eva dialled back her reaction, focussed on the important thing. "What was in it, this safe I don't know about?"

"A chess set Dad doesn't even play with." Lily, trying to justify herself.

Eva couldn't hold back her almost shriek. "This is about a chess set?"

"No," he jumped in. "It's about what's in one of the pieces, information that's been keeping us safe."

"From this Society?"

Charles shook his head. "Now's not the time."

"Now's exactly the time." Eva snapped.

"It's complicated."

"I think I can keep up."

Charles looked at Lily, shook his head again. He was right, Eva could have screamed. Lily shouldn't hear whatever this was, she already understood too much. Eva pulled it back to more general ground.

"The piece is lost, you can't get it back?"

"It was my wish stone," Lily said. "The whole point is to

lose it. It was Anya's idea. You take a token, something little that you can carry around with you, you make a wish and, when you lose it, you wish'll come true. I didn't know."

"Charles, something so important you couldn't have put it in a safe deposit box?"

"No, they're not safe." That word again. "We have to get off the street. I'll explain, I will, but later."

"Come on, sweetheart." Eva took Lily's hand, and they followed Charles into a street the mirror image of the one they'd just left, more two storey flat fronted, square houses, yellow brick with dark painted wooden window frames and doors.

Eva's coat smelt of the man burning. Every waft from the cutting wind blew his death throes at her, a punishment for what she'd done.

At least wherever they were walking seemed to be a nice area. At the last house at the far end of the cul-de-sac, Charles didn't knock on the front door but took a couple of steps onto the short front path and looked up.

He waited.

This was his plan?

"Mum, I want to go home."

"I know, sweetheart. We just have to wait while Dad does whatever he's here to do."

"Eva, Lily, come here."

They joined him on the path and he pointed at her and then his left hand, at Lily and mimed a pregnancy bump.

"Playing charades, that's what we've walked all this way for?"

Exactly what Eva was thinking.

Apparently Charles' charade was too difficult for the person in the house to guess. The front door remained closed.

Charles pointed at his watch and gestured an oval around his face. Eva had no clue. Some kind of code?

"We're freezing, Charles." She tried to hurry it along.

He strode up to the door and knocked.

"Is this CJ even home?"

He nodded.

No handy letterbox to shout through, so Eva took her growing anger out on the door.

"Eva," Charles chided, "you'll just make things worse."

"Will getting in there make us safer?" When he nodded, Eva banged harder, yelling. "Open the door."

She nearly hit the man who did. He was around her age, immaculately groomed, in a white linen shirt over white linen trousers, small rimless glasses. She'd have said he was a yoga guru, apart from his socks, brown with smiling pumpkins lined up in neat rows on them.

"My husband said you can help us, can we come in?"

Charles cut off his retort. "I'll forget about the extra you took in fees. But because you did that, know I'm in deep." Charles looked at Lily, began again. "I was counting on the right amount for something serious. Now I'm short, I'm on the hook for it. I don't have an issue with your higher fee, but you should have told me. As of now, I'm overlooking it." His cryptic comments were the open sesame they needed. The man stood back to let them into the narrow hallway. "CJ, my wife Eva and daughter Lily. We need your skills, of course I'll pay."

"Follow me." CJ led them into the warmth of what was probably the master bedroom in the surrounding houses, but in his was like something out of a sci-fi movie. Banks of hi-tech computer stuff took up racks along two of the walls and an enormous desk with four different size monitors straddled the other side of the room.

"What do you need?" he asked Charles.

Charles looked at Lily, back at CJ. "We need new passports, ours are broken."

CJ stared at Eva, his gaze roving over her bruises and grazes and the not so white dressing now. "Hers will be extra."

Charles nodded. "That's fine."

"It's not fine, we're not using our savings—"

"No, we're not, this is my money."

Another of the ties that bound her and Charles together as a couple, as Lily's parents, snapped.

"Your money? When did we become that couple with his and hers? What did you do, Charles? Is this why The Society's after us?"

"The Society's after you and you came here?" CJ's voice was low, his words measured into a threat.

"I can explain." Charles said.

"I wish you would." Eva couldn't help her sarcasm. She saw Lily's face. "It's okay, sweetheart, no one's after us. The Society is Daddy's new bank, and he didn't pay a bill. Isn't that right, Charles?"

"Yes." He nodded confirmation. "That's all this is. My friend, CJ here, didn't pay me everything I thought he owed me and I was supposed to give it to The Society so now they want the rest that I owe."

"But I don't owe you, do I, Professor?"

"No, it's a misunderstanding, that's all."

Lily looked from one to the other of the lying adults. She was far more astute than they gave her credit for, but maybe this time she just wanted things to be normal, to feel safe. She nodded. "Okay."

"And you're going to sort things out so your bank doesn't come after me." CJ added.

"I am." Charles' promise didn't sound sure of itself.

CJ got busy at the keyboard, typing in a cryptic conversation between him and a machine, network, someone. He pulled down what Eva had thought was a projector screen but was a curtain of two halves, bright green, bright blue.

"We're not doing this."

"Eva." Charles hissed-whispered, a parent telling their naughty child to behave themselves. "You want to go to India," he challenged her, "this is the only way."

"We're not using," she mouthed the words, "fake passports." She could sense her retaliation cracking open a distance between them she'd never wanted to feel again.

"I need your passports." CJ intruded into her sadness, alarm.

Charles held his hand out, but Eva shook her head.

"It's okay, sweetheart." Eva pulled Lily into a hug, reassuring, calming. Tired and confused already, she and Charles were adding to it. And neither could budge without—

She felt rummaging in her backpack, and CJ was catching the three things Charles threw at him. Snip, snip, snip and CJ had cut right through the covers of their passports before she could even protest.

"Now we've got the histrionics out of the way, stand in front of the green."

Eva looked at Charles. Charles did as directed, and CJ took his photo.

"Next."

"How can we pay for this?"

"I'm using an emergency fund." Charles said it like it was obvious.

"An emergency fund of thousands? How many is this blowing?"

"Lady, there's no blowing here, I'm the best."

"It doesn't matter how good you are, there's no way you can fool biometric scanners. No offence."

"Then you have no idea what you're talking about. If your husband's using me, there's a very good reason why. I'm not cheap."

"You have to trust me, Eva." The more Charles said it, the less she did.

"Trust that we're breaking the law?"

"It's the same thing as you in the lab."

"What's going on?" Lily's looking from one to the other of them sped up.

"I'm not using a—"

"Let me explain something to you." CJ pointed at Lily and shook his head, gesturing that Eva should follow him into the hallway. Eva closed the door behind her, catching him up downstairs beside the front door.

He moved so quickly she had no idea it was coming. Grabbing her hair, he pulled her head back. She felt something cold, hard against her taut throat.

"Who the hell do you think you are?" he hissed. "You don't come in here throwing around names that get people killed. Worse than that, you don't insult my work. I don't need to beg people to come to me, it's the other way around. Right now that's your husband, but no matter how hard he begs, he can't say anything that would make me help you." His threat was loud against her skin, making goosebumps rise at the back of her neck, her stomach churn. "I know people, you say anything about where I live, they'll visit you but they won't be as nice as me. And with that lovely daughter..."

Eva tried nodding, but he had her tight against his shoulder. "Glad you understand. You're leaving, don't come

back, don't knock on my door, do not dare disturb my neighbours again. Your husband and daughter are still in here
with me, remember that."

With a wrenching, he yanked his hand out of her hair
and propelled her outside onto the street. The front door
closed with her on the wrong side of it.

26

Eva held the back of her head where it felt as though CJ had pulled out a huge chunk of her hair. She stared at his closed front door. Charles would follow, he'd bring Lily, they'd come right out.

She crossed the road to stand behind a parked car, far enough away she hoped she wasn't an ongoing threat to that, that—who the hell did he think he was? She pulled in a breath that didn't have enough oxygen in it, let it shudder away.

They'd come out.

But the door stayed closed. One minute, two, three, four. Eva lightly stamped her feet, stepping side to side. A weight pressed at her chest. Charles wouldn't leave her out there. They were a team. Eva shrugged herself deeper into her down coat, but the hug she needed from it wasn't warm enough, wasn't reassuring at all.

The door opened. Eva stood still. They were coming. A single figure closed the door, the sight of her bright red bobble hat catching at Eva's throat. Lily ran over to her.

Eva gathered her into a hug. "You okay, sweetheart?"

"No, what's going on? He's a horrible man. What's Dad talking about?"

"I have no idea."

How long should they stand there waiting?

With every second that passed and Charles stayed on the other side of the closed door, Eva could feel an unravelling of them, as though an integral thread of their relationship was fraying away to nothing. Then, unanchored, they'd be adrift, the scaffolding on which they'd built their marriage collapsed in a heap of unknowing and mistrust. They were supposed to be forever, their reunion seven years ago had promised it, their wedding vows underlined it.

Frost had begun icing patterns on car roofs and windscreens when she allowed herself to acknowledge the unwanted truth and took Lily home, arguing with herself all the way. But there was nowhere, no one else. Eva's mother would put up with them for a couple of days, maybe even be pleased to see them, for the first hour anyway. Charles would understand where they'd gone.

But she didn't have to stay there. The relief made her legs feel weak. She could take Gordon up on his offer now, with no Every Drop work she could help him. Gordon could protect her, he'd said. They'd be okay, they just had to get through tonight.

It took until they'd turned into their road before Lily agreed to stay with their neighbour for a few minutes.

Eva rang Hugo's doorbell. "So sorry to knock so late."

"Eva, Lily, sweetness, it's no trouble, Cynthia is being quite the diva, aren't you, pet?" Hugo rubbed the ears of the dog he clutched in his arms. "So am I. It's far too cold to be standing out there waiting for her to do her thing."

"Hey, Cynthia," Lily ruffled the tiny dog's chest.

"Is it okay if Lily sits with you for a little while, I just have to run a quick errand and it's a bit late to drag her around."

As if on cue, Lily yawned.

"Of course, she can help me with the diva dog. I've got some flapjack I made earlier, all vegan, not so naughty." He winked at Lily. "Take as long as you need, we'll be good but can't promise there'll be any flapjack left if you're too long."

Lily smiled at Hugo, but her gaze at Eva tightened.

"I'll be quick, promise." Eva hugged her. "Thanks so much, Hugo."

When he'd closed his door Eva prayed the distance of bricks between his house and theirs would be enough to keep Lily safe, just for the few minutes it'd take her to pack.

Trying to be fast, silent, wanting to be far away from there already, she fumbled at the front door lock, let herself in.

Their house felt as it always did, if anyone was in there she couldn't tell from the hallway. She peeked in the lounge, a quick in out. Ridiculous, what would she do if she saw someone?

Still, she checked the kitchen diner and every room upstairs. All empty. Eva sank onto her bed, lay on her side, laid her hand on Charles' pillow. How different things were now than the last time she'd woken up there.

How did Charles know CJ? What work did he do for him? How could there be a part of Charles' life she knew nothing about? And then, in the replaying of his cryptic conversation with CJ, it hit her what he'd said, what it meant. He'd said he owed money to The Society. Charles, her stolid husband, obsessed only with his work, had paid a group of assassins. Her mind floundered to make sense of it. Who had he wanted killed? Charles, who have you become? She closed her eyes against the sadness.

Charles' urgent voice reached for her. Eva sat up, 2:00 am the alarm clock told her, she'd slept for—Lily!

Eva got up to go downstairs but from where he was pacing in the kitchen, something about it—his tone?—made her cautious, on edge, before she'd got halfway along the landing.

"Tell him he will speak to me if he knows what's good for him. I realise that you're an exceptional gatekeeper, but this is a life-and-death matter. Why else would I be calling. . .Get him out of it, he'll want to speak to me. . .He'll be more angry if you don't."

Who was Charles not happy with? Who was she now, eavesdropping on her husband?

Eva glanced at the front door, superseded by the remembered image of the green one she'd grown up with. Her and Daddy creeping into the house like cartoon characters trying to be quiet, fingers on lips, exaggerated tiptoeing. His eyes crinkled from his smile at her, "you can learn more from listening than talking." But it had only been Mummy in the lounge, on the phone, having a conversation Eva didn't understand. Daddy didn't want to go in and surprise her, so they waited in their half-frozen crouch, while his face changed until she reached for him. He swept her up into his arms, taking her back to the front door, opening it quietly, closing it loudly, calling out to her mother that they were home.

Eva understood as little now from Charles' end of the conversation as she had her mother's then. He stalked through the hallway out of the front door, closing it behind him.

Eva picked up the landline and pressed redial on the last number. When it was answered, she slammed it down.

Charles, what have you done?

27

"You know what time it is?" Nancy had never woken well in the middle of the night.

The sound of her grumpiness reached right into the heart of him, made him smile. "It's Charles."

Her gasp made him hope, she hadn't slammed the phone down.

"I. . .How did you get my number?"

He'd always had it, memorised it, followed it as it had changed, her address, her work. He hadn't been able to let her go all the way. But, careful, he mustn't make her bolt. "I need to speak with you. It's urgent."

"You're speaking right now."

"Not on the phone. I'll be at the all-night-café in Armstrong Street." He pressed down the peeling corner of one of the stickers plastered on the back wall of the phone box. It popped up again. "You still take your coffee black, twist of sugar?"

"No sugar these days."

"You might be grateful for it. Please, Nancy, it's red important."

To him, the silence between them didn't feel awkward, rather the recoupling of a shared past, two shared pasts. Was it the same for her?

"Red important?" No panic, a simple clarification.

"Yes."

The café's florescent lighting was a beacon in the empty street, Charles' footsteps the soundtrack to this ungodly hour as he walked towards it. The sparse traffic hum from the closest arterial road barely intruded there. No other sound to worry about. He opened the café door and stepped into the warmth, welcomed by the smell of bacon and coffee as though it was already breakfast time. A group of taxi drivers occupied the safest table, backs to the end wall, their cabs parked outside in a factory production line.

Under the guise of using the gents, he checked out the exit, a door past the toilets, no enclosed courtyard. Good. Funny how he thought he'd forgotten all that.

"Just tea?" the lad behind the counter looked like Charles had told him why he was there when he ordered. "Our bacon butties are legend, yeah."

"Too right, Rajiv, I could go for another one." The taxi drivers started a chorus of 'and me'.

Too noticeable not to after that. "Then I'll have one too, thank you. And a black coffee." He'd be optimistic.

He took a seat and waited, staring at the TV screen, the silent BBC News 24 with the yellow subtitles turned on. The odd sentence transcription could have been a good distraction, the gobbledygook that appeared on the screen funny even on another day.

And then nothing was funny. The assassination of Hunter Malone has been claimed by a group called The Society. The ticker tape dropped the bombshell on him with as much concern as it had proclaimed that The Met Office forecast this would be the coldest October for a decade.

Charles had never heard of them before Tony instructed them, and now they were everywhere. Why would they assassinate Hunter? He wasn't anywhere in the picture for failing to pay them. Unless—they guaranteed a remove to their clients, the one thing Jed would insist upon. People didn't change. Plausible deniability had been the guiding principle of his entire life.

Tony, so sure you'd hit upon the perfect solution by hiring a hit on the President while he'd ordered the same on us. He would have appreciated that irony.

Duncan, because he would have responded to Charles' red important messages if he had just gone away out of his own choice, Hunter, now Tony, they were getting closer. Hurry, Nancy.

His bacon sandwich was crumbs on the plate, the dregs of his tea long cold, and he'd moved to the safest seat when the bell on the door tinkled.

His insides somersaulted, the last seven years evaporated, and Nancy was there, sitting opposite him.

"You look good." Glorious, beautiful, the years apart wore well on her.

She shook her head, short, sharp, fast, like she was shaking water out of her hair. He'd forgotten she did that. "You don't get to say that." She peered at the cold coffee. "So confident I'd come?"

"I hoped. Rajiv, could I have another tea and coffee?"

"First name terms already?"

"The bacon butties are legend." Charles whispered.

"You want a bacon butty with that, lady? They're legend, yeah."

"Just coffee, thanks." Her smile creased into more wrinkles now, framing her eyes, at both sides of her mouth, lighting up her blue eyes.

"How 'bout you, guvnor, annuva?"

"Just the tea, thank you."

Nancy pulled off her bobble hat, she'd caught her black curls back in a ponytail, slipped her coat off onto the back of the wooden chair. A forest green jumper underneath, her favourite colour. "Why am I here?"

Charles' new passport in his shirt pocket pressed against his chest. Come with me, let's run away together. The words she'd wanted him to say seven years ago were right there. He couldn't hold them in. They whispered into the no-man's-land between their lives. Dynamite.

She let go of her coffee mug, reached for her coat. "You're seven years too late."

Charles held a hand out, hovering over the table. "I'm sorry, I didn't come here for that."

He'd meant to woo her, wean himself from Eva, and still he had things to action, to complete, but his heart galloped ahead of his logical mind. Why shouldn't the time be now?

"That's not your red important." Her eyebrows arched a warning that it had better not be.

"No, no, I mean it, with every fibre of my being, but I understand I have to earn your trust. I will ask you again, but for now I came to warn you. You've seen the news?"

She stayed in the chair, reaching for her coffee again. "Hunter."

He nodded, "Hunter killed, who could have got close enough to do that?"

"It wasn't the Russians?"

"Duncan hasn't been seen for almost a month."

She nodded, digested, waited. What he'd told her so far

didn't add up to red. So he dropped his bombshell. "Tony died from a heart attack."

The significance of that alarmed her. "Could it be an actual heart attack?"

Charles shook his head. What the news had shown him altered everything. He dropped his voice, "We need to get out, it's urgent. I've been working to a plan, it's nearly complete. I wouldn't have told you yet, not until it's ready, but," he spread his hands, "I'm not in control of the timetable now. What I can reassure you of is that I have a way for us to be safe and financially secure so we can disappear beyond his reach."

Nancy sipped her coffee. He felt the weight of her decision making. Decide the right way. Please.

"He has long arms, deep pockets," she told the pot of sugar sachets, turning it half anti clockwise, back clockwise. "If I'm doing the same old routine, living at my apartment, going to work as always, how can I be a threat?"

"Tony, Hunter, Duncan, wasn't that what they were doing?"

"We don't know their deaths are linked."

"We don't know they aren't."

"You're not thinking about your wife." Nancy's emphasis on the word was no more than he deserved. "What about your daughter?"

Of all the grey areas, this was the one he'd wrestled with the most. And he still had no answer. If he offered Lily the choice, she'd choose her mother. Knowing that didn't make it easier, make him not wish it were otherwise.

"He's made us all targets, Nancy. It's better if we just disappear."

"If I were to say yes, Charles, how could I trust you wouldn't leave again?"

He hesitated. Said out loud the justification for what he did to Nancy, what he would do to Eva, and by extension to Lily, it sounded cold, heartless even. In his head, in his heart though, it was all too tangled up with emotion. His motives were pure. Had always had Nancy behind them. Leaving Eva for Nancy had been the choice of his heart, leaving Nancy for Eva had been a duty for his and her future together.

He was repeating his own history by going back to her in a strange symmetry, an ever decreasing circle of their two lives until there was just him and her, joined by the tiniest symbol, the largest illustration of trust, a wedding ring. And he'd thought he was a pure scientist, no poetry in his blood. Nancy brought out the best in him.

He placed his hand over hers. This time she didn't draw away.

"I'm a cliché. Everything I've achieved has been for you, for us, leaving you was the hardest thing I've ever done." He nodded at her raised eyebrows. "You know me, all of me, deeds and misdeeds. Bigger than everything else was the pain of walking away from you. To do it again would break me."

He'd said it, laid his heart out on the table. Would she trample it or lift it up? He could scarcely breathe. His fingers on hers felt the lightest tether to his dreamt of future.

"I want to believe you," she said, "but I need time."

Time, it was perhaps more than he deserved, but it was the one thing they didn't have.

Nancy murmured her truth. "You broke my heart, it never mended right. I don't know how to trust you again." He held his silence, needing her to fill it. "Give me twenty-four hours. You have a number where I can reach you?"

Inside, Charles soared. "I'll call you, if that's all right?"

She smiled. What that did to him. How he'd missed it. "It's okay. I'll speak to you tomorrow." She put her coat and hat on. "Maybe not the middle of the night again. Try a civilised hour, around nine."

"I'll walk you home." Charles' feet tangled themselves up in his chair, the one next to him, the table leg, while he watched her, not willing to let her out of his sight.

She held a hand out to him and he grasped it, a drowning man hanging on to a lifebuoy. He was grinning as though he had won the Nobel. Hell, no, this was better than that. This was all his dreams coming true. And when his royalties started flowing, any day now, he could buy the security that would have come with the high media profile of the prize-winner.

"It's okay, you're a bit of a liability. Besides, you need to sort out Rajiv."

Their fingertips lingered together a long moment before breaking apart as Nancy left.

"My man, respect." Rajiv's reaction was so surprising, Charles fist bumped the hand he held out. "Made me totes emosh, worth doing the night shift for that right there, yeah."

So much for being inconspicuous, under the radar. But right then Charles didn't care.

28

The second mug deposited on Charles' table by the young guy manning the all-night café stopped Eva dead. She'd been so careful, but Charles had noticed her anyway? Was he calling her bluff? She traced the handlebar grip on Lily's bike with her gloved fingertip. He didn't play games.

Eva moved further into the freezing shadows behind a parked car on the opposite side of the road, jabbing her calf with the pedal. Lily was safe at Hugo's. His scribbled note through the door that he'd put her to bed, so they'd see Eva in the morning, a lifesaver.

She recited the reassurance over and over, trying to ignore the concrete cold leaching from the pavement up through her boots, a way to justify watching her husband.

It had to be for her, the drink, because it had to be cold by now. Clearly no one else was coming. Should she show herself, let him know he'd—As the woman entered the spotlight of the cafe's lighting, Eva knew she was who Charles waited for. She propped Lily's bike against the shop front behind her and stepped out from the camouflage of the parked car to see his face better.

Oh, Charles.

His expression, his hand hovering between him and the woman. How could he? Weren't they everything to each other?

The weight in her chest, the crushing of her heart, not felt since he walked out of her life twelve years ago, told her otherwise. The frigid air gnawed at Eva's hand, telling her to put it back in her pocket, that her heart wasn't going to shatter, didn't need her to hold it in place.

Charles, what are you doing? You can't. . .Eva could scarcely bear to watch his apparent truth in the way the woman and he held fingertips, drew apart.

The tinkle of the café bell rang loud in the silent night as the door opened on the woman leaving, the night moving on while Eva tried to hold her heart together.

The truth in heeled boots was walking away. Eva's numb feet step-limped, step-limped behind her into the next street, past a row of closed restaurants and nail salons. The woman turned the corner, the distance between them growing. Did she know about Eva, Charles' wife, about Lily?

"Hey!" Eva's yell surprised the night, made the woman jump. A glance behind her at Eva's all-in-black figure made her hurry away faster. "I just want to talk."

The woman didn't.

Eva sped up, gritting her teeth, trying to weight bear on her right leg. But rushing round the corner, a spectacular agony tore through her. Her knee gave way as if it wasn't there and she keeled over onto the stack of rubbish bags at the kerb. Her short, sharp cry sounded like a scream in the quietness. Clasping her knee, she screwed her eyes shut, seeing flashes. Hard edges dug at her back, into her side, as she rolled on the unsolid surface.

The woman was at the door of a small block of flats, the white ball of fur on the top of her hat bobbing up and down as she wrestled with a difficult lock. Eva wasn't that terrifying. She yanked off her beanie that her stitches had forced her to wear instead of Lily's cycle helmet. The bright beacon of her hair should reassure.

The chink of dropped metal and a cry—surprise, fear? —then the woman was running towards her. Eva elbowed her way up out of the grip of the rubbish bags. The smell of rotten food greased into her nose, whipping the churning in her stomach into a frenzy. Pushing, shoving, her hands disappearing into hard-edged crevices between slithering masses of food waste, Eva wrestled to be free.

The woman's heels rat-a-tat-tatted as she ran down the middle of the road. Then a new sound, London intruding. A car. An everyday, expected thing, until the crump. The terrible deadened sound of metal smashing into human, a half-strangled scream, the falling, falling, breaking of bones, ripping of skin, the almost unremarkableness of the car accelerating away.

Oh God, oh God. A whisper of a moan urged Eva, hurry. Her elbow jarred through the bags' contents, smacking onto the pavement.

Footsteps coming from where the woman had tried to get into the building. A long stride, rushing, not rushed. Someone else to help, thank God.

Eva's useless knee dared her to trust it.

Her mirror image dressed all in black knelt beside the woman. The man cupped her face; he knew her? Did she need mouth-to-mouth resuscitation?

"Is she okay?" Eva's question jolted him.

She rolled onto her side, levered herself up onto her hands, an awkward press-up.

He moved both gloved hands, one over the woman's nose, one over her mouth and her heels made a different sound then, a desperate drumroll.

"What're you doing?" Eva asked, struggling to get upright, awkwardly on her good leg, not trusting her damaged knee. "Hey!"

She took a step towards him. Her body screamed at her to run, get away, but she closed the distance between them with another awkward step, another.

"Leave her alone."

She sounded as authoritative as you'd expect an injured 5'3" woman to be when facing off against a man who looked like he'd just stepped off the cover of MMA Monthly.

He rolled up to standing, interlaced his gloved hands, pressed the palms towards Eva. Any hope she had vanished as she recognised him.

29

How was he there now?

Eva fled out of the street where the woman lay still in the road. The next was just as deserted. But by the first pile of rubbish, a gift. Eva snatched up a bottle from the box of glass recycling, rapped it on the pavement.

"You can't get away from me." He toyed with her. "Even without a bad leg, even if you hadn't killed my buddy."

Eva ran faster, harder in a clumsy limping that jarred her spine, screaming, screaming, screaming. She lunged for the end of the street. The man who'd taunted her from outside the fire exit door at Charles' lab sauntered behind her. His slowness, his assurance he'd catch her and make her pay, made her frantic efforts feel pointless.

"I might have made it quick, like for the other woman. But for what you did to him, I'm gonna make it real slow."

Her jacket hood cut into her throat, jerking her to a clumsy stop. Her throat was already raw. Someone must be able to hear her.

"I'm gonna make you scream like he did, you'll beg me to die."

Pretending both knees had given way, making her a surprising dead weight, she dropped to the pavement. She heard the air moving past her as his punch skimmed just above her head. He kneed the air out of her lungs, knocking her onto her side.

"Go on then, you're so hard. You think you can suffocate me too?" she wheezed.

He grabbed her by her throat and squeezed.

"Coward." she could barely force the word out.

He leant closer over her, closer. Close enough.

She snapped her arm up and stabbed his face with the broken-ended bottle. Again, again, until his grip loosened. He roared with fury at her. Eva jabbed with everything she had, catching his open mouth. She dragged her weapon through his skin. Warm drips splattered her face. Her grip on the glass was slipping.

She dragged in a raggedy breath and twisted away from him as a punch rocketed towards her, connected with the pavement. He yelled louder, rocked upwards, holding his ribboned face. Eva rammed the bottle at the side of his neck, scrabbled to her feet. Fled away from him.

Ahead, a beacon of safety. She burst through the café door.

"Call the police!"

"What's occurring?" The lad behind the counter looked up from his phone. "Holy crap."

"It's not me, it's not my blood. There's a woman out in the road, she was knocked over, I don't know if she's okay."

The guy got busy on his phone. "I know what time it is, listen, yeah, I've got a lady in here covered in blood, says there's another one knocked over in the street. You'll call it in and all that cop stuff?. . .Innit. . .Yeah, I can do that." He hung up and gestured at the phone. "My cousin, he's a copper, he'll sort it out."

"I need to check her—"

"You need to sit. Here," he was in front of her brandishing a handful of what turned out to be freezer bags. "I have to bag your hands for evidence. It's okay, he'll be here, he only lives round the corner. He'll check the lady, do all his cop stuff. You let me, yeah?" He gestured with the bags. Eva nodded. "Sit, come on."

She sank onto the chair as though her knee had given way again and held out her bloody, shaking hands.

"I'm Rajiv, what's your name?"

"Eva." She focussed on Rajiv, not looking at the table where Charles had broken her heart.

Happy that he'd done a good job of encasing her hands in the freezer bags, tied at her wrists, Rajiv brought her a cup of tea that looked like it could dissolve the straw in it.

"Strong and sweet, my mum swears by it. Tell you a secret, yeah, tastes crappy but it works."

They both looked up at the sound of more than one siren. "See, my cuz has got it."

Customers came and went, a surprising number considering it was still the middle of the night, tea and coffee drunk, bacon sandwiches, the smell of which made Eva's stomach churn harder, eaten, all satisfied with Rajiv's explanation, 'incident, yeah'.

"Eva," her name pulled her from her half-dozing state. "Are you hurt?" The man sitting opposite in a bright blue down jacket asked.

"Detective Elliott? Smith, I mean."

"Are you hurt?"

"The woman?"

He shook his head. "No visible blood on her, so where did this come from?"

"The man I saw kill her, he attacked me. Did you find him?"

"There's a unit outside, they'll take you to the station where you'll be forensically examined for evidence. Then I have a few questions."

Eva put her hand out to cup the empty mug, the freezer bag reminded her not to. "I couldn't save her, I would have, even though." She couldn't make herself say it, but that half sentence was enough for DI Smith to pay her more attention until she had to ask.

"Am I under arrest?"

"One thing at a time."

30

Eva stared at the table in the police station interview room at which she was sitting. Its hard rigidity looked ridiculously inviting. She wanted to cross her arms on it, lay her head down. She put her fingertips over her eyelids, rubbed them. It was going to take a lot more to get rid of the grittiness.

A sudden knocking at the door jerked her into her present. Thud, thud, thud.

"Eva, open up." An urgency not quite muffled through the wood.

She did as asked and DI Smith burst into the room, depositing two vending machine cups onto the table. He flicked his hands up and down.

"Coffee, not that great, but it's hot. Milk, no sugar, right?" She looked her surprise at him. "I watched you make us a drink."

"That's observant of you."

"That's what they pay me for. So," he closed the door and sat opposite her. "talk to me. You've had an extraordinary week, you've been around more murders than I have."

Eva focussed on the coffee. If they'd discovered the man who'd come after her at Charles' lab, he wouldn't have tied it to her yet. Either way there was no explaining that. Self-defence again, but from some shadowy secret order of assassins trying to kill her. Who would believe that? His next question would be why, and she couldn't tell him something she didn't know.

"Tell me why you were there in the middle of the night, when you're struggling to walk."

"I didn't—I forgot it." She went to rest her forehead in her hands, remembered her stitches. "I used my daughter's bike. I left it there, outside the café."

"A bike ride, that's still going to need some explaining."

She let her explanation drop onto the table, each word destroying something inside her. "I followed my husband, he's having an," she whispered the most terrible word as if it could make it untrue, "affair."

"With the victim?"

Eva nodded, swallowed hard. "I realise that makes me a suspect, but I didn't hurt her, I just wanted to talk to her. It sounds awful and you probably don't believe me."

"So tell me what happened." With a weighty sense of déjà vu she gave her statement while he wrote it down. His face remained deadpan, impossible to tell what he was thinking, where the questions would go next. Eva's gaze dropped back to the tabletop, the pen looked small in his hands.

When he'd read her the events of the night, encapsulated in the dry black and white of her statement, and had her sign it, he sat back in his chair, watching her.

She had to ask. "Are you going to charge me for what I did to that man? I carved him up quite a bit."

"From the look of your neck I'm minded to believe it was self-defence, but we'll see once we've accumulated all the evidence."

She touched her throat, another soreness. She was a limping injury.

"Once we've been through the CCTV footage from the area, we'll have a better idea of how things played out. In the meantime, don't leave the country."

She shook her head; he didn't need to know she couldn't.

"I'll take you home, you're probably still in shock, so go to bed. In fact, I'd say stay in bed for the rest of the week." His smile was more surprising.

Eva hesitated outside her front door. This was her home, it should be her sanctuary.

It would be again, once this was over. Part of finding out what the 'this' was might be found inside, if Charles had come back. And, if he hadn't, that confirmed her worst fears. Then how would she find him? Should she try? She hiccupped in a breath, her throat closing, nothing to do with her bruising.

Why had he done this? A surge of anger settled around the weight in her chest. She rammed the key in the lock, raised a hand at DI Smith in his car and let herself in.

The mess everywhere surprised her all over again. She threw her keys into the glass bowl on top of the tiny hallway cupboard. The tinkle summoned Charles to the top of the stairs.

"Eva? What are you doing here?"

Up the stairs, each step seemed to grow higher as she climbed them.

"Where's Lily?" he asked.

"Hugo's."

She searched his face, but Charles looked no different to how he had at CJ's when they'd last been together. Had she been seeing only lies since he came back to her, was that why she hadn't known?

"Who is she?" she blurted it out.

"Who?"

"The woman in the café, the black-haired lady you met." She said them as though they were just words, but each one splintered something inside her. He looked shocked, at least, sideswiped.

"You followed me?"

"If it makes you feel better, I wish I hadn't."

There was something different about him, a nervous energy fizzing through his veins. She was used to him pacing while he thought his deepest thoughts, but this was different, more. He fidgeted with the banister.

"Are you having an affair?" The word hit her hard, said out loud, but she had to hold herself together.

"No, nothing like that. I knew Nancy a long—"

"I don't need her name."

He nodded once, message received and understood. "What do you want to know?"

Nothing, everything.

"How long have you been seeing her now?"

"I haven't. It's not what you think, Eva."

"What is it then? I saw the way you looked at her."

"I. . .I needed to. . .The Society's after her, too. I had to warn her."

"They were, they just killed her."

The words punched him. She'd been too cruel, bursting out with it like that, wanting him to hurt like she was. But at the look on his face, she smothered her softening apologies.

"You love her." Her stunned whisper gathered strength, her pain hitting out. "You're in love with someone else." The pressing double weight of grief and betrayal on her chest stopped her breathing enough. In her heart it crippled her, in her mind paralysed anything else.

He loved that woman.

"How?"

Eva gave him a wide berth on her way to their bedroom.

"How?" Almost animalistic, his howl of grief and pain crammed into that one short syllable.

"She was run over, then a man suffocated her."

"You know this for certain?"

"I saw it happen, he tried to do the same to me."

Charles whirled away from her and ran down the stairs. He didn't care?

Eva closed her eyes as though that might shut it all out. She wanted to sLeep more than ever, not for the rest she needed but for the oblivion it promised. But Lily would be getting up soon, time for her and Eva to leave. And figure out how to explain why her dad wasn't coming too.

Eva stopped in her bedroom doorway. What? A brown holdall she didn't recognise was on their bed, and on the floor beside it, one of their big suitcases zipped up. Charles was leaving? Not what she thought? He was leaving. It was everything she'd thought, dreaded.

Downstairs he was slamming doors, Eva got in the shower.

She leant her hands on the tiles, bent her head, let the water pummel away the man's blood from her hair, from everywhere she hadn't been able to wash at the police station. She watched it swirl away down the drain as though it might take her pain away with it. Her gaze traced the patterns in the woven bracelets on her wrist. What would you say now, Daddy? How would you make this all better?

Dressed in leggings and a fleece, Eva inspected her neck. DI Smith was right: as clear as if he'd painted it on, the imprint of the man's fingers, all swabbed, photographed and measured at the police station, was bruising. She stuck a clean dressing over her stitches and went into their bedroom to pack.

"We have to go now."

"I see you're all ready to do that." She gestured at the luggage.

"Eva, after Nancy we're next."

"Lily and I are leaving soon enough. You can leave, it's clear that's what you want to do."

He grabbed her arm; she pulled it away. "Just go, Charles."

"Listen to me, they've planted something on the gas inlet pipe outside, some kind of timer. It could go at any time, make it look like we died in a gas leak explosion. We have to get out. Now. Get Lily, next door is still too close."

Eva hammered at Hugo's door while Charles warned the neighbours on the other side.

"Get out, there's a gas leak." Eva screamed over Hugo telling her something about Lily and breakfast.

Lily appeared at the kitchen doorway, holding Cynthia. "Lily, out quick, run!"

She did.

"Out, go, go." Eva pushed her from behind. Hugo, Charles and the other shocked neighbours following.

Halfway up the street, their charge petered to a halt. Was this far enough away? Should they tell more neighbours? Eva looked back. Their houses as solid and safe as always, brick exterior, curtains closed in the lounge bay window, the ones in their bedroom open. Built at the end of the Victorian era, these houses had survived the best efforts of the Luftwaffe during the Blitz. Solid, invincible almost, they'd witnessed generations come and go, the rise of the cars that now clogged the roads, the climate emergency that made the residents appreciate the plane trees planted at the kerbside. Yet they weren't safe from a fanatical group?

Charles had left their front door open, another departure from his methodical self.

"Have you called it in?" A neighbour asked.

Who to? Bomb squad, police, MI5?

"Do we just have to stand here?" Lily asked.

"You said no time to get anything." Eva pointed at the unrecognised brown holdall in Charles' hand.

"There isn't."

"What's in there that's so important?" It had to be more than clothes, the way he hefted the weight of it.

"We should go, we shouldn't be outside watching when it goes up, we want them to think they've succeeded."

"Shouldn't you have shut the front door then?" Eva looked at Lily. "Wait there."

"Mum, where're you going?"

"I'll be just two minutes."

"You might not have two minutes." Charles pointed out.

She knew where her father's memory box was, she'd need only one.

31

It wasn't the boom action movies had taught Eva it should be, but the drawing away from her of all the air, as if their house had inhaled it. A crumpled collapsing inwards and then the house sighed it out again in a concussive wave that knocked her backwards. Another collision with unyielding concrete.

She lay where she fell expecting a rain of debris to sear her skin, stab and maim, like in her father's photo. But maybe he had a hand in directing it away from her because nothing hit her. She staggered to her feet, her ears ringing a loud silence.

Their house had imploded into a tangled mass of bricks and wood, plastic, roof tiles. Fires sprouted where the gas fire had been, where the oven was, spreading over the debris, seeking anything flammable. The houses on either side were okay, if not leaning towards the mangled mess that had stood between them for so many years, as though bowing to their fallen neighbour.

Lily, Charles and the others got to their feet, their shocked faces popping up on the other side of parked cars that screamed their indignation at the disturbance in flashing hazards and beeping.

"Mum!" Lily screamed.

"Stay there, I'm coming."

Lily hugged her tightly enough to hurt. She was safe, that was the important thing. Eva's memory box, it was gone, nothing left except for the bracelets she could feel on her wrist, the tiniest of comforts.

A far away siren penetrated the fog in Eva's ears. No more police questions.

"Thanks, Hugo, for having Lily last night. I'm so sorry about this." Eva waved a hand at their street, they'd all have to be evacuated while the non-existent gas leak was checked out, while their homes were made safe.

"I was going to redecorate," Hugo stared at his house. "No excuse now."

"I'm just taking Lily to find a toilet."

He nodded, distracted by a wriggling Cynthia, staring at the shocking scene as though he could wish it into being normal.

Charles followed them while Eva limped past the coffee house to the internet café at the top of the high street. She chose the biggest chocolate extravaganza for both of them and looked the question at him.

He handed her a couple of twenties. "Just coffee, I'll be back in a moment."

Eva barely processed his words, what his absence might mean. "Go wash your face, sweetheart."

When Lily rejoined Eva, her face lit up at the pile of marshmallows, cream and chocolate sprinkles in the biggest mug the café had. Oh, to be eleven and believe everything was right in your world no matter what happened. And that, despite all the evidence to the contrary, your parents had everything under control.

Eva couldn't help herself. She'd bought the minimum fifteen minutes of internet time and opened a Google tab, closed it, tried again on DuckDuckGo who promised no tracking. She'd pretend she didn't know someone like CJ could probably still follow what she was doing. It wasn't a secret anyway.

She didn't have to go any pages in this time to find mention of the unrest at Tirupudur. It was hard to see the scenes of desperate people pulling the aerial network of water pipes down, the precious resource it carried being spilt onto the shacks and into the dirt. Fury spilled like the water through the streets, fuelled by old fears the people had believed forgotten. Betrayed and frightened, Eva understood why they were so angry. She needed to get out there.

Charles reappeared while she clicked into the next article.

"What's happening?"

"More sickness at Tirupudur, there's fighting, people are angry."

He leant in closer and peered at the photo of the unrest. "They shouldn't be pulling the pipes down, they're keeping them safe."

"They think it's the water that's making them sick."

"They shouldn't be pulling the pipes down."

Eva closed the browser. It felt like torture not being able to do anything, to show them Every Drop was only trying to help, to push to get samples tested, to figure out what was causing this. To fight it.

"There you are." Charles held out a box to her. A knee support. "I thought it might help, make things easier for you."

"Thank you." The stiff formality of strangers hurt, but she didn't know what they were now.

"We can't stay here." Charles murmured when Lily went to get another serviette and a packet of crisps.

"Let her be, she needs to eat, to—"

"I meant in the UK."

"I can't go anywhere, your 'friend' took care of that."

"I persuaded him to do you a passport. We all have new ones."

"Fake ones." Eva couldn't keep the snap out of her voice.

"Does it matter if they get us out of here?"

"And go where, with what money? Your emergency fund will stretch to that, will it?"

Lily looked at them as if she could see the tension that curled between them. She placed the change coins on the table like they were made of dynamite.

"Can you get me some of those, sweetheart?" Eva lightened her tone. Lily nodded, went back to the counter.

"Can't you get one of your big shot donors to help?" Charles asked.

Eva sipped her drink. "I can't take advantage of a donor."

"You're not at Every Drop anymore."

How did Charles not look any different to the man she loved on the outside when his entire personality seemed to have changed?

"That's irrelevant."

"Not even to keep Lily safe?"

"Here you go, Mum." Lily handed her the crisps with a smile.

"Thanks." Eva pulled her to her and kissed the top of her head.

Lily nodded, nestling closer. "I knew you'd prefer salt and vinegar, I got pigs in blankets."

"You knew right." Eva hugged her tighter. "You okay?"

"I'm good, I'm with you." And that was her simple truth, the trusting warmth of Lily next to her, the slow crunching as Eva watched her taste testing each side of every crisp to find which had the strongest flavour. Eva would do anything to keep her safe. Paying an extortionate amount to the café owner for use of the landline was nothing at all on that scale. Breaking her code of conduct, the rules of her sabbatical, her word to DI Smith, less still apparently.

"Addison? It's Eva Janssen."

"A pleasure to hear from you." But the pleasure wasn't Addison Clarke's, it belonged to intense hazel eyes.

"Luke?"

"Addison has his calls diverted to me while he's overseas. Can I help?"

"I don't…"

"Try me."

"I was wondering if it would be possible to hitch a ride with him the next time he's flying out of the country, me, my daughter and husband." He might not have noticed her falter over that last word. "But if he's already overseas."

"He is but his jet isn't. Where do you want to go if the world's your oyster?"

"Tirupudur near Chennai in India." She hesitated, but Addison probably already knew. "I'd like to check out what's happening at the Every Drop sites, it's a way of looking out for Addison's investment too, but anywhere out of the UK would be great."

"Let me see what I can do."

32

Luke's seeing what he could do opened doors she'd never expected to walk through, right out onto the tarmac apron, where a half dozen private jets gleamed in the rays of cold sunshine.

"Oh my God, are we going on a private jet? This is so cool. You have to let me get a photo of this, Dad."

Charles handed Lily her phone. "Just the camera, no internet."

Luke came down the steps of the closest gleaming plane. He smiled and held his hand out to Eva, drawing her in close, murmuring in her ear. "I quite like being your knight."

Eva snapped a glance at Charles, but he was more interested in checking the number on the tail.

"Hello, young lady. You all excited for your trip?" Lily nodded and grinned at Luke so hard you'd never know anything awful had happened to them that morning. "Let's get on board then."

The inside of the plane was more than she could have dreamt of. She rushed from seat to seat, undoing tables, reclining, straightening up, opening cubbyholes, stroking soft leather. "Wow, this is all so cool, Anya's going to be so jealous. Everyone's going to be so jealous."

"I just have to go over a couple of things with security. Passports?" Luke held his hand out to Eva.

With a flick of the cover he'd see she wasn't Sara Peyton and Lily wasn't Madeleine. Charles had gone through the biometric scanners at security while Eva's insides squirmed and her heart beat 'criminal, fake ID' against her ribcage all while she smiled at passport control and agreed that Madeleine Peyton was her daughter, keeping a hand on Lily's shoulder to guide her through the subterfuge.

Eva placed hers and Lily's on Luke's palm but rested her fingertips on them. "It's probably not a good time to tell you they're not. . ." She dropped her voice, felt herself sagging. "I'm sorry, someone blew up our house this morning."

"Hence travelling light." She nodded, even that an effort against her new bruises and scrapes, delayed shock and the exhaustion the promise of comfy reclinable seats had released in her. "And the hasty exit."

She nodded again, waved a hand at her front. "And the fetching look of building dust."

Luke looked at her passport. "It's a good one, I won't tell if you don't."

"Thank you, I'm—"

"You're not going to apologise again, are you?" He smiled, teasing her, but she couldn't help being defensive. "I'm not normally so helpless." The word stuttered out of her. She hated even the sound of it.

He touched her arm. "Take a seat. Last-minute security check, then we'll be out of here."

Lily was still road-testing everything in the cabin.

"Lily, calm down and strap yourself in somewhere."

"Sir, can I put your bag in the hold?" A woman in her early twenties looking catwalk perfect, everything manicured and hair sprayed away, held her hand out for Charles' holdall.

"No, I need to keep it with me."

"Of course, but I need to stow it in one of the cabinets for take-off." He relinquished it like he was Lily giving up her phone.

"Last minute security check, can I take your passport?" Luke asked Charles.

"Is it necessary?"

"If you want to take off. As the plane's representative, I have to call in the passenger details, additional measures. The pilot's a little busy finalising the fuel stops."

"Where are we going?"

"Chennai, as per Eva's request. Three stops en route. Eva's explained." Luke soothed. "It's fine, they're good, Charles."

"Maxwell Peyton, you mean."

Eva looked at him, that was the name he chose? Something grated at her.

"Maxwell." Luke held his hand out and Charles placed his passport in it.

Luke exited the aircraft.

While the air hostess readied them for take-off and Eva got Lily to sit still long enough to fasten her seatbelt, Charles threw a hasty "be right back" at them and followed Luke out.

"Bet the food on here's out of this world." Lily laughed at her joke. "Mum, that's funny."

Eva tried. "It is. What do you think they have?"

"Bet they have champagne, they've got to have champagne."

"You're not having champagne."

"Not for me, but in the billionaire books they always have champagne. Is the man who owns this a billionaire?"

Eva made the right noises at Lily's chattering, laughed when she did, all the while peering out of the window. Where were Charles and Luke?

"Take your seat please, otherwise we'll miss our take-off slot." The air hostess told Charles as he got back on and walked towards the cockpit.

Where was Luke?

Eva got out of her seat to look out of the hangar-facing windows on Lily's side of the plane. Was that—?

Running down the steps to the tarmac, around the rear of the plane, she gave the fired-up engines the widest of berths.

Just in sight from the plane, it was what she'd thought she'd seen. The upturned sole of a shoe, in which was a foot belonging to a leg, belonging to an unconscious Luke.

33

"Luke? Can you hear me?"

It was an automatic response to get to her knees to help him, even though Eva's body protested. More soreness from last night, this morning. She put her fingertips on his neck, his pulse beat against her touch.

"What happened?" Stupid question while he couldn't answer her.

No obvious signs of injury, no blood pool spreading out beneath him, no sweat on his face, no clamminess on his palms.

"Hello?" Eva walked around the stationary plane in the hangar, "anyone here?" Her voice reverberated in the immense space as she scanned the walls looking for a phone. The pilot, of course, he could radio the tower to get help. "Luke, I'll be right back. I'm just getting you help."

Out of the hangar, the space she walked through was unexpected. Where—What? Eva bolted three steps, five, until that becoming all too familiar star bursting of pain through her leg warned her to slow down. But not now.

Even running flat out, there was no way she would catch Addison's plane pulling away from her, taxiing towards the end of the private area.

She pushed herself after it. She couldn't see if Lily's or Charles' faces were pressed against the windows, hands hammering at her to save them.

Faster.

She gritted her teeth against visions of a car mounting the pavement, against an unknown deadly something lying in wait to blow up their house. The Society winning, after all. Eva stared so hard at the plane as she limped after it, willing it to stay in one piece, to not turn into a fireball, that her eyes ran.

Lily, no.

No, no, no, you can't take her.

Eva pushed herself harder, harder. Her mind screamed Lily's name. A siren from somewhere behind her; someone had seen her running onto the airfield like a terrorist. Good, they'd have to ground the plane. Eva turned to hurry them up, but it wasn't airport police, a fire engine, anything that might help, anything that made sense.

A silver van shot past her. Eva stumbled, pain flared, her knee only being held together by the support Charles had bought her. The runway was so far. But even as the plane rolled forwards for its take-off slot, she ran. Past the van as its doors opened and two men got out.

"Stop the plane," the words fell out of her, a tangled mass of not enough air, too much emotion. "Stop it, Lily!"

She limped on but something snaked around her, foreign hands that gripped and pulled.

"Eva, stop."

"Let me go. I have to stop them."

The man held her hard, barrelling her towards the van.

Making herself limp against him, rigid, trying to jump away, push herself off him. But he'd been trained for better efforts than hers.

She was in the van. The side door slammed to the roar of the jet thundering past them, lifting skywards, wrenching Lily away from her.

34

Eva lay where she'd landed in a rolling darkness. A light turned on above her, yellow holding back black. They'd carpeted the interior, the sides and roof too. Just her in the large space.

The leaning of high-speed corners and the forces of hard braking and quick acceleration eased. Out of the airport, she guessed, into regular traffic, but it was only a guess, no visual, no auditory clues. Who soundproofed their van? Eva shivered. Who were these people?

Stay aware, Evie.

Daddy, I'm trying.

What can you do?

She couldn't change what the plane was doing, where it was going. She pushed hard at the tsunami of panic that threatened to overwhelm her. Not now.

Lily. I'll find you, sweetheart. But first she had to get free. Think.

Stay aware, Evie, the most important thing. It had saved her father once when he'd been thrown into the back of a van on assignment, seized as currency. When there seems no way out, he used to tell her, you searched for the unexpected, always the best weapon.

His bedtime stories to her then had been a game. Pop quiz, Evie, what do you do if? But she'd never been terrified for her daughter in those games, her baby girl, an innocent. Eleven years old, heading into the abyss of words Eva couldn't think about. Breathe in, out, count it. The numbers, just think of the numbers. Banish the known truth, skipping at the edges of her reason, that some men paid fortunes for pre-pubescent children. Charles was with Lily, he would protect her.

The van stopped. Eva crab-crawled to the side door. No lock for her to undo on the inside. She hit the sides but the sound barely reached her ears, deadened to a flatness that no one would hear on the outside of the panels. So organised and thorough, they must do this a lot. She swallowed.

The brake lights. By sabotaging her knee support, she could use one of its hinges as a screwdriver. She ran her hands over the panels as the van drove off again. But her arm buckled, and she face-planted the rough carpet. A wide curve, a big roundabout?

Her captors had thought ahead of her; both brake lights screwed behind a wire cage she couldn't get her fingertips into, and the screws, too flush to reach, needed an allen key.

Eva sat back against the corner that gave her the best leverage behind the driver.

What now, Daddy?

His child had never been in danger, he'd only had to think about himself when he was. The van lurched forwards, braked quickly. The distance between her and Lily was the furthest it had ever been since Eva had first felt her kick inside her, the fluttering butterfly kisses of Lily's 'hey,

Mum, I'm here', since Eva held her tiny form, overwhelmed that this life was in her hands, since Eva had promised she'd be all the parents Lily would ever need. Always there for her, she and her baby facing the world together.

Eva mustn't cry, it wouldn't help anything. She made herself pull it back. Be aware. Look at it like an analyst. Okay, she spelt out in her mind what had happened on the airfield.

The hostiles had incapacitated Luke, not important enough to take? That made sense. Every unwilling hostage was a potential problem, needing resources to restrain, keep alive. So why split them up and take her somewhere different from Charles and Lily? Double sites, double teams, where was the sense there?

When her father went missing, he had the Army looking for him. No one would miss Eva, no one would guess at why she'd disappeared, no one would look for her. She was on her own.

The world was a big place, Lily one small child. Eva couldn't get a breath. Pins and needles prickled in her hands. She had to stay able to function. Not enough oxygen. Lily. A darkness hovered, all seduction, no pain there, no worry, no dread, no terror, no facing making it all worse.

Her hands were clawing in on themselves, the edges of the darkness at the corners of the van solidifying, a curtain falling over this nightmare reality.

What had they injected her with?

Cramp tore up her left calf muscle. Eva screwed her body up against it, a living rigor mortis. No injections, there'd been no time for anything like that in their snatch and grab of her. A panic attack, she must be having a panic attack. Out, she had to breathe out, slow it all down.

Be ready, that was all she had. Too late now to be

wishing she'd taken Gordon's long ago offer of a field position and all the useful training that came with it, self-defence, offensive fighting, getting out of situations like this with a paperclip.

Eva felt her weight against the panelling behind her increasing as the van nosed downwards, a steep slope, taken cautiously. Parking ramp?

Slow driving, manoeuvring, then the engine switched off. Wherever it was they were going, they'd arrived.

Eva positioned herself in front of the side door. It would open to her left, where would her abductor stand? Further down she'd guess to accommodate the sliding door.

Slam, slam, the driver's door, the passenger's, the two men were out. She was wearing flat boots, no heels for stabbing. No keys, no jewellery apart from her wedding ring, her engagement ring. No help to her at all.

The side door clicked and began its path back through the runners. Eva shot out, a bruising misjudging of the widening gap. Her feet to the tarmac, her knee paying the price, hobble-sprinting away. Just away.

"Hey!"

"Bloody hell—"

Eva wove her way round the cars parked in the underground garage. The overhead lights in the concrete-edged space did little to dispel the menace personified in the running feet searching behind her.

There, the raised kerbs of the streamlined passage for cars out through the exit. A black-arrowed white sign pointing to the right. Eva followed the directions, but the metal latticework of a shutter rolled down and locked to the floor barred her passage to freedom. Swipe card activated. Only a steep concrete-sided access road on the other side. No one to hear her scream.

She whirled away from the exit, searching for refuge amongst the cars parked nose to tail in the crowded spaces.

35

"**E**va!"

Eva leant against a pillar. If her knee would have let her, squatting behind the boot of the dark-coloured grimy car beside her would be better. Not being here would be better. Being held hostage alongside her daughter would be best.

"Eva, it's okay, you're safe now."

A woman, a voice she recognised? Out of its place and time, her mind floundered to identify it. Nora?

"Eva, come on out. We can't figure out where your family's gone while you're hiding down here. Gordon's giving you resources. I'm too damn old for a chase around the garage. I've got coffee on."

It really was her, standing in the middle of the car park.

Eva let Nora wrap her in the briefest of hugs, pulling away before she burst into tears.

"You're safe now. We're beneath our building. Sorry about the snatch and grab but we had intel you're a hot target."

"Lily, do you know anything?"

"Not yet. Come on, you look like you need one of Gordon's whiskies. We had to pull the guys off assignment to get you, hence the van, not a comfy car where they could have explained."

"I wouldn't have gone with them if they had. Lily and Charles are on that plane."

"We know, we're on it. Come on."

Nora deposited Eva at the ladies on the first floor. "First things first, take a shower, looks like you have half your house on you." Nora nodded at her surprise. "There's clean clothes in there," she gestured at the long locker beside the shower door. "Debrief next, two doors down on the right, I'll leave the door open. Take as long as you need."

Eva stood under the powerful stream of hot water. If only it could wash away everything out of kilter in her life. The pummelling on her bruises wasn't so bad, and as much as every graze stung, they were nothing compared to the tear at the heart of her, the ache in her arms to hold Lily. And Charles. She couldn't even go there. Thinking of the last few hours, dwelling on what she felt—no, she only had one focus, Lily.

Nora waited for her in the meeting room. "There you go, get that down you." She pushed two mugs across the table. "Start with the whisky. It's better than tea for shock."

It burned Eva's throat, made her shudder even as she embraced the warmth it spread through her, the unknotting of the fibres of her being. "Is there any news on the plane?"

Nora shook her head. "Too soon. I won't insult you by telling you not to worry, but we're working on it. Why weren't you on the plane?"

"I saw—what happened to Luke, Luke Fox? Did you get him too? They knocked him out in the hangar. He needs medical treatment." She looked around as though he might have materialised next to her.

"The guys only got you, Eva."

"Someone needs to check on him."

"Finish your whisky, give yourself five minutes. We're all playing catch up here."

Eva downed it, a longer shudder rippling through her that made Nora laugh. "Still not a fan?"

Eva tried to smile back. "I'll stick to G&T."

"Tell me about the plane, we might be able to get it grounded when it stops to refuel."

"It belongs to Addison Clark, maybe to the Clarke Foundation, rather than him. Luke Fox was with us, the guy knocked out in the hangar. He's been working with Addison. Flight crew, I'm not sure how many were on the flight deck, one steward. Charles had some ridiculous idea that it was too dangerous to take a commercial flight, that there'd be a border alert for us. He got us fake passports."

"Since when does your husband practise tradecraft?"

Eva spread her hands, steadier now. "I have no idea. It seems that I don't know him at all. He has secrets I can't even guess at."

Nora laid a hand on Eva's arm, her bright red nails stark against the black of Eva's fleece. She squeezed in an 'I'm here for you' way. "We all have secrets."

But Eva's weren't going to get them killed. "How did you know where I was?"

"If I told you, I'd have to kill you." Nora smiled at the age-old joke, underlining that, as at home as she felt right then, Eva was an outsider. "What's the plane's destination?"

"Chennai, India. Three stops on the way.

"How's our guest?" Gordon filled the doorway of the meeting room.

Eva tried a smile. "As good as you'd expect."

"We'll get our best people on it, we'll find them."

Eva nodded. She was lucky, she had access to resources that would help find Lily. In the meantime she could punish herself with the worst imaginings or she could give back.

"Use me while I'm here. You've got me as a captive audience, let me do something. I can free up someone else so they can find my daughter."

Gordon smiled as he slapped a folder down between them and sat opposite her.

"Am I so predictable?"

"Not quite, bit longer and Nora would have won our bet. She thought it'd take another hour before you offered." There was something comforting about being around people who knew you better than you knew yourself. "There's been another high-profile incident today, Aleksandr Oblov, collapsed in a London street."

"The Russians are killing off their own?"

"He's not dead, as far as we can gather, but we're not in the loop on it. This is Five's territory. Oblov's bodyguard took him home and there's been no reports of emergency services attending the property, we assume he's there, recovering." Gordon slid a piece of paper towards her, his fingers holding it face down. "Eric wanted to ask you about this, still time to walk away."

Eva made a spiral motion with her right index finger, and he turned it over. She emptied her mind, pulling on her analyst's training. Lose the preconceptions, the bias. What could she see in the copied photo? A row of shop fronts, a high street. Three Union Jacks fluttered to the right, obscuring some shop names.

"You have a magnifying glass?"

Nora produced one, watching while Eva ran it up and

down the picture in regimented rows, taking in the thatched cottages, yellow hatched markings on the road that led to an out of shot school. A perfect English village.

The contents of the shop windows told her what they were, a butcher's, bakery, post office, outside of which was a red pillar box, neighbouring a pub. The Red Lion, the most common pub name in Britain, it could have been anywhere in the country. A row of little cottages marched off the edge of the page.

It looked a nice place, a safe place, far away from assassins. Eva shut down the panicking spiral in her mind. What was she seeing?

Gordon passed her another photo, a small garage with two petrol pumps, a hairdresser and corner shop in that one. A building that could only be a village hall ran off the page on the right. The flags waved to the left, the other side of the street.

A man and woman walked along the pavement, but the image's resolution wasn't good enough to make out their faces.

Gordon handed her another page, the middle portion of the one she already held blown up beyond confusion. The surprise of a much younger Charles linked arm in arm with a dark-haired woman stabbed at Eva, their smiles hurting. It was her.

Focus, be professional. What did she see? Charles visiting the woman in her home village? She peered at his face through the magnifying glass. He looked so young; it had to be before his PhD, before he went to Uni even. He knew Nancy before he ever met her. She didn't want to think about that.

"Any idea when it was taken?"

Gordon shook his head.

It was simple enough maths.

"Charles looks about 18, so it's around the millennium. But it's not. . ." she peered at the photo again, minutely inspecting their clothes, the things in the shop windows. They didn't quite fit. "Where is it?"

"There were no satellite co-ordinates in what Eric dredged out of the archives." Nora said.

She moved the photo to the side, unable to not ask. "Who's the woman?" Trying for nonchalance.

Gordon spun the file round for her to see a closer shot, Nancy Seymour, the caption said.

"I saw her last night, she was killed right in front of me." Eva touched her neck.

"Do you know why?" Nora asked.

"Charles has been. . .I thought he was being paranoid." Knowing everything might help them find him and Lily so Eva asked. "Have you heard of The Society?"

"What's that?" Gordon asked.

"A group of assassins after Charles."

"Why?"

Eva blew out a breath. He'd told her half-truths, started sentences, but never finished them. She shrugged. "He wouldn't say."

"We've heard the name more frequently." Gordon said. "How does Charles know it's them?"

Eva shrugged. It didn't hurt so much, even after today's extra bruises, perhaps the words would be easier too. "He owes them money. I followed him. He met her in the middle of the night to warn her about them, he said, but he didn't say why they'd be after her. When she left, I followed her, but she was knocked over, then suffocated. The man tried to kill me too, but I was lucky. The police have the full details if you need them, you can use the e-fit I did with them."

"Did you hear her speak?"

Eva shook her head, she'd almost called her. But she had called Tony, who was also dead. "Aleksandr Oblov, you said. Is it the Russian spelling A-l-e-k-s-a-n-d-r?"

Gordon nodded.

"They're connected, Charles, this woman, an Aleksandr, the Russian spelling, and a man called Tony who just died. I don't know his surname." She thought back to the other names in Charles' hidden phone. "Hunter, what are the chances it's another? Rory, Ted, Duncan, people who mean something to Charles. This Society, they could be after all of them. What happened to Oblov?"

"We don't know enough."

Eva pushed the close-up of Charles and Nancy aside. Nancy, not such a British name. "Background on the woman?"

"Works for the European headquarters of a global mining company, not senior enough for leverage there."

"And their shared history?" Eva forced herself to ask, to look at Gordon for the response.

"No intersects we can see."

Which told its own story, given how they'd been together. How Charles had looked at her. "What do you think this is?"

"We're not sure, but we have this." He showed her another photo of the street, clearer resolution, and, in the zoomed-in image, not much had changed in the shop windows. The satellite shot showed a man just holding onto a thin ribbon of white hair at the back of his head, talking to Charles as he looked now. He'd been there not long ago.

"Is it a charm school?" Eva shook her head. "Twenty years ago, maybe?" She looked at the more recent photo. "But now?" That's ridiculous.

She looked at Nora then Gordon.

He played devil's advocate. "Even then, with globalisation, what need is there to train operatives to pass as British citizens?"

"Has it changed," Eva asked, "their raison d'être? It might be old school spy craft, but the endgame of those running them must be the same: to infiltrate the enemy and operate incognito to further their own state's interests? Question is, who's our enemy here?"

"Indeed." Gordon nodded.

Inklings made concrete, the way Charles had told Luke his fake passport name, Charles' life or death phone call. "Jesus." Eva breathed.

"Unlikely to be him." Gordon said.

She could understand now why Eric had come to see her. During the Cold War, it had been one of their best kept secrets that the Russians had been training operatives to pass as American for years. But something about these photos was a bit off. Something Eva couldn't quite place. Could it? No, but it was the only answer that made sense. But no sense at all.

What was that saying? Eva would bet dollars to doughnuts Eric had reached the same conclusion as her.

"It's definitely not the Russians, there are too many flags. The Russians aren't training there to be British, the Americans are."

36

I t would be quicker to walk. Charles was counting out notes for the fare when the battered taxi leapt forward in the jolting kangaroo style that seemed to be the only way the driver knew how to drive. Elbow on the lowered window, he smacked his palm on the roof of the car, his ring tapping out a metallic 'and we're off' in time to the vehicle's lurching.

Charles fanned his face with his passport. Funny how it didn't feel strange to be travelling as Maxwell Peyton again. He knew it might raise troublesome questions, but it had felt too compelling to not use it when CJ had asked for his new name.

Lily looked everywhere. "Dad, look! Did you see that? Did you see it? An actual snake charmer, with a snake. They really exist. I thought it was a made-up thing. Dad, Dad, did you see it?"

"No, but I'm sure we'll have time to come this way again."

"You have to let me take a photo of it." Charles' smile at her enthusiasm felt wrong. A heavier thing than all the trickery and planning. He stared past palm trees and motor-bikes and Eastern-influenced buildings, seeing only black curls and dark blue eyes, ringless fingers on a white table-top, a heart-stopping smile. Hearing the hope held within the words 'give me twenty-four hours', smashed with Eva's abrupt 'she just died.'

The logical part of his brain saw the irony that his wife, whose heart he'd been preparing to break, had instead broken his. His other half raged at her—she should have saved Nancy, and at himself—he should have warned her earlier. Then he'd be as excited as Lily being there and at a future together.

His breath shuddered out, not now. Time enough to grieve if Terry let them in, gave him the space he needed. It was a small mercy being with Lily, Charles didn't have to pretend so hard he was okay. And she wouldn't ask him pointed questions he couldn't answer.

"I wish Mum was here."

Except anything about Eva.

"Well, you know her work."

"I know, I'm not a kid," she said as though she were. "I still don't get why she couldn't have said goodbye."

"We had to take off right then, so we didn't lose our slot."

"We could have waited for the next one, then Mum might've been able to come too."

"You see that?"

Lily followed Charles' pointing at nothing.

"What?"

"Keep watching, we might see it again."

"How can I look for something if I don't know what it is?"

For then, at least, Charles had circumvented the problem of his excuses for Eva.

The driver stopped like he'd run into a wall. "Is here."

They walked to the end of the street where it dead-ended in a series of stone bollards. Terry had always liked his privacy, being off-grid, foot access only would have sold living there to him.

A gaggle of people spilled out of a street food café, windowed walls covered in yellow paper, shouting animated streams of Arabic above the general din. Sun-bleached stone reflected heat back at them from the pavement and the road. It felt wholly foreign.

The passageway between buildings took them out of the direct sunlight into a cooler, hushed world, where their booted feet traced the footsteps of a thousand years of people. A handcart ahead of them made its jerky way, being pushed by a teenager behind, pulled by one in front. The one at the back, tall, skinny, white shirt pulled out over jeans, sleeves rolled up to show sinewy arms, turned around and smiled at Lily. Charles flicked a glance at her, but her stream of chatter didn't falter. He checked behind them, it could just be that she looked foreign. It could be something innocent, nothing to do with Charles.

A woman in a doorway to their right dressed head to foot in dark navy, embellished with a silver pattern, paused in her hitting a rug against her yellow rendered doorway to frown and shake her head.

How had he not thought? He stopped.

"We there?"

"You have a scarf?"

"You cold?" Lily laughed. "You know I do, we just came from winter."

"Put it over your hair."

"You're kidding, it'll be boiling."

"It's accepted practice that women here don't show their hair. Put it on until I can get you a summer one."

"You don't—"

"Lily, it's discourteous not to respect local custom. We're the outsiders here, so we will follow what's accepted. You need to cover your head."

"Easy for you to say, you don't have to." She pulled it out of the pocket of her coat she was carrying, a silver glittery wool scarf. Poor kid.

Charles set his holdall down between his legs, pressing his calves against the bulk of it to hold it while he helped her wrap the scarf on. She accused him with a paler version of his own eyes while he tried to tuck away her long hair.

"It'd be easier if I just wore my hat." she sulked.

"Good idea, not much further."

"Better hope I don't pass out with heat exhaustion before we get there."

He stopped himself calling her out on all the times she'd gone out in an inadequate cardigan or denim jacket in the rain or freezing cold. Instead, he took her hand to hurry her past the two teenagers who'd stopped to watch them.

"How long till we get to the hotel?"

"We're not staying at a hotel, we're going to your uncle's."

Lily didn't pick up his distinction, going to was very different to staying with. He had to hope the years between them had mellowed his brother enough to at least let the past remain there. He knew he couldn't count on Terry being open to them staying in the same space while Charles got his bearings, his future settled. But a payment should be enough of a sweetener.

"I don't have an uncle."

"You've never met him, my brother, Terry."

"Uncle Terry?"

"Yes, Lily. Uncle Terry." It sounded strange. The most unlikely person to be an uncle. Left here or right? The labyrinthine streets, Terry's defence, were almost proving beyond him. The street view he'd memorised kept wavering away behind dark curls, the parting kiss of fingertips.

"Why didn't you or mum tell me I have an uncle? Do I have any cousins, and an auntie too? Can I take this off yet, I'm super hot." She looked behind them. "There's no one here to see me."

That was where she might be wrong. Charles turned them right, trying to follow a circle as he'd learned, but in the boxy alleyways it was difficult. He was sure they weren't being followed. And the proximity of the surrounding buildings was its own defence against spying drones.

Could they mobilise so quickly? The second the pilot had filed Charles' revised flight plan, the stop watch timer had restarted until The Society found him again. But getting people there, that would take even them time.

"We've been down here already." Lily pointed out the obvious.

"I've gone wrong, I remember now where it is."

"Dad."

"Come on, aren't you looking forward to meeting your uncle?"

It would be an interesting reception for both of them.

Back to the junction where he'd taken them in the opposite direction on purpose, still no sign of anyone. It was eerie, in such a noisy, busy city in these narrow paths being cocooned in a subdued silence. But the buildings carried a weight, beyond the bricks and cement, concrete and stone of which they were constructed. The possibility of spying eyes weighed heavy.

The doorway was tiny, easy to walk right past. It was the

red tile painted with the out-of-place words that stopped him at 'Riad Lucky Eight'. Set at the bottom of three steps down from the path, a wooden door was fastened by a padlock. Charles' luck was holding, with Terry out, he could get what he came for and leave without having to see him. Best all round, everything considered. Charles placed his holdall down to open the combination lock. Terry, did you still believe?

8, 2, 8, 4, 8, 8, good luck numbers according to the Chinese and Terry's superstition. Charles pulled on the padlock. Good luck for him too - it clicked open.

"In you go," he gestured to Lily to proceed him.

They walked through a dim entrance hall that opened out into an interior courtyard, an oasis in an urban land-scape. Lush tall plants leaned against a terracotta painted wall on one side. The middle was taken up by a hexagonal plunge pool; the inside painted an inviting brilliant blue. The riad climbed two floors above their heads on the four sides of the courtyard.

Terry had got all this from gambling? He'd never been so lucky when Charles and he had been speaking. Or had he branched out?

"Wow, my uncle lives here?"

"Terry, it's Charles." His call for Lily's sake, she hadn't realised he couldn't have locked the door on the outside from the inside. They listened to the silence. "He's not home."

She pulled her hat off. "Can I paddle my feet? I'm so hot."

"Tell you what, you help me find what we came for and we can both swim. How about that?" Lily nodded, watching the hypnotic water. "You need a swimming costume first, so the quicker we find it, the quicker we can get one, before the shops shut." The way he'd get her out of there.

"Suppose so." she sighed.

He left her searching on the ground floor while he climbed up to what he assumed must be the bedroom level. Terry was still a slob. The number of arguments it had caused when they'd shared a bedroom, the perennial trail of his dirty clothes, crumpled and screwed-up pieces of paper on which he sketched his world, bits of stubby pencils Charles was forever standing on, piles of pencil sharpenings that breezed all over Charles' things. Terry had learnt nothing. His bedroom wouldn't have been out of place in a look at my wonderful house magazine if he bothered to put things away. The reality was more like a crime scene photo after a vicious burglary.

It sped up Charles' search, not having to be careful.

Lily's scream reached for him, echoing up through the courtyard. He flew down the steep curving stairs two at a time, tripping on the mosaic tiles, lunging for the banister to stop himself falling.

"Lily, what is it?"

37

The Covent Garden entrance of the Royal Opera House was still how Luke hoped: no body scanners, and, now the evening's performance had started, just the odd member of staff to check latecomer's handbags. Sloppy, long may it last.

Who would he choose?

Now he was in his mid-thirties, the youngsters looked like they were still at school so approaching them to help was just creepy. He breezed past the young girl drifting near him, aiming for the older woman cleaning her glasses on a corner of her blouse. A tall guy with spiked hair walking up to her looked him up and down. Luke looked good in a tux, but it was nice to be reminded. He stopped, looked around him, I'm lost, help me. The guy was over to him in a nanosecond.

"Can I help you, Sir?"

"I'm a little late, any chance you could let me in before the intermission? I'd be very grateful."

"Well, it's policy—"

"I'd be this grateful." Luke held his hand out and,

surprised, the guy grasped it. His eyes widened as he felt the folded note in Luke's palm. "Opera's not my thing, but it'll be the end of my promotion hopes if I don't show. My puppy didn't want me to leave her, so here I am, having left her and now I'm late." Was the puppy thing too much? Not judging by the usher's sympathetic face and nodding. Luke tipped the balance of his indecision. "If I can slip in behind my boss, I can pretend I was there all along. You know how it is, us little people against the big guys."

He nodded. "What seat do you have?"

"It's so embarrassing, her PA couldn't find my ticket, but I don't want to get her in trouble either. My boss has the box closest to the stage."

The usher looked up and down the still corridor. Strains of the performance reached them as he dithered. "Oh, come on then. You have to live dangerously every once in a while."

Luke laughed, if only he knew.

The usher paused outside the first door in a row of many. Unguarded, better than Luke had hoped. "Wait for one of the longer notes before you go in."

Luke smiled again. "Thanks so much."

He waited for the usher to drift away, two backward glances Luke pretended to not notice, then out of sight before he withdrew his Glock.

As the notes on stage soared, he opened the door the tiniest amount, waited long enough for anyone who'd caught the sound of the lock disengaging to look behind them and discount it. He slipped inside the box and stood in the shadows, appraising.

Only two people, that was surprising. Husband or bodyguard?

In one motion Luke was down on his knee on the left side of the Director General of MI5, furthest from the companion, hiding the gun pressed against her shoulder from everyone in the neighbouring box, stooping to whisper in Anna Bailey's ear. "You and I are going to have a chat. You co-operate, I don't pull this trigger. It's that simple, understand?" She nodded, waved a hand at the companion's interest, everything is okay, this is expected.

Luke handed her an earpiece, a twin of the one he was wearing, which she put in her left ear. He dragged a chair close to her. The chorus was winding up now, the noise level rising.

"What do you want?" Straight to business

"Why is MI5 killing people?"

She whipped round; he reminded her with pressure on the Glock that she needed to keep her place. Not them, as far as she knew. The problem with a many-headed beast was that the one holding them in check didn't always see what each part was up to. Until it was too late.

"It's an outfit called The Society."

What he thought she might say, but she appeared to believe it. "Who told you that?"

"It's on the news."

"Who's pulling their strings?" A slight shrug halted by the pressure of the barrel against her. "You think I have the inclination to play twenty questions?"

"We know nothing concrete."

Luke pulled a photocopy out of his tux pocket. "Look at it."

The row of faces, the matches to the names he'd found in Banks' little black book, looked out of the page, a low-tech identity parade. Red crosses over Tony Banks, Duncan Leadbetter, Hunter Malone, Nancy Seymour. A young Charles Buchanan, Aleksandr Oblov, Jed Carson and two other men were unmarked, all alive as far as Luke was aware. All apart from Jed Carson, the photos Gordon Stamford had shown her while Luke watched.

"The kill list, yes?" It took longer for her to respond this time. "Don't make me repeat myself."

"Your guesswork leaves something to be desired."

"Last man standing?" It was only a questioning whisper, but Bailey tensed. Christ. No matter how good they were, no one was going to get close enough to the US President to kill him—he would be the survivor. That would kill his re-election chances next month if it came out. Was it in retaliation to Tony Banks instructing The Society to kill him? How had Jed Carson found that out? Did The Society have a security breach?

"Are you actively assisting?" Luke had to prod her again to get her to answer.

"We're actively not investigating."

"Seems you need to decide just how special the relationship with our friends across the pond should be. This meeting stays between you and me. It serves to show you I can find you anywhere, you'd do well to remember that. One last question, Eva Janssen, Buchanan's wife, is she a target?" He followed his hunch.

"I don't know details but I believe we can count her as active collateral, a warning to Buchanan."

Luke moved the Glock down beneath Bailey's bare arm, its barrel level now with her heart. "Tell whoever's listening, I don't like to share. She's off limits, she's mine."

38

"Lily, where are you?" Charles found her sobbing and screaming near the pool. "What's the matter?"

She clung to him, hysterical, the only comprehensible sound she made was calling for her mum, over and over, until he had to tell her enough. A glance into the small square enclosed room she'd looked in explained for her.

He led her up the stairs to the second floor into another bedroom and wrapped her in the red blanket he retrieved from the floor. "I'll be right back. I'm just going to get you a drink of water."

In his search of the main bathroom cabinet and the drawers in his brother's bedroom, Charles had to trust his schoolboy French. His hand paused over the tap in the kitchen. He'd read that the water was safe there, but it didn't hurt to check. There were no plastic bottles in the fridge, none in the tall cupboard in which Terry kept his food, no empties in his bin. It must be.

"Here you go," he lifted Lily's hand and dropped two sleeping pills onto her palm, "these will help." He didn't know what else to do.

"I want Mum," she wailed.

"I know. But I'm here with you." He sat beside her, letting her cry herself out on his chest until she sagged against him, her breathing even, regular, no more hiccupping sobs.

Charles laid her down, felt her forehead. Not overheating, good. The plunge pool-cooled breeze from the courtyard wafted around the whole place. It was an ingenious design.

She looked so young. Lily, his unexpected bonus seven years ago when he reunited with Eva. Just growing into herself, Lily was losing the childish roundness from her face, as it became more heart-shaped. Her cheek bones would reveal themselves in a year or so if she was going to take more after Eva than him. Longer eyelashes than either of them, his brown hair, Lily's potential tallness from further back in their family trees. All to play for still at eleven-years-old. So young, too young for this week's traumas.

Lily, I'm sorry.

On what looked like a church pew, out of place in a room painted sandy yellow with terracotta stars decorating the ceiling, tumbling down the walls, lay his brother. Flopped sideways he stared at a point beyond where Charles could see, a bluish tinge to his open lips.

Lily should never have seen this.

Terry had clearly enjoyed the sweet pastries and fried street food more than the spiced vegetables. And probably the local spirits. Past his brother's out of shape body, past even the ridiculous—was that a sarong?—he wore in place of trousers, his garish yellow shirt nailed Charles' gaze. Or rather, what peeked out of its open collar. Charles undid the next two buttons, steeling himself more against Terry grabbing at him to stop him, than what he might find. Terry's killer had gouged a message into his chest, the curving number Terry had lived for.

The jagged eight was raw, his skin puckered with what would be horizontal ribbons of blood streaming down it, if he were sitting upright. They'd carved it when he'd been alive.

Yes. Charles caught himself. It wasn't a celebration that The Society hadn't beaten him there, that Terry's death was nothing to do with Charles' problems. An unfortunate coincidence, that was all this was, a warning instead, as stark and clear as if they had written the actual words: honour your debt.

No smell of decay, no insects Charles could hear or see. The tiny fireplace would be their conduit, the molecules of the odour of rotting flesh already rising beyond the rooftops their invitation. Terry's arm was cool, not cold. Maybe only so many hours since he died. Been killed.

Killed. The killer had replaced the padlock on the outside of the door, and Charles had smeared his fingerprints all over it. He might only have minutes before the authorities arrived and a Moroccan prison would never be a good place to be.

Bolting for the front door, checking the ornate spyhole, he swiped up the padlock from the standing sentry cabinet beside the door where he'd left it and wiped it on his shirt. He found a key in a drawer which locked the door, leaving it in place to make it more difficult for other key holders. Bolts at the top and bottom slid across smoothly, ramming into holes in the substantial doorframe. It might withstand a few attempts to batter it down. The warning it would give was all he could hope for. Because until Lily woke up, they were trapped there.

Charles stood for a moment in the master bedroom.

Terry's killer, killers, must be responsible for the mess, may have already found and taken what he was looking for. On its surface it was valuable enough to have been stolen as restitution but no common thief would understand its true worth. Terry was beyond Charles' apology for rifling through the things his brother had chosen, things he'd found memorable enough to keep. The shift in how it felt, voyeuristic now, uncomfortable, wasn't enough to make him stop either. His and Lily's lives were too important.

Charles reached the top of the even steeper stairs leading to the roof terrace. The call to prayer was ramping up from a whisper of suggestion to an urgent instruction blared across the city as each mosque passed it on. Beside the open door to the outdoors, tucked into the tiny landing, stood the twin of the ornately carved wooden cabinet from the entrance, its doors open. Skewed beneath a battered Scrabble box, it was right there, Charles could hardly believe it. He opened the drawstring bag beside the chess board and shook the contents onto the floor, a waterfall of black and white chess pieces. Innocently tumbled with the others, the one he'd come for, the white knight. It was a work of art beyond its value to him, sleek, smoothly cast in a metal that mimicked the quicksilver of mercury. He snatched it up, gripped it in his fist.

Too huge for the moment, his emotions propelled him out on to the terrace.

He was back in control.

This ought to have been a moment of celebration, it should have heralded the rebirth of the life he wanted, the sharing of it with his one love. Charles stumbled onto a lounger. The vastness of the deepening twilight sky mirrored his loss: unfathomable, all-consuming, encompassing everything he could see and hear.

Harder to lie to himself beneath the coming night's impassivity. Harder to pretend that he could reunite with Eva.

But he had Lily. And now he could keep her safe. On the table beside him was a plate holding several peach stones. He picked up the knife Terry had used, sticky with dried juice, and levered off the knight's base. He peered inside but couldn't tell.

In the bright light from an anglepoise lamp beside a clunky desktop in Terry's study, Charles' euphoria was surprisingly weak, heart-breakingly so. There it was, as he'd placed it all those years ago, the evidence that would buy his and Lily's safety. Until his new payday happened, at least, and then that regular income would guarantee them wanting for nothing lives and the best security money could buy. But it should have been for three of them.

Now his knees wobbled, his stomach threatened to rebel. He squeezed the chess piece, imprinting his guarantee on his palm that he wouldn't share the fate of Tony, Hunter and Nancy.

Blocking Terry's number—let them believe he was still in London—Charles dialled the one he'd called yesterday. Had it only been yesterday?

"US President's office, Chief of Staff, Dennis Wakeman."

"Hello, Dennis."

"Who is this?"

"The royal pain in your and his arses."

"You're gonna have to be more specific."

"You don't recognise me? How 'bout now?" Charles tried to let go of the accent they'd taught him, but he'd had excellent instructors. His drawl just wouldn't any longer. "It's Charles Buchanan, Maxwell Peyton." Here to sabre-rattle.

"Maxwell, calling to threaten some more? I heard you gave Allouette a hard time on the phone yesterday."

"I'm not threatening anyone, I'm trying to help you. Put me through to Jed."

"That's Mr President to you."

"It's Mr President thanks to me."

"He's not here."

Of course he wasn't. "I'm not in a mood to play games."

"Don't you watch the news? He's on Airforce One."

"Patch me through."

"No can do, you're not high enough priority."

Did Jed know Dennis was busy hammering nails in the coffin of his future?

"Ask him this, then. Where's Duncan Leadbetter? Why was Nancy Seymour killed? Why are you going after my wife?"

"We're not 'going after' anyone."

"Call it off, I know what's going on here and it stops now. My family and I are off-limits. If I sniff a hint of you coming after us, I'll release the data from the fuel contamination," Charles tightened his grip on the knight, let his insurance hang between them, swelling to fill the distance across the Atlantic. "I'm sure the senator Jed pushed under on his way up the pole to power will be real interested to learn about it."

"You're not holding any cards here." Dennis growled down the phone.

"Senator Mack Hillard III might think otherwise. The Attorney General, Congress, the Senate, the American people, I think you'll find I'm holding quite a few. Consider yourself warned. Oh, and Dennis? Having Nancy killed was a big mistake, you'll regret that."

Charles slammed the handset down. Now he just had to come up with a way to get out of the target The Society had on him.

39

———

Any of the three camp beds in the basement were comfortable enough, and the room was dark and quiet. Eva had a blanket and pillow and was secure a floor below the airlock at the entrance to 37 St George's Grove, all the creature comforts needed for sleep. But there was no rest for her aching heart and arms, desperate to hold Lily. Not when her frenzied mind fed the battle between the 'what if' scenarios her brain kept running and her logical mind trying to convince herself Lily was okay.

It was too late to call the airfield again and no one was going to know more than they had the first three times she'd spoken to them. Addison's Executive Assistant, if she was even still at work, would tell her that he was still unreachable, as he had been on the five times she'd already tried.

Eva dropped into and out of sleep, until her crash into dreamlessness was profound, disorienting, and made her late.

The office that sported Big Brother scrawled on a Post-It

on its door refused to let her in, even when she swiped her temporary access pass. It opened when she tapped on it.

"Eva, right?" She nodded at the guy who opened it. "You're with me today. Iago, yeah, trust me, I've heard it all before, I know Othello was the black dude. In case you can't tell, my mum wasn't a Shakespearean buff. She wanted a good old English name for me, but it all got a bit lost in translation, Iago's Welsh, in case you were wondering. Take a seat."

He waved an arm that was thicker, more muscled, than her thigh under his navy blue jumper. "You won't have worked on this kind of system before, state-of-the-art." He emphasised each of the words as though he'd invented it. Maybe he had.

"It looks impressive."

She sank onto the chair, looking from one to the other of the screens wallpapering the wall behind the long office desk. Nothing on any of them was distinctive enough to hint at where the cityscapes in various degrees of daylight and different weather were. Its official name might be the Surveillance Division, but the Post-It note had it more accurately.

"Where do you want to go for me to show you how this baby works? World's your oyster."

And Lily, the pearl in it somewhere. Eva could watch all available feeds for the rest of her life and still never find her. She didn't even have a starting point. That Addison's jet hadn't landed at their first fuel stop on the way to India was fuelling her slow-burning panic.

It might help to focus on something else. "Is it possible to watch remote areas?"

"Sure, if we have a bird above it."

"How about thirty odd miles south west of Seitu township in Ethiopia?"

"That's pretty specific but no probs, let's see what we've got round there."

"Could you see what you had there a week or so ago?"

"Time travel?" Iago rubbed his hands together, pulled up his sleeves with a flourish. "Now you're cooking."

He explained each step as he zoomed in and tracked around the remote area away from the township. He fed the co-ordinates of the water supply Every Drop had tapped into his computer program and waited for the archive to pull up recent footage.

"How long do you keep it?"

"I've got an algorithm. It calculates the likelihood of ongoing interest based on activity in the area, current and developing threats."

"That's impressive."

He ran his hands over the wall to wall desk at which they were sitting. "Yeah, she's pretty sweet." He peered at his desktop. "You might not think so, nothing for that place in the archive."

"Could you try one more?"

After an elevated threat level in the broader area earlier in the year, the algorithm had saved some footage of the water source used for Tirupudur. While the archive sorted and retrieved, Iago showed Eva how to work on her brief, but it was hard to focus on finding Aleksandr Oblov's wife with the time lapse backward journey in India playing out beside her. Sometimes in night vision, sometimes in bleached-out equatorial sunlight, every frame showed an area desert-like in its activity.

Eva set up an alert through the London hospital network for Kathy and Aleksandr Oblov. Tracing the footage of him being taken ill backwards and expanding the search to cover the entire street, the most suspicious person Eva could see anywhere near him was his bodyguard. He was huge, mean-looking, a man you'd cross the road to avoid, not inflame by going after his boss.

Kathy Oblov was a ghost, an anomaly with no social media presence, barely any online footprint that Eva could find. No sightings of her or her husband since his collapse in the system trawl so far. No call to emergency services or the police to respond to a sudden death at their home address, so he must at least still be alive.

"How's it going?" Iago asked after a while.

"I'm not finding anything on Kathy Oblov. If she's had enough plastic surgery, would facial recognition still be able to find her?"

"If she's different on enough of the right points on her face, it could be like looking for a new person. You're thinking that's why?"

"It's the hobby of a lot of oligarch's wives."

"I'm glad I'm happy kicking a ball around. It's a good shout, I can run some permutations through a couple of channels. Grab a coffee, it'll take a while."

But Eva didn't understand what he was saying to her. The archived screen stole her entire attention. She froze the image. Twilight where Every Drop's contractors had tamed the underground freedom of groundwater into the network of pipes that carried life to Tirupudur, time-stamped the day the first reports of sickness came through.

She leapt up. "I have to go out, I'll be right back."

'RIGHT BACK' must have morphed to 'she's taking a long time' to 'where the hell is she' by the time Dario joined her.

"You might want something stronger." He nodded at her ginger beer on the table between them.

"I was thinking the same for you." The largest coffee the wine bar did was only a couple of mouthfuls, so she'd ordered him two.

"I feel like we should have met under the clock at the station or on a park bench with identical briefcases." He placed a memory stick beside her drink. "I downloaded it yesterday."

"Getting psychic in your old age?"

"Vaishali was promoted yesterday to acting CEO." Eva nearly choked on her drink. "With ownership of the accounts."

"Do you still have oversight?"

He shook his head, downed one of the coffees. "That's why I downloaded everything yesterday."

"What about Letitia?"

"She's doing Vaishali's job."

"Our accountant is doing social media and donations?" The bottles of wine artily arranged in cabinets behind the bar looked enticing. "On whose say so?"

"Stuart did the 'development chats'." Dario hooked air quotes around his sarcasm. "With the full weight of the Board." He shotted the other coffee. "Apparently. He also vetoed the idea of water purifiers. Not allowed to source any, not needed is his excuse."

Not needed? Cost was driving that decision, people's lives being expendable again. Eva's hand closed around the memory stick. She had no proof of his thinking, but what it contained might show it. "Thanks for this, I'm sorry to put you in this position, but this is why." She gave him her print out, finished her drink while he ran the magnifier on his phone over the black-and-white image.

"One person."

She nodded, not maintenance. It could only be what it looked like, the single figure near the beginning of the pipe network with some kind of upside down container, the thin end pointing into the water stream.

Dario looked as if she'd accused him of being the person in the image. "Sabotage, why? We're only doing good there."

Eva sighed. "I know, you know, our competitors know, at least I thought we were all on the same page." Tiny doubts were solidifying in her mind. She pocketed the memory stick, hoping it would prove her wrong.

"I'll let you know what I find." She gave Dario the switchboard number of Gordon's unit. "Call me if you need me."

40

"Got that ping." Iago's welcome back to the surveillance room could have been him quoting from an obscure Shakespearean work for all the sense he made to Eva.

She corralled her whirlwind thoughts to focus on him. "Ping?"

"Yeah, the Oblov's car. Involved in a crash near The Shard. They've been taken to St Thomas' A and E, both still breathing."

"What happened?"

"Just got the heads up about it. Let's have a look see." Iago wielded his mouse and one screen responded. A police car blocked off the road feeding the crash site.

"That must be theirs." Iago paused over the black Range Rover crashed into a traffic light pole that was losing its fight to stay vertical.

"I'll go and question them."

"You going off again, forfeit is doughnuts, proper sugar, pack of six, raspberry jam, none of that custard crap."

"Deal, where's Nora's office?"

"You don't have access."

"Is security this tight at Vauxhall Cross now?"

He shrugged. "Barely get over there, we have everything here and I'm not senior enough to warrant summonsing over." He grinned at her. "Thank God. What do you need?"

"To give her something."

"You want me to?"

Eva shook her head. "I can knock."

"Come," Iago led her to the top floor and bellowed through the closed door opposite Gordon's. "Nora, you up for a visitor?"

After a few seconds, Nora appeared in her doorway. "You saved me from myself, I ignored my last 'get up and move around' alert, want to join me for a cup of tea? Stairs are always good for my step count."

"I can walk down with you, but I've got to get to St Thomas'. Iago found the Oblovs, admitted after an accident." Eva's question was hard to ask, but she had to. Rip the plaster off, faster was always less painful. "Do you know any good forensic accountants?"

Nora raised her eyebrows. "That's a non sequitur." But she nodded. "We have a couple of bodies who do accounting, they can forensically audit."

"It's private, I mean, not to do with what I'm doing here." Eva made herself say it. "I want Every Drop's accounts audited."

"Leave it with me, I'll see what I can do."

Eva held out the memory stick Dario had given her. "Accounts as at yesterday."

"You're sure about this?"

She nodded. "You shouldn't find anything suspect in there but I have to be know." She took a breath, went with a deep unacknowledged hunch. "Can you cross reference any payments without a clear audit trail to Stuart Worthington?"

"Your Chairman? Of course."

"Doughnuts." Iago reminded her as she passed him going down the last flight of stairs to the exit.

"Six, proper sugar, raspberry jam, no custard crap, got it."

Eva's limited pass worked better at opening doors outside St George's Grove, she was okayed to go straight to the ward where Kathy Oblov was.

The woman in the hospital bed appeared to be sleeping. The bedclothes rose in a rectangular protrusion above her left leg, they'd placed her hands on the blanket by her sides.

"Kathy Oblov, there you are."

She leant closer, scrutinising Kathy's face. Very heart-shaped now, a smaller nose, a few abrasions marred her perfect skin, so smooth and taut it was amazing her chiselled cheekbones didn't cut right through it. The points of reference on this Kathy Oblov were all different to what Eva had been searching for, no wonder she hadn't found her.

That perfume? Eva leant closer, her nose almost touching Kathy's skin. Where? She breathed it in again, sweet, then smelt it once more, bitter. Eva closed her eyes, too strong. She sat back and let the answer find her. Was she sure? She hadn't even noticed it then, not really, but now, oh God.

Eva limped to the nurses' station. "I need a doctor for Kathy Oblov. She's been poisoned. She needs an antidote immediately. Where's her husband? He'll need the same."

"We'll have to wait for her doctor."

There was no time. "Can you call them? I can explain it."

"They'll be doing rounds soon."

"She'll be dead soon. Was she unconscious when she

was admitted?"

"She's been in an accident, big trauma. We'll wait for the doctor."

Eva left the ward searching for that most elusive of things, a public pay phone. Her reverse charge call was accepted right away.

"Gordon, it's Eva. I'm at St Thomas', Kathy and Aleksandr Oblov were in a car crash. She's been poisoned, and probably he has too. I thought nothing of it when I said goodbye to Eric, but he had the same bittersweet smell on him. It's got to be the same poison. The nurse won't listen that she needs an antidote."

"We're still unsure what killed Eric. You're sure about this?"

"I am."

"I'll call the hospital director."

"Do you want me to stay here with them?"

"If either of them are up to talking, an idea of what happened would be helpful. Good catch."

Not really. She hadn't understood it when she'd hugged Eric goodbye. It had been right there for her to pick up, but she'd been so obsessed with getting back to the office she hadn't given it any thought.

Heavy steps, beyond her injury, took her back to Kathy's ward. The hospital director moved fast. A flurry of activity just a few minutes later pushed her outside the curtain, yanked closed around Kathy's bed.

Eva waited at the mercy of her guilt. And overlaying every breath, every thought, two syllables, Lily. Until a level of urgency, of snapped instructions and the running in of a nurse with a crash cart brought Eva slamming back into her present and Kathy Oblov's struggle for life. Eva didn't need any medical knowledge to understand she was losing.

There was an inevitability about it, the hurried but calm workings of the team, one step then another to keep their patient with them. A desperate last-ditch attempt until Eva heard the pronouncement.

"I'm calling it. Time of death, 11:52. Thank you, everyone."

"Can you tell me how Aleksandr Oblov is, Kathy's husband?" Eva caught a doctor rushing out of the cubicle.

"Are you family?"

Eva dropped her voice. "I'm a consultant working with MI6."

The doctor tightened her ponytail, checked her watch. "So I understand from the hospital director."

"We believe both Mr and Mrs Oblov have been targeted."

"I can take you to him." She logged in at a mobile PC station. "Can you tell me what you find out about the poison?" She held out her swipe card so Eva could read Dr Asha Chakrabarti. Her photo showed her long black hair down, her beaming smile a long way from the tired frown she now wore. "It's my field, but I've never seen anything like this."

"Like what? Please, we need to catch the people responsible. Kathy isn't the first to die. Anything you can tell me could make the difference to us stopping it happening to anyone else."

She nodded, took a second to compose her thoughts. "Mrs Oblov was stable but poorly before we administered hydroxocobalamin, it's effective in treating cyanide poisoning, and the smell from her pores led us to believe that's what it was. But from the way she went downhill, I believe the antidote triggered her body's collapse."

41

Dr Chakrabarti tapped at the door to a private room and went straight in. Eva followed. Aleksandr Oblov lay in the bed, a mirror image to his wife, minus the broken leg. A large man on the other side of the room cut off his phone call and rose from his seat, tense, his hand reaching towards his suit jacket. Dr Chakrabarti held her badge out for his inspection, used to his overprotectiveness already. Eva recognised him from the CCTV footage as Oblov's bodyguard.

"I'm a friend." Eva said when he turned his gaze on her. "I've just been with Kathy."

"I don't know you."

"I'm a new friend." Eva dredged up the rusty words, hoping he was as Russian as his boss.

"From Russia?"

She shook her head. "I'm really sorry to say that Kathy died."

He nodded, more a digesting of what the new order would be going forward than anything else.

Dr Chakrabarti gestured at the bed, "I just need to check something."

She bent over Oblov and sniffed the skin of his face, his breath, his neck. "Is it the same?" She asked.

Eva copied her. "It's not as strong. He could have had less, or been dosed after his wife, but, yes, it's the same."

Dr Chakrabarti considered for a moment. "It's very hard to just not treat him but, having seen what just happened, I'm not going to, at least not right now."

"You must treat him." The bodyguard straightened up in full-on intimidation mode.

"He hasn't been poisoned," Eva floundered, what was the Russian word for primed? "He's been given something that makes it seem as if he has, but the antidote will kill him. It's what killed Kathy."

"How do you know this?"

"It killed a friend of mine."

"I'm going to advise Mr Oblov's medical doctor of the—I don't even know what this is. We need to figure out if we need to try to flush it out or let nature take its course." The doctor murmured to herself, rationalising. "A nurse will be in to take bloods." Back to normal practice, her voice was firmer. She looked at the bodyguard. "Are you staying with the patient?" He nodded. "I'm going to update his notes, but don't let anyone give him anything until they clear it with me." She held her pass out for him to read her name again until he nodded and she left.

"I'm not wired, not armed. You can check." Eva held her arms out to her side. Treat this as though he were an airport official rather than a man who could put her through the wall.

His hands patted her down, no lingering, just searching out weapons, a quick sweep with the little finger sides of his palms between her breasts, down her midriff. Not his first rodeo. He stepped back from her. "Who wanted your friend dead?"

Eva shook her head, the burden becoming heavier each time she thought about it. "Not my friend, me." Then a sideways hunch, the only connection in this was her but through her, Charles. "Does the name Charles Buchanan mean anything to you?"

"Why?"

"He's my husband, he's being targeted by the same people."

"Who?"

"They call themselves The Society."

The bodyguard was silent, utterly unreadable. Eva had run out of ideas, another warning to not let the doctors give Oblov the antidote was all she could do.

As she reached the door, the bodyguard stopped her. "A man I didn't know came to see Mr Oblov recently. There was difficult talk about money and a debt. The man talked about Charles being involved, it could have been your husband. Mr Oblov agreed to help." He looked at his boss, back at Eva. "If The Society is involved, I need reinforcements."

"You know of them?"

He nodded. "They will try to get you again."

"I know, they blew my house up."

"Yet you stand still."

She nodded. "Yes, I'm still standing." Running towards the bullets. "Do you know how to get in touch with them?" He considered for a while. "My daughter could get caught up in this, she's only eleven, she doesn't deserve that."

"The sins of the fathers."

A sudden surge of fury stained Eva's worry about Lily. Whatever Charles had done would not get her daughter hurt, she wouldn't let it. Maybe that flash of anger was what he was waiting for. The bodyguard produced a pen out of an inside pocket in his suit jacket and tore a strip from the paper detailing the ward's daily menu choices. He searched for something on his phone and wrote it down.

"This is how you get in touch with The Society."

Eva looked at the long string of letters and numbers suffixed by .onion. Was this a wind up?

"It won't connect, it'll redirect you but if you follow their breadcrumb trail, you'll reach them."

"Thank you."

She reached for the door handle when he stopped her again.

"A word of warning, before you use that," he gestured at the note in her hand, "be sure you want to come to their attention."

42

"You sure this isn't a wind up?" Iago asked exactly what Eva had thought as he frowned at the copy of The Society's contact details she handed him.

"Apparently not."

"And these are the guys Oblov's bodyguard said are after his boss?"

"Something like that." It wasn't exactly a lie, it was probably the same poison, something that elaborate wasn't an easy over the counter purchase.

Iago typed in the URL, hit return. Error flashing in the middle of the screen wasn't what she'd hoped to see.

"He said it wouldn't go straight through to them, that it would redirect." They watched the unchanging message. "What about a general search for The Society, would that work?"

"It might, but I'm not risking this system on a trawl through the dark web. I'll pass it to our tech team, they've got protocols, stand-alone systems for stuff that looks dodgy."

But she couldn't wait that long, one minute more was too long. She had one other option, but was it going too far?

"Where's my doughnuts?"

"Where's the closest place to get some?"

"You forgot."

Eva nodded. "I forgot, the whole poisoning thing was distracting."

"There's a Sainsburys not far, a wicked bakery the street over, though the good stuff'll be gone by now."

"You had lunch?"

He grinned. "Can always eat another lunch. Food's my language of choice."

"I'll remember that."

NORA POPPED her head round the door before Eva had finished her baguette.

"It's going well then if he's had you on a doughnut run already."

"I'm not sharing." Iago reached for the bakery bag.

"I'm not asking, I've got a raw cashew nut bar in my desk calling to me louder than your sugar addiction." Nora checked her fitness tracker on her wrist. "And definitely not today." She gestured at Iago's kingdom. "It's quite something, isn't it?"

Eva nodded. "Things have changed a lot since I was here, well, there," she waved a hand as though pointing at where she'd worked in Vauxhall Cross, MI6's public headquarters, the Legoland building, as it had become known. "But one thing's the same in the work, one step forwards, two back. Walk with me to the kitchen?"

"Coffee, since you're going." Iago said.

"You're not tied to that chair." Nora followed Eva out of the surveillance room. "What's up?"

As perceptive as ever. "What's the process to get an unlocker?"

"QM Provisions, same process for everything, has to be signed off by a signatory once they've reviewed the case, then you just sign it out, sign it back in. What're you thinking?"

Eva filled Nora in on the morning's events at the hospital.

"A two-part poison? Our opposition keeps getting smarter."

"I'm thinking that while the Oblov's bodyguard is otherwise occupied, I could take a look around to see if I can figure out how they were poisoned."

"Breaking and entering's still not policy."

"It's only breaking and entering if you're breaking something. With an unlocker it's just like having a key. I recognised it, the smell on them both, I've smelt it before, when I said goodbye to Eric."

Nora sighed. "You've got to do it then, haven't you?"

EVA WALKED UP THE STREET, which the Oblovs now called home. Londoners had nicknamed this area Red Square, nothing to do with the architecture but everything to do with the fact that the extortionately expensive houses were only affordable to oligarch level bank balances. Most of the Russian ex-pats would have bought their way in waving the twentieth-century equivalent of suitcases of money that the UK had been happy to stash under the bed of the banking system, no questions asked.

She rang the doorbell at the electric gates of the Oblovs' mansion, probably one of the most impressive in the row, eight zeroes worth, maybe nine these days. Eva's first press of the buzzer on the pillar beside the electric gates wasn't answered. Another one, to make sure. She stared up at the tall gates, getting over those would be—

"Hello." Someone home, helpful.

Eva summoned up her rusty Russian, "I'm a friend of—"

"I don't speak that." The woman cut her off.

Eva tried her best I'm a Russian speaking English accent. "Kathy is my friend, I need to get clothes for her at the hospital."

"Mrs Oblov has died."

She already knew? Eva wailed, a caterwauling perfectly pitched to draw attention. She grabbed hold of the gate bars as though they were the only things holding her up, shouting her distress louder still toward the neighbours, shouting over the woman's reasoning on the intercom.

She couldn't yell loud enough for anyone to hear past all the shrubbery and locked-up frontages, but she was attracting awkward should we do anything about the mad woman glances from the few passers-by. She swung herself from side to side on the gate, making sure all the cameras watching her got a noticeable performance.

It popped open. Eva rushed inside, up the driveway to the huge front door at which a middle-aged lady stood.

"Poor Kathy," Eva wailed, "I can't believe it, I spoke to her yesterday. But Aleksandr?"

"He's in hospital, he'll be coming home. Viktor is with him."

Eva nodded. "Good. I can collect clothes for Aleksandr? I must go, how you say, make him feel better."

The lady nodded. "I can get what you need, you wait there."

Eva sniffed, rubbed at her nose. "You have handkerchief?" Burst into loud sobbing again, wailing for Kathy.

The housekeeper sighed. "You must be quiet."

Eva pushed the volume higher.

"Come, come." The housekeeper ushered her inside and deposited her in an immaculate lounge that was bigger than the downstairs of Eva's house used to be. She closed her eyes against her last image of it.

Eva counted what she hoped was enough seconds for her to have reached the first floor, before padding through the enormous hallway to the kitchen. Wow, no excuse to be a terrible cook in there. Every gadget imaginable lined one wall, filed away in individual cubby holes behind glass doors.

To have escaped notice, the poison had to be tasteless, odourless. She checked the bin, the bag inside was empty.

Peering through the windows, there was nothing as pedestrian as a dustbin outside, but on the ground lay a disposable coffee cup. An odd place to leave it, or, so used to being cosseted, the drinker didn't bother putting it in the bin.

The back door was unlocked, giving Eva the chance to step outside to look at it. Wouldn't it have been neat and tidy if it bore the Coffee Espresso logo? The generic brownness of the unbranded cup meant it could have come from anywhere.

"What are you doing?" The housekeeper rapped Eva with her voice.

"Whose drink was this?"

"You need to leave, I'm calling security."

43

"I'll be honest with you," Eva dropped her accent. "I'm not a friend of Kathy's. I'm working on this case as a consultant for the security services. Kathy was poisoned, so was Aleksandr. He may not live. If he dies, you lose your job. Help me figure out what hurt them. Who brought this in?"

The housekeeper opened one of the dozens of kitchen cupboards to show Eva a leaning tower of twin cups. No one here worried about saving the planet. "The Oblovs make their coffee here." She gestured at the huge gleaming coffee machine.

"Did either of them eat or drink anything from outside the house yesterday?"

She shook her head.

"Do you eat and drink here?"

The woman nodded, her eyes widening, her hand flying to her mouth as she realised what Eva was actually asking.

"The Oblovs aren't the first to be poisoned in this way. May I?" Eva gestured at the gap between them. The woman looked totally confused. "I need to make sure you haven't been affected."

At her vigorous nodding, Eva stepped close and sniffed her cheek. "Thank you. I just need to make a phone call."

"Have I? Have I been poisoned?" Her eyes filled with tears.

"Not exactly, but you have ingested a drug. It won't harm you if you do exactly as I say, okay?" the woman looked like she might die from a heart attack first. "It's vital that you're not given hydroxocobalamin, you understand? You're quite safe unless you're given that drug." Eva hoped. "That's what killed Kathy. Aleksandr hasn't had it, that's why he's still alive. Do you understand?"

Tears ran down the housekeeper's cheeks, but she repeated the name of the drug at Eva's insistence until she said it fluently. Eva sat her down in the lounge and called the situation in to Nora, adding that someone needed to check the bodyguard.

She sat with the terrified housekeeper until the house got busy with the arrival of the police, CSI, paramedics and a couple of guys who didn't ID themselves but came in unchallenged. MI5, potentially Six.

The waiting gave Eva a lot of time in which to argue with herself. She had too much evidence to the contrary now to not go with her Plan B. She shifted on the sofa, the housekeeper clutched her hand tighter. "I'm not going anywhere." Eva reassured, "until I know you'll be safe." And then she'd have no choice but to do what she didn't want to.

While she watched the efficiency of the authorities evaluating what this might be and how to deal with it, something tickled at the edges of Eva's mind, something she already knew. What was linked? But the more she questioned it, the further away from her the feeling fled, further still as she explained the situation to the paramedic examining the housekeeper.

"Repeat it back to me, please." At his look Eva added, "I need to be sure for when you hand her on so please humour me."

The paramedic repeated her words exactly. "Though the patient is presenting with the appearance of having ingested cyanide, it's a priming agent. And administering hydroxocobalamin will be fatal."

Eva nodded. "Dr Asha Chakrabarti at St Thomas' knows about this, she's treating the owners of the house. This appears to be a two-part process, the hydroxocobalamin, potentially any drug, could finish it."

"Got it." The paramedic shifted attention to the housekeeper.

"You'll be okay." Eva squeezed the stricken woman's hand and let the officer in charge know she was leaving. It felt good giving her contact details as SIS, a sense of belonging she hadn't realised she'd missed.

The bus deposited Eva close to her next destination. She watched the house from the street corner. No sign of anyone in there, but there hadn't been the first time she'd been there.

She'd do anything to keep Lily safe, that was all this was, looking after her baby girl. She could do that.

As bold and confident as possible with her limp and her churning insides, she walked up the front path and knocked. And again. CJ probably wouldn't let her in out of choice. That was what the pick gun—she'd had to start again with the requisition form, using its correct name—was for. One more knock, ignored. You don't have the choice, CJ, you're going to help me.

She pressed the front door, almost immoveable in its

frame. Starting with the deadbolt, she inserted the tool's pick into the lock, a quick press and she heard the unlocking she wanted. Same procedure in the top lock and open sesame.

Eva stood in the hallway and listened. Was he home?

She steeled herself. The closest door to her had a lock on it, the bar in the big screwhead beneath the handle was vertical – cloakroom unoccupied? She tapped the chrome fitting. What was she doing? He wasn't likely to have electrified it. Grasping the handle, cold against her skin, she pulled it downwards and opened the door.

Nothing breathing in the tiny space.

Eva tiptoed to the one on the other side of the passageway. Heart thudding in her head loud enough to cover any noise she might make, tensed against a rough hand in her hair, something cold and sharp against her skin, she peered into the room.

Empty. A huge painting surprised her, CJ had seemed too angry to even know Buddha's name, but the room was almost a shrine to the East. He needed to study harder.

She tiptoed towards the last door downstairs and peered into the space beyond it. Kitchen: sage green units all around the room's periphery minimised the space he could be in to one cursory glance. Not there.

Eva let go her held breath, looked up the stairs.

Softly, carefully she placed each foot on the next step and eased her weight onto it. One, two. . .seven, eight. . .twelve. Thirteen would take her onto the landing.

Three doors up there, closed. Silent.

Thirteen.

Eva padded to the first door, CJ's office. He could be just the other side of the wood, headphones on maybe, his knife within easy reach. How much of a threat was the pick gun in her hands?

Eva opened the door.

CJ wasn't in his office.

She whirled around, no one behind her.

She eased over to the next door. CJ's bedroom, empty.

The last door was a repeat of the downstairs cloakroom, lock in the unlocked position. A quick check of the bathroom and Eva could breathe properly. No one there but her.

She walked into his computer room, the auto-closer on the door shutting it behind her. Every screen was blank, no keyboards out. The winter light wasn't reaching very far past the half-drawn blinds. Eva sat in the captain's chair at the bank of monitors and waited, her fingers unfolding and refolding the piece of paper that held The Society's contact details.

The hiss started quietly, a disturbance in the air that Eva scarcely noticed. From nothing to everything in a few seconds, raucous, threatening and, when she bolted for the door, malevolent in every way. Eva grasped the handle, but she tumbled to the floor into darkness.

44

Eva woke as though she'd set her alarm wrong and had been asleep only a couple of hours before it went off. She dragged her eyes open. Sage units, strange kitchen. CJ's house. A bolt of adrenaline tore through her, firebombing the vestiges of the sedative he'd knocked her out with.

She flexed her wrists, but the cream cable ties holding them together on her lap were immoveable as they looked. Her ankles were also tied, one to each of the two metallic spindly front legs of the hard chair on which he'd propped her.

She blinked hard, swallowed. The wooziness might be receding, her thirst not so much. There had to be knives in the drawers. She leant forward, tipping the back legs of the chair off the floor, but it was weighted weirdly and pulled her back onto its seat. The clunk of the legs brought CJ into the room.

"Is this how you treat all your clients?" Her voice was a lot steadier than she felt.

He leant against the units opposite her. "Only the ones

who break in." In black jeans and jumper today, black socks with green aliens on them, he seemed to be a man big on co-ordination. Something in his hand. He threw it up and down, a metronomic game of catch. "How do you have one of these?"

The pick gun.

"Don't you?"

"Pissing me off isn't going to get you released."

"Pissing me off isn't going to go well for you." she retaliated.

"How did you end up with the Professor? You're not exactly his type."

She didn't want to hear what was fast becoming a truth. "I want to hire you."

He cupped his free hand around his ear, "You know, if you listen hard enough, I'm sure you can hear the echo of what I said the other day, nothing's going to induce me to help you."

"You don't want to be paid for a job, fair enough. I'll go elsewhere."

"You wouldn't know how."

"I have one of those," she nodded at the pick gun, "one that tackles deadbolts," thank you, Nora, for pointing out what Provisions had stressed about how good it was, rolled up in the warning don't come back without it, "you think I can't hire a hacker? I bought your line that you're the best. But this job is simple enough for me to choose someone else."

"You're at a bit of a disadvantage." he gestured at her.

"You think I came here without a plan? My people are expecting a check-in, it doesn't happen, well, I'm sure you can guess."

He laughed, a belly laugh. "You don't honestly expect me

to buy that? No phone, no ID, no keys. Oyster card, bit of cash, not promising for me to believe anything you say."

She shrugged. "Your funeral."

Eva hoped CJ was reading her silence as nonchalance, unconcern, not the chorus of what was she going to do that was actually hammering through her mind. She tried to pretend he wasn't studying her, not squirm beneath his gaze.

He placed the pick gun on the worktop beside him. "What's the job?"

"I want you to open a URL for me."

"A URL? You don't need a hacker for that."

"This isn't anything run of the mill." She paused, he hadn't been happy when she'd mentioned their name before. Saying it now might get her thrown straight out, or worse. Mustn't think about the 'or worse'. "I'm trying to get in touch with The Society. Before you say no," she cut him off, probably about to say exactly that, "you should understand that they're after Charles and, if they get him, well that's the end of your paydays." She glanced around the room. "What's the time?" Looked CJ deadpan full in the face, "only you can't afford for me to be late for my check-in."

"When?"

"What's the time?"

"Ten past four."

"Fifteen minutes. Name your price."

"I have all the money I need."

"Great, what don't you have?"

"I'm set."

Now what? She'd been convinced money would sway it. She fought down the urge to panic. She couldn't let him read any weakness in her lies, her anger that he was wasting time.

"Okay, I'll go elsewhere. You need to untie me."

He held her gaze. She tried to keep it blank, to not panic that this could be a life and death decision. Lily.

He walked out of the kitchen.

"You realise we won't be replacing your front door, don't you?" A last try.

"No battering ram's getting through that."

Eva laughed, forcing it to sound less like hysteria, more like she was driving this. "A battering ram? You think we're amateurs?"

He sauntered back in.

"They're on their way already," Eva ad-libbed, "my back-up, and the one you need to be worried about is the one who used to study IEDs for the military. He loves a big bang."

"IOU for me to do what you want, if you call them off."

"I'm not making any calls until you untie me."

"I can make you, you're forgetting I have the upper hand."

"Do you?" Eva smiled sweetly. "Charles said you're good, but enough that you know my code word for everything's okay and the one to blow this place wide open? That's pretty impressive." Eva faked a yawn, though her heart was hammering so fast she was surprised he couldn't see her rocking to its beat. "Untie me, I'm leaving."

"An IOU." CJ insisted.

"Untie me."

He bent down behind her and snap, snap, her legs were free. "IOU."

Taking a gigantic leap into places she didn't want to be, Eva agreed. "You have two requests only, I have one veto."

CJ considered. "Fair enough. Two requests, one veto. It's their details on the paper you had on you?"

Eva nodded.

He picked it up from the worktop, ran up the stairs and she heard the fast keying of someone who'd used keyboards for most of their life. Silence, more tapping.

She stood up slowly, the effects of the sedative almost gone now. She focussed on the sound of him typing as she walked upstairs, if he was occupied, he couldn't knock her down them.

"You called your people off?"

Eva held up her bound wrists. "I'll need to use your phone."

"I have other fail safes around this house if you act out any stupid ideas."

"Why would I do that, you're doing what I want." She held her wrists out and he snipped the cable ties off her. He pulled a mobile out of the many drawers and handed it to her. "Don't make me use another one on you."

Eva went through the charade of a raid-pausing conversation until she reported in, once she'd left her current location, with her broken mobile voicemail. A crazy message if anyone thought to look for it, if she was never seen again. At least there was a record of where she'd been.

"They're talking to me." CJ gestured at one of the screens on his desk. She'd have to take his word for it, the scroll of text covering most of the page was gobbledygook to her. "What do you want them for?"

"To find out who instructed them to kill Charles Buchanan and Eva Janssen."

CJ typed, interpreted the answer. "They're asking if you have a job for them."

"Did you tell them what I said?"

He typed again, "there, twice. . .same response."

"Try this, I want to buy out the contract on Charles Buchanan and Eva Janssen."

CJ consulted the screen's response. "You can't afford it and it's not their way."

Their way? They killed people, now they were clinging to ethics?

"How do I stop them murdering my husband and me? I'm listening."

CJ typed as though he was trying to break the world speed record. "They'll give you a task, acquit yourself well, and they'll consider cancelling the contract."

"What do they want me to do?"

"Find out who killed Hunter Malone."

"Do I have their agreement that Charles and I are safe while I do this?"

CJ typed. They watched the screen. Who was on the other side reading it, holding her and Charles' lives in their hands?

The screen flashed blue then black.

CJ shrugged, "guess that's a no."

45

This time being on the outside of CJ's house was a relief, the long walk to the bus stop a chance to think about what Eva had learned. And not think about what she'd agreed to.

It was the Sherlock Holmes question: if you eliminated the impossible, even just the improbable, whatever remained was the truth. Therefore, if The Society wanted to know who killed Hunter Malone, they hadn't. Unless it was a test to see how resistant to scrutiny their safeguards were. She could second guess this for ever.

Eva got on the bus, tapped her Oyster card at the console and climbed to the top deck. She sat in the front where Lily used to pretend she was driving, as if that could make her materialise beside her. Eva smoothed the fabric of the seat next to her, remembering the patterns Lily used to see in it—Lily, where are you?

Eva closed her eyes, her fingertips on the fabric grounding her in her painful here and now. I'm finding you, baby, I'm coming.

Being back under the SIS umbrella loosened controls,

changed priorities, so when Eva made it to her desk, the email she'd wanted from the police was already waiting. The e-fit of the man who'd attacked her stared out at her from the monitor. It surprised her, the rise in her heart rate. His likeness couldn't hurt her. And she'd hurt him back. He didn't look quite like that anymore if the amount of his blood that had splashed over her was anything to go by.

Eva searched for the phone number she needed. It was a precarious tightrope between how she wanted to help Gordon and Nora by finding out about the charm school, in case that was what had cost Eric his life, and pursuing her own agenda, in case it was that. They weren't tangled together exactly, but they intersected.

She dialled the number.

"Eva? I didn't expect to be speaking to you again."

"Nor me you, and you're still in Moscow, you must really like it there."

Beatrice laughed. "Or they're punishing me. Jobs in this Embassy aren't exactly on the list of cool assignments."

"But still the most interesting?" Eva remembered Moscow had been Beatrice's first choice of posting and she'd studied very hard to make herself the best candidate.

"Indeed. What brings you back to SIS?"

"I'm consulting on something, I'm sending you an e-fit, can you see if he was anywhere near Moscow before the Hunter Malone assassination?"

"Interesting. Sure, fire it over. Is he a suspect?"

"If not for that, for a murder here. Do you have any leads on the ground?"

Beatrice blew out frustration. "Not really, all we're finding is smoke and mirrors, which makes me wonder. There's an official state investigation. We all know that means nothing, but the word is that they're appeasing the Americans."

Which meant they weren't behind it.

Eva pulled out the file Gordon had given her – he was right, Eric had sourced little on the charm school, but he hadn't known Charles. Eva grabbed paper and pen and brainstormed what she knew about his connections to the USA. He'd told her he'd interned there in the summers during his first degree, spent time there during his PhD, but he went just about everywhere in the world all the time to attend academic conferences.

She set the SIS search function loose to worm out details it would have taken her days to cross reference while she went to make a drink.

Gordon poked his head into the kitchen.

"You want one?" Eva asked, dropping a teabag into her mug.

"Heading out for a meeting, how's it going?"

"I might have something, a little sideways, but it's looking promising."

"I have news for you."

"You found them?"

"Not quite. Charles knocked out the man you saw unconscious in the hangar. Only he got on board the plane, no hostiles involved."

No hostiles. Eva rolled that around in her mind. No hostiles, no trafficking ring, no assassins. Tension leaked out of her, Lily was safe with her father. But Charles knocking Luke out, commandeering the plane—Charles making them take off without her?

"Are you certain? Could Charles have been under duress?"

Gordon shrugged. "No one else was seen anywhere near

the plane. Of course he could have been contacted remotely, but it's unlikely, where's the duress?"

So she was going down the right route.

Back at her desk her search had given her the titles of all the conferences and symposia Charles had attended since he qualified, the titles of which were beyond her or sounded as boring as hell until she got a rogue result. Double checking her search instructions showed her it wasn't the system at fault, but her knowledge of her husband. Charles was a chemical engineer, with the world to choose from. Why would he attend a psychology conference in London every year?

Psychology, he didn't even rate it as an academic field. So if not what, then who? She set the system searching, watching it flick through the new parameters she'd set.

When the phone rang, she answered it almost absent mindedly.

"It's Dario, thought you'd want to know they sacked me."

"What? They can't do that."

"Apparently Vaishali can, I'm undermining her authority, not following her orders."

"Every Drop's not the military, we value everyone's opinions."

"Not anymore."

Eva felt the pain of betrayal sharpen inside her. "How did you upset her?"

"She wasn't upset, she was, it was weird, it was more like she was terrified. I'd told her I was going to see our pipe suppliers. Things are getting worse at Tirupudur since they dismantled the aerial network but at Seitu, where it's intact, things aren't as bad. It's probably a wasted trip, but I wanted to rule it out."

Eva should have been watching it, shouldn't have abandoned the people she'd sworn to help. Pressure pushed at her, another weighty priority to juggle. She massaged her temples around her bruise. The dull residual ache from whatever sedative CJ had used on her was blooming into a full-on stress headache.

"I'm really sorry, Dario." She should have been there to look out for him. "Leave that with me, I'll go. There's a whole procedure Vaishali must follow. It's on the employee pages, protocols, termination plans, numbers of employment law specialists. If there's anything I can do, let me know."

Time only to talk herself out of the urge to get on the phone to Vaishali when the system told her it had completed its new search. The cursor blinked at her, waiting for her next instruction.

One man had met Charles away from the psychology conference, a dinner reservation for two. CCTV confirmed it, both men had arrived at and left the restaurant separately. Eva clicked onto the public-facing profile of Professor Louie Steinman, gripped the mouse.

He was older, maybe some margin for error there in a looser chin, under-eye bags, age-spots and a thin halo of white hair. Eva closed her eyes to check her memory, opened them looking directly into the Professor's eyes. No doubt at all.

46

———

Eva shuddered, she was safe. It wasn't him. She looked again at the photo of Professor Louie Steinman on her computer screen, past the mild-mannered professional façade. In his eyes, even in the pixels, albeit watered down, she recognised the same cold brutality she'd seen in the man who killed Nancy Seymour and tried to kill her.

Eva's desk phone made her start like a gun had gone off beside her.

"Eva, Beatrice from Moscow. Got an ID for you. Your e-fit was pretty accurate." Eva wasn't surprised, she'd never forget that face. "Brett Steinman entered Russia on a tourist visa two days before Malone's assassination."

"He used his real passport?"

"He went to the US Embassy twice. I pulled a favour; he has dual nationality, British and American. I'm waiting for their CCTV footage to see if it was him, if he rigged the car then."

"In the Embassy compound?"

"None of us were in crisis mode, clearly we've become

too complacent behind our walls. We're all looking at threats outside them, none of us expect it to be one of our own. I've got a request in for the street footage near the Ambassador's residence but the Russians like to watch anything we're interested in first so it takes time. I'll let you know if I find anything."

Eva paged through Louie Steinman's university profile. A public lecture at 7:30 pm was more than she'd dared hope for. She knew where he'd be and how to get close to him, somewhere his neanderthal of a relative wouldn't be. And she had an in through Charles. She shuddered. She couldn't rely on Beatrice in Moscow turning up anything on CCTV quickly enough to confirm what they suspected. And Eva was sure The Society only dealt in absolutes. It wasn't as though Professor Louie Steinman could hurt her in a public lecture hall. Eva could handle an old man.

She climbed the stairs to Nora's office and knocked. No answer. Should she bother Gordon with it? She'd give him the choice. But he didn't answer the knock at his door either.

If she went now, she'd have the chance to take care of another of those heavy priorities first.

"You can't see Mr Mills," the middle-aged woman wasn't even trying for reasonable, "without an appointment."

She held up one finger on Eva's reply and coughed before she picked up the ringing phone. While Eva got Mrs Hyde, the caller got Dr Jekyll.

"Pipemaster UK, trademaster specialist, we value every customer. How can I help you today?"

Eva took her chance to dive through the side door that

must lead to the warehouse. The vastness of the space beneath bright lights was surprising. It stored a sober rainbow of black, grey and white pipes brightened by orange on one side.

As she stepped away from the door, the MD appeared as though she'd triggered an alarm. "Mr Mills, Eva Janssen, CEO of Every Drop." She injected enough authority into her introduction that he would never guess she was jeopardising her future by being there.

"You should make an appointment."

"I shouldn't have to be here at all."

Long sideburns and hair poked out from beneath his white hard hat. Dressed in a god-awful brown checked shirt and an orange hi-vis vest, he could have walked right off the pages of a magazine's homage to the seventies. He gestured at a rack behind her, frowning at her boots. "Health and safety."

Eva put on a bright blue hard hat. "I'll take responsibility for my toes."

He held out his clipboard. "Care to sign to that effect?"

She grabbed it and did.

He took the clipboard back and checked. "There's nothing wrong with our pipes. You need to be looking at the supply."

"We are. I'm just here to understand. Other agencies use your pipes for water transportation in the developing world?" He nodded. "And they're all manufactured in the same way."

"Same as it's always been done."

"Can I see what we buy?"

He looked at her inadequate boots but led her to a run of thin black pipes that filled the centre racking. "Water pipes that get buried have a greater diameter but suspending them we're limited by the weight factor, water's heavy."

"Remind me how these pipes differ from the regular ones." It had been at Every Drop's inception that they'd struck the golden idea of using the space above the slums to get the water in.

"The material is thicker, more rigid, the pipe diameter narrower and the span shorter, overlapping joins wider." He slapped his hand against the pipe at his waist height. "These aren't for you lot though, haven't had the compound added."

"The compound?" Eva forced a laugh. "I'm the Chief Executive Officer, not the Chief Operating Scientist." She plucked a title from her imagination. "Remind me."

"To stop them getting brittle under the UV rays. Fearful sun out there. We dip the pipes in it before they're shipped out. No one complaining about that, are they? We're following your regulations."

"No, no, that's fine, that part of it."

"You might want to think about selling it on, no one's got sick from your pipes. Only thing that's different from everyone else's orders is your compound." He winked at her. "We might have to charge more to add it, seeing as it's a desirable element."

"It sounds like our scientist in charge needs a bonus. Which one was it, who instructed you?"

"I don't remember names, more of an accent guy myself. Daughter's a budding actress, what I haven't spent on accent coaches. The man who comes in is a shoe-in for a Royal."

Eva's mind flicked through a list of Every Drop staff. No one spoke like that. "Where does the paper trail go for this? The extra cost?"

"To the bloke who's been in the news, wittering on about how your water is saving everyone. Should at least mention us." Mills complained. "Wetherington, like the toffee, that's him. Without us adding the compound, you've got nothing. It's not him who comes though."

"What does he look like, the man who does?"

"Nothing stands out about him, brown hair, eyes, average height, weight, bit of a beard going on. Insists on being here when we do the dip, brings the compound with him every time. Bit anal like that."

Those four words told her exactly who. Charles, hurting her again. How was he involved in this? What were he and Stuart doing?

Eva sighed. In the scheme of things, what she wanted didn't matter. Doing the right thing was more important. "I want you to pause the next shipment until I personally give you the go ahead."

Mills looked at his clipboard as though his sheet of paper could tell him what to say. "That's irregular. Your lot's been on and on about speeding it all up. We've been paying double overtime to get it done to your timetable. And we can't just store it here, you know."

"I understand that, but we can't proceed with any new installations while people are falling sick, you must see that."

"We're not a charity, space is money." He took his hard hat off and ran his hand over thinning hair.

"I don't want to be heavy-handed here, Mr Mills, but I must insist you pause the shipment, pause all shipments until the sickness passes. I'm sure there's nothing wrong with your pipes, but we must make sure, mustn't we? I'll be telling the media you've been very helpful on this."

He gave a curt nod. "Wetherington won't like this. Been banging on about time is of the essence." He did a lousy impression of Stuart.

Eva shrugged. "He doesn't have to."

47

───────

Eva followed Professor Louie Steinman from the lecture hall. He walked slowly, less swinging his ancient briefcase with each step, than gripping it tightly so gravity didn't pull it from his grasp. No strength in those hands with which to strangle her. No resilience in his leg muscles to chase her. She was safe, even if the well-lit campus was only dotted with a few students and people taking shortcuts through the grounds.

She slipped inside the access-controlled building he entered before the door closed after him. His back to her, he seemed focussed on which lift would carry him up to the next floor. When the doors pinged open, she was already in the stairwell.

His puffing and sighing led her along a corridor where he rattled a key in a lock and a door squeaked open. Professor Louie Steinman, the name plaque confirmed. They could have moved him to the ground floor.

A glance inside the office to confirm he was alone and Eva went in after him. The room smelt old, stacks of journals, folders, yellowed papers everywhere.

"Interesting lecture." She announced herself.

He looked up at her from where he was stacking papers into his briefcase. She had to hide her shudder. The man who'd tried to kill her was all too clearly visible beneath the professor's crumpled features.

"What's yours then, your learned prejudice?" his voice was surprisingly strong, his vibrant address hadn't been just the product of a good sound system. His clipped English accent was very different to the broad London his relative spoke.

"I've never really thought about it." Though that people shouldn't kill other people probably topped the whole of her belief systems. "I should imagine I have many."

"A little more of an enlightened view than the normal denial," he peered at her. She held his gaze while he checked out her healing grazes, bruises and dressing on her forehead. "You're not a current student."

"What makes you ask that, because I'm mature?"

"What makes you ask that, a learned prejudice?"

"How do you know Charles Buchanan?"

He snapped his briefcase closed "I'm late, you'll have to excuse me."

She followed him out of the messy office, which he locked and checked twice. "I can walk with you. You had dinner with Charles during the symposium in July, it's odd that he attends every year, it's not his area of expertise."

"Academic colleagues collaborate all the time, it's not geographically or subject specific, there are tangential inter-sections across all fields."

"Let me." Eva held the door to the lift lobby open.

An ancient ring tone warbled from his inside jacket pocket. He fumbled out a phone and listened. "Come up."

He returned it to his pocket, "another student, no rest for the conscientious."

He dawdled back to his office, Eva with him.

"I'm Charles' wife. He's gone missing, I'm trying to find him."

"You should have said. Charles and I have been colleagues for a lot of years." He gestured for her to precede him inside. "He interned with me in the States during his PhD. For an engineer, he has some interesting ideas on the psyche." He did? Eva was beginning to wonder if he was a twin and had switched places with the one she'd never met. "You're American?"

"You sound surprised."

"Your accent is misleading."

"Or a learned prejudice." The professor looked at the doorway and Eva recognised the back of his head. How had she not noticed it earlier when she'd been following him? His thin halo of white hair, he'd been in the last photo she'd seen of the charm school, talking to Charles.

Footsteps from the corridor stopped outside his office. Eva followed the Professor's gaze and looked right at the man she never wanted to see again. His face was a mass of angry weals swollen against spider-leg stitches, his expression as stunned as hers probably was.

"Is this her?" the Professor asked.

The killer nodded, took a step inside.

Eva's insides somersaulted.

She held up a finger, mimicking Mr Mills' secretary, as though that would stop him tearing her apart. "You look worse than me, I probably should apologise for all that," she waved her finger in an oval at his face, "but really, what the hell were you doing? Did you not think we'd be watching you?"

"You're The Society?" Professor Steinman asked. Did she imagine a hoped-for querulous tremor to his voice now? "You said you're Charles Buchanan's wife."

"I can't be both? Charles is two people, isn't he." Her bluffing grabbed at a breadcrumb trail made whole. The Professor's look confirmed it, him too. And why so worried? Unless. . .trying to reason it out was like trying to knit spaghetti. Instead, Eva took her gamble in both hands, ignoring that she was on a crumbling precipice. "Why do you think I'm so busy looking for Buchanan? You let him get away, your attempt at a gas explosion was pitiful." Eva sighed. "You see, Professor, I do have a prejudice but it's hard learned, it's why I don't work with amateurs."

"Brett, deal with her."

Eva took her second gamble of the last minute. "You want to go again?" She looked at the killer. "I'll repay the favour better this time, I'm prepared today."

She could maybe get through the door ahead of him. But he'd be on her before she got halfway down the corridor, and she was completely empty-handed. The papers on the desk were useless as a weapon. The Professor had no handy paperweights or letter openers, not so much as a stained tea mug.

"Open the window, Dad." Steinman's son looked at her from the open doorway. "I know what you're thinking."

Eva could feel hysteria bubbling up inside her. He had no idea unless it was all the swear words.

"I'm sure you don't but go ahead, we can play guessing games."

"We're only one floor up, me throwing you out there isn't likely to kill you, but it's enough for what's that lovely euphemism? Life-changing injuries, but that'll only be a problem until I pay you a visit in your hospital bed. I'll even let you choose - heart attack like Tony Banks? Suffocation like Nancy Seymour? Bomb like Hunter Malone?"

"Finished?" Eva raised her eyebrows at him. "Like I said, amateurs. Here's another learned maxim for you, Professor. If you want something done, do it yourself." Steeling her knee, she whipped around the desk, swept up the office chair. It was surprisingly heavy, but somehow she hefted it high enough that the act of letting it go crashed it through the window.

Steinman's son roared and charged after her, but she grabbed his father, spun him in between them. "Stop or he follows."

"You wouldn't."

"I'm The Society, you really think I'm here to be nice? We don't take kindly to what you've done."

He stopped. "It wasn't our idea."

Eva's mind raced faster than her heartbeat, trying to put the pieces together so they made sense. "Then why do it?"

"To obfuscate clearly," the Professor's breathing was faster, shallower, but still he struggled against her.

"Who instructed you?"

"Brett, stop poncing about and deal with her."

Eva pinched his neck hard, shutting him up as he became lightheaded. She shuffled him round to keep him her barrier between her and Steinman Junior, backing right up to the gaping window. The professor's legs became weaker, he sagged. She released her hold on his neck and reached behind her, pincer-grabbing one of the shards of glass left in the frame. But it had stayed there for a reason. It resisted. The Professor straightened, pushed against her. Eva pinched his neck again, harder.

"I have your father's life in my hands, literally. I'm pressing on his carotid artery, just enough to make him lightheaded at the moment. But I'm not a doctor," her hands were cramping, his weight on her too heavy. She loosened her grip. "I don't know how much pressure is too much, will cause a stroke, brain damage, how long he can stand for me to do this. How far do you want to push it?"

Eva felt the wall of the office against her right shoulder. The gaping blackness of the car park below pulled at her. Freezing air flooded the hothouse room. It was a standoff until she grew too tired to hold the professor up, until she misjudged it, until he retaliated or until the son charged her.

Lose, lose.

48

Eva stared at the killer as though her gaze could hold him there. He looked from her to his father, to the desk, still nothing there to use as a weapon, to her. He took a half-step inside the office.

"I'm warning you." she growled.

The blip made her start. Outside, it was a car being unlocked.

"Help," she screamed, "Call an ambulance, Professor Steinman's having a heart attack. He needs help. His son Brett Steinman is in here with me."

The man looking up at her from beside his unlocked car was already on the phone, directing his colleague to the first floor.

"You might think you can disappear," Eva told Steinman Junior. "But we're after you. You need to be made a lesson of. Who instructed you?"

She squeezed harder at the Professor's neck. He sagged against her and his legs gave way.

"Who instructed you?" She glared at Steinman Junior

but he stayed silent, ready to pounce, just looking for his chance.

She lost her battle holding the Professor vertical and she landed on the floor with him. She tensed against another onslaught from his son but he'd vanished.

The Professor looked harmless, an old man collapsed. 'Deal with her.' She'd done what she had to.

She had never been so glad to see anyone as she was the guy who charged into the office on his phone summoning campus security and first aiders.

The shaking hit her as the man who'd made the 999 call rounded the office door and a security guard made the room too crowded.

Eva manoeuvred her way out even as the siren of incoming help tore in through the broken window. She tucked her hair in the neck of her f

ce, kept her head down as she limped away from the campus. Her heart hammered at every bush and parked car, every corner and doorway, every likely place for ambush until she found a cab. The cabbie who took her back to St George's Grove definitely wasn't Steinman but still Eva's heart thundered a warning at her the whole journey that she wasn't safe.

Her adrenaline-fuelled strength left her as she stumbled out of the airlock and slumped onto the bottom step of the stairs, not entirely sure she shouldn't be running for the ladies.

"Eva, come on up." Gordon's voice filled the corridor. They still worked long hours there.

He buzzed her into his office and pushed a whisky across his desk before she sat down. "You look like you need it." He let her sip at it. "Tell."

It fell out of her, a dam bursting, everything that had

happened since she'd met Eric, the things she'd done that would haunt her. She left out her deal with CJ, embarrassed that she'd agreed to something that could burn her.

"That's quite something. So next step, you need to contact The Society to tell them what you've found?" Gordon asked.

Eva opened her mouth, closed it again. She didn't know how, hadn't thought to ask CJ.

"Let me get someone on it. We've been looking at this group for a while, you appear to have an in, it'll help us get past their firewall at least."

"But it's not just them after Charles, someone else instructed Steinman, told them to pretend to be The Society."

"I'll get a team after him, we'll get eyes on his life, question the father. Leave it to us, Eva. You've done enough."

The whisky was unknotting her, soothing her. "I just need to know they've cancelled the contract on Charles, he's all Lily has to keep her safe right now."

"Addison Clarke's pilot has confirmed Charles paid a sweetener to change their flight plan from Chennai to Marrakech, two passengers, one man, one child. Extra to not report the change until he arrived back in the UK."

"Marrakech? But Charles hates the heat."

In a heart-breaking second, she realised her terrible new truth. Morocco was what, four, six hours away. He hadn't contacted her, no email, no questions about how to reach her, call for her to join them.

A sharp panic punched Eva in the stomach. How could she possibly find them if he didn't want her to?

49

Hypnotic in its exotic rhythm, the early morning call to prayer broke into Charles' on off dozing. Like an aural flame, it touched the nearest mosques, and the azans rebounded around the city in a compelling round robin.

Leave? Stay? His steps to Lily continued the battle that had raged in him all night. The semantics, the likelihoods, the possibilities. His logic had deserted him, leaving his head a tormented, messy jumble of shattered dreams.

Still asleep, her breathing was easy and calm. Where should they go? The chess piece, rather the information inside it, was it the shield, the protection he needed it to be? Was his threat enough? Jed's office would protect him regardless of what he did. Charles needed his information to do the same for him.

It should never have come to this. After everything Charles had risked for him, Jed should have trusted him, all of them who'd put him where he was. Jed the Judas paying Charles his pieces of silver carefully packed in the leather holdall, the culmination of years of expensive, no questions asked, here want another grant, research. And now he might not live to see his brilliance pay off?

He found himself in the courtyard, slumped onto the tiled edge of the pool. He had asked for the wrong payment. For all those years, he'd got it completely backwards. Would it have mattered if he'd sacrificed the acknowledgement of his academic prowess? If the world believed he was just another scientist? His empty future told him no.

Nancy, with her gone, all that he'd imagined had been snatched away, lost forever, no chance to turn the clock back and put things right as he'd planned. No happy ever after. Charles sobbed for it all.

When he fell quiet, he stayed there, sitting on the cold tiled floor, against the raised side of the pool, letting the gentle shush of the circulating water soothe.

There he was off-grid, as safe as possible, especially while Jed believed him to be in London. His gaze strayed to the closed door. Terry had probably thought that. Ironic really, his distrust of the modern world and all its tracking— no online poker for him—hadn't killed him. He must have bought his demise instead with the turn of the wrong card, mahjong tile, the faltering stride of a horse.

Tendrils of something rotten reached for him, Terry's reminder that he was still there. Charles needed to get rid of the body. The body, they'd hardly been brothers to each other for a long time, but it still felt wrong calling him that.

He stumbled to the kitchen and drank two glasses of water in quick succession to relieve his cried-out headache. He tipped away the half of the third glass he couldn't face. The clear stream splashed into the sink, droplets bouncing up from the hard surface onto his skin. His index finger circled the drops. Water, the elixir of life, unless you were able to manipulate molecules, unless you were a god.

Would he? He could, he should. Round and round, his finger burst the fragile shapes on his hand, pressed hard against his bones.

The idea was wild. But perfect. And why else would he have found his way there at this time? Charles would take a last lesson from Terry – if Air Force One was on its way to Africa or Europe, anywhere on this hemisphere that was reasonable for Maxwell and Sara Peyton to travel to, that was Charles' winning coin toss. If it was going elsewhere, so be it. His money train would go far in Marrakech, and it would only help Lily to learn Arabic. It didn't even need to be a zero-sum game, revenge not lost, only postponed.

He ranged through the TV channels. Terry apparently hadn't worried about fitting in, his satellite choices were English only. BBC World News stopped Charles' channel hopping. The flash from his past smiling at the camera as though he was the greatest statesman on the planet, Jed Carson. Beaming harder still as he climbed the steps to the open door on Airforce One, before giving the expected wave and disappearing inside.

The shot panned back to the studio. "President Jed Carson leaving the USA yesterday on his way to Marrakech in Morocco, where the G20 leaders are meeting for a summit into technological advances to further progress for the human race."

Not just Africa or Morocco, but Marrakech. Charles had won the coin toss.

"The programme commences with a dinner this evening," the reporter went on, "hosted by Per Larsson, the Chairman of the Nobel Prize Committee. Much of the work being showcased here will be contenders for Nobel prizes next year."

Per was going to be there, Charles had won blackjack.

The luck that had got Terry this riad was rubbing off on him. Lucky Riad Eight indeed.

The screen split into two halves, on the left the rich warmth of an African sun, on the right the false cheeriness of LED lights in the London studio. "What's on the agenda for the summit?" The couch-seated presenter asked.

"This summit is an addition to the normal programme of G20 events and could be badged G40 because of the number of nations attending. Morocco was selected as host, given its recent advances in technology driving the extension of a reliable and safe water supply to its people."

"It would seem a perfect time, given the unrest happening in areas where the water is making people sick." The studio presenter commented.

"The water isn't making people sick, you stupid woman." Charles snapped the TV off.

"Dad?"

"Hey, sleepyhead. How are you feeling?"

Lily rubbed at her eyes. "Hungry."

"Me too. How about we go out for breakfast?"

"What about . . ." Her gaze swivelled to the balcony beyond the fluttering long curtains, to the courtyard below.

"Don't worry about that. The police will deal with it and we don't need to be here while they do."

"You spoke to them?"

"I know this isn't the best start to our holiday, but. . ." he lost the rest of his words. There was nothing to say to make things better for Terry. "There's a nice shower in the main bathroom, go freshen up and we'll go out."

"Can I call Mum?"

"I don't know how to call her, her phone broke."

"Well, she's at work, you said so."

"Of course, silly of me to forget."

How could he have her knowing where they were, about his brother? And he couldn't have her challenging him about what happened at the airport, about leaving her behind, in Lily's earshot.

And Lily, what about her? Eva would want her back. He didn't know if he could give her up; she was all he had left. Could he reunite with Eva? There was only that one meeting with Nancy that she'd seen. He could sweet-talk her again, but did he want to?

"There's a phone here, Dad." Lily called him into the room Terry had used as an office.

Charles dialled the 044 for the UK and keyed the zero at the start of the London phone number that international calls didn't require. After the third time of it failing he suggested trying later. "Phones don't maybe work as well here."

"What about my mobile? You still have it, don't you?"

"It's not working, I don't think you have international calls on it."

"Can't we get them?"

"When the phones are working, we can try. Now get washed up and let's go eat. Mum will understand."

While Lily did as he asked, Charles woke up Terry's PC.

In his personal email account, he selected one of the oldest unsent drafts with the subject line 'Your car insurance renewal'. Buried in the bumpf at the bottom amongst the insurance company's details, he found the phone number. For what it was worth on this call, he blocked Terry's number and dialled.

He hadn't even finished wondering whether the number would still be valid when it was answered.

"CJ, it's Charles Buchanan."

"No more favours, Charles. I know you were listening when I told you that."

"Last one, unless a locked door on a different continent is too much for you. It's a tricky job, it has the potential to draw some real heat and a lot of fireworks afterwards, so it needs to be very untraceable. And obviously it's not an unpaid favour, you can bill me."

"Did you know your wife came here, she wanted to contact The Society."

What was Eva playing at? If she found out—there'd be no reconciliation, even if he decided he wanted it. "Did she, contact them?"

"I did, she's finding out who killed Hunter Malone for them."

"She paid you?"

"Not yet, she now owes me a favour."

Eva, what have you done? You don't make open-ended promises with people like CJ. And having anything to do with The Society, she was playing with the devil.

"I'll bill you double. That work for you?" CJ was asking.

"Yes."

"Glad we understand each other, now where's the door?"

50

'I know more secrets than a Catholic priest', the spook humour on the mug into which Eva poured her first coffee of the day must have been something else, it almost made her smile. She stared at the froth's bubbles popping, trying to corral her thoughts into something more than panic. Knowing they'd flown to Marrakech hadn't helped. If they were still there, Lily was one in a million people. And if Charles had moved them on, one in seven billion.

"You're looking better this morning, how are you doing?" Nora pulled Eva out of her reverie.

Eva shrugged, slopping her now lukewarm coffee over her hand, over the laminate flooring she'd been staring at. She put the mug down and pulled off a piece of blue roll to mop up the puddle.

"Another?" Nora asked.

"I'm good."

"And I'm the boss." she said.

"Aren't you?" Eva's lips aimed for a smile but what she couldn't quite manage, Nora made up for, hooting even louder than the noise of the coffee machine grinding the beans.

"I'll tell himself you said that." She wiped at her eyes.

"He's aware, trust me."

Nora frothed the milk, the hissing steaming filling the silence with all the things Eva couldn't bring herself to share because then she'd have to think about them. Nora jiggled the milk jug back and forth over the dark liquid in their mugs. "I can never make it pretty but as far as coffees go, best in the capital I'd say. Hmmm, what do you have here then?" she turned the mug anti-clockwise, back again. "Looks like the monster from the deep." She rinsed the jug, wiped the machine down. "Lily will be fine, she's with her dad, not a kidnapper or worse." Nora studied her. "Ah, that's why you're worried. He doesn't know, does he?"

"Know?" Eva's pretence melted away beneath Nora's look. "How did you?"

"She looks like him, doesn't she, Vincent? In the video of her you showed me."

Eva could only nod, ridiculously close to tears. It was the first time she'd ever acknowledged to anyone else that Lily wasn't Charles' daughter. "I'm surprised you remember him."

"I remember everyone, especially the good ones."

"He was, wasn't he?"

Nora checked the biscuit tin. "Someone remembered, vegan cookies. Come." Nora handed her a coffee and took her and the biscuits into the room Eva was using as an office. "Let's take a minute. You want to talk about it?"

Eva read and reread the inscription on the mug. Her secret was out. What would it hurt to give all of it away? "It was just after Charles dumped me. Vincent was exactly what I needed then, fun, a way to find me again."

"And then he got sent back to Belgium. You never told him?"

How to summarise all the soul searching, the sleepless nights, trying to reconcile not telling Vincent, the wondering if Eva could be enough for her unborn baby. It had been a lot for a twenty-one-year-old to wrestle with. And while she struggled for the right thing to do, Lily arrived. A squalling whirlwind that made her whole, completed her life, filled her heart.

"I didn't know what to do, I, things were already so. . ."

"You don't have to justify your decisions to me." Nora smiled at her. Were her daughters and grandchildren aware how lucky they were?

Eva sipped the hot foam. "I should have told Charles the truth when he came back into my life, saying we should try again, but he was so happy when he met Lily, I couldn't take that away from him. The timing was so close from when we split up, he never questioned that she wasn't his. I thought he might have guessed when we tried for another baby and it didn't happen but, if he did, he never said." Eva sighed. "Ensam är stark, my father used to tell me that. Alone is strong." She'd believed him until she'd been a single mum trying to juggle the hours the intelligence service demanded and then, once she inherited her father's money, trying to set up Every Drop. "It makes me sound weak."

"No more than the rest of us. Don't we all want someone to share things with? Humans aren't meant to be solitary creatures. Charles'll look after Lily, Eva. He would, even if he knew."

But would he though? Eva didn't recognise the Charles of this last week as the man she'd married, the man she thought she loved.

"What are you going to do now?" Nora asked.

Eva wanted to lay her head on the table, go back to sleep. "What can I do?"

"You're not helpless. Agents aren't our best resource, you remember? And you're not without anything you can use. So what are you waiting for?" Nora laid her hand on Eva's. "You know what to do."

Eva nodded, she did, at least where to start.

Addison Clarke's Executive Assistant put Eva through to him and this time she didn't get voicemail.

"I was wondering when you might ring."

"Luke? You're okay?"

"Yeah, hard head. How're you? Any news about your daughter? I heard you missed the flight too."

"I saw that you'd been hurt, I got off to make sure you were okay."

She heard a smile in his voice. "Your turn to be my knight."

"Not so much, I was—" Impossible to explain being picked up by the intelligence service. "It's a long story. But you're okay?"

"I'm okay. How can I help?"

"I wanted to ask Addison if his pilot knows where Charles was going in Marrakech. He has no ties there. . ." That she was aware of. "Does Addison hate me, for Charles taking the plane?"

"Hate you, why? He said you could use the plane, the plane was used. No deal there."

"But you being knocked out?"

"Now why would I tell him about that and ruin my macho image? Addison's about to leave town, off to Marrakech for the summit on technology driving water safety as it happens. Seems like I can give you another lift."

51

Luke waited for Eva on the tarmac by the hangar. "Let's hope we go somewhere today."

Addison was sitting in one of the seats facing the direction of travel, every inch the man in charge of his destiny. Making it before he was Eva's age would do that, she was sure, give anyone an unshakeable confidence. Now, at around fifty and, according to his official bio, in the prime of his life, he was keen to give back.

"Addison, I can't tell you how grateful I am. Sorry I'm so late." No need to bother him with the trifles of Nora having to hurry a passport issue to Mach Ten.

"It's no problem, the summit doesn't start until tomorrow and I'll be there in plenty of time for the dinner. Sit yourself down." Eva dropped into the seat next to him. "A drop of the good stuff always helps the flight I find. Stephanie." He gestured at the air hostess who produced a tray holding a healthy measure of an excellent whisky Eva would guess in three crystal glasses. Luke buckled himself in opposite Addison and took one.

"How do you two know each other?" Eva asked.

"We have a mutual friend." Luke held his glass up. "Cheers."

"Skol." Eva replied automatically.

"The Vikings did a fine toast." Addison approved. He let her drink, watched her shudder before hitting her with the question. "So, Eva, tell me, what's gone wrong at Every Drop?"

"Apparently I trusted the wrong person."

"I wondered about your choice of Stuart Worthington for Chairman, but my position doesn't give me permission to stick my nose in that far."

Eva wasn't sure she was talking about Stuart. "This happened on my watch, any fallout is on me."

"You need to know the worst case because only then can you deal with it." Addison was right.

Running towards the bullets.

"Is there time before take off to make a quick call?"

He nodded his agreement.

Luke handed her his smartphone.

"Thanks, international okay?"

"Go for it."

"Eva, are you going to brighten our Christmas?" Her godfather always sounded as though she'd made his day by calling.

"I'm doing my best, Per." If she found Lily. When, when she found Lily. "I'm on a plane, about to take off, but I wanted to ask you to explain it to me, the science of Charles' submission, in layman's terms."

"Sure. It's a two-step process," Per parroted her own words back to her that she'd told Dr Chakrabarti and the paramedic who tended to the Oblov's housekeeper. A two-step process like the poison primer and the antidote, like the compound applied to Every Drop's pipes and whatever the saboteur had put in the water.

"It's an ingenious idea, with so many application possibilities," Per was saying.

"Did it come from the White House, the intel that he'd plagiarised the work?"

"I can't confirm that."

"But you can't deny it either?"

Per laughed, "You're Mathias' daughter. I'll see you soon."

"You will, Lily and I will be there for Christmas." Eva would find her.

How, the thought hammered at her as the plane took off, Lily's favourite part of the journey. To distract herself, Eva picked up one of the brochures Addison had discarded. The tap gushing water in shades of black and grey on the cover felt like a pointing finger.

"Morocco's done some interesting things that Every Drop might want to emulate." Addison nodded at the one she was flicking through. "The Moroccan president is all over YouTube proving how safe their water is. He's a thirsty man, if the publicity is believable. That's part of the reason we're going there, photo ops and all that. It's a couple of years away, I'd guess, in terms of investment capability, but it's worth thinking about it for long-term planning."

If Every Drop survived that long, if Nora's team found nothing untoward in the accounts, if, if, if.

To keep herself from throwing up, Eva read furiously. It had been her best defence against the bleakness that haunted her childhood after her father was gone. 'Don't be like him', every time her mother snapped her favourite saying, Eva would fill her mind with the words on the page of whichever book she grabbed. 'What are you crying for?' That question made Eva shout them in her head. 'He didn't love us anyway. Look how he left us', Eva silently screaming any written salve in a frenzy over and over to block out her mother's hateful words. A pathetic plaster stuck over an amputation.

Addison was right. It was impressive how Morocco was making strides to change from a desert state to one with water available for everyone. Rolling the tech they were installing out worldwide would end the worst of the world's water problems. Their sideways-thinking solutions were ingenious.

"Do you want me to redress that?" Luke nodded at her forehead when she put the brochure down.

She padded it with a soft touch. "I guess it probably needs changing."

They took the seats nearest the cockpit, leaving Addison to work undisturbed, turning them to the inside, facing each other.

"How's it looking?" Eva asked when Luke took off the dressing.

"Like you took a fall. I'm no doctor but it seems to be healing okay, you might get away with just a small scar." He cleaned up around her stitches with an antiseptic wipe. "You know you're more than the sum of your parts." Her gaze snapped up from her lap to hazel eyes, close to hers. "Just an observation. You're more than Mathias Janssen's daughter, CEO of Every Drop, Lily's mum." He laughed away the intensity. "Apparently I'm more than Luke Fox too, psycho-analyst or too much whisky at altitude. But while we're being honest, I think you forget you're Eva too. You should try putting that first."

She laughed it away. "So what do you do when you're not psychoanalysing or working with Addison?"

"Or practicing my Florence Nightingale?" He leant closer and whispered dramatically. "If I told you, I'd have to kill you."

"How did I know you were going to say that?"

"You want some company in Marrakech? Addison's going to be busy at the summit. I've been here a couple of times. I speak the language, it might help."

"It may get. . ." What? She had no idea.

"Sounds like just my type of thing." He winked and then dabbed the clean dressing onto her forehead.

As the plane began its descent, Eva glimpsed a snake of green, vibrant against the barrenness of the desert landscape. Stark white against the redness of the soil, a collection of what must have been mega-sized rocks precisely placed.

"It says 'God, country, king'" Luke translated.

Squares of greenery interspersed amongst large tracts of desert that lined the approach to Menara Airport swelled to fill the landscape beneath them. The plane was heading towards a dense jumble of square buildings crowded as far as she could see. How could she find Lily in there?

She'd only just stepped onto the tarmac into the welcome warmth of the North African sun, than a call to prayer rang out, the exotic richness of voice that underlined how foreign was this city that held her daughter.

Addison's car pulled up outside the Hotel Adina where the G20 summit was taking place. The fountain display that welcomed them rivalled anything in Las Vegas, one desert state catching up with another. Behind the pool was a circle of security she wouldn't want to be on the wrong side of. Each guard looked like he could take her and Luke on with one hand and half an effort.

Porters materialised to deal with Addison's suitcase and

look questions at Eva and Luke over their lack of tipping opportunities.

"You're very kind, Addison. I can't thank you enough." Eva held her hand out to him.

"I think we're past that." He leant forward and kissed her on the cheek. "I'm here until the day after the summit if you want a ride home."

Eva watched him pass through the security cordon and go inside, shielding her eyes from the glaring sun, looking at each of the closed windows as though she could somehow see past them into the rooms beyond to locate Lily.

A brief conversation with the hotel reception told Luke neither Charles Buchanan, nor Maxwell Peyton, were staying there, just summit attendees and their entourages.

Eva watched security move a couple on who were posing for their Instagram moment in front of them. She could feel the bite of the sun on her skin, its ferocity pressing on her un-hatted head, roasting her in her English winter clothes.

"Any ideas on where they might be?" Luke asked. Eva shrugged. "You'll be no good to Lily with sunstroke. Let's get a mint tea while you're thinking."

The mint tea was a brilliant idea, the baklava more so.

"Not strictly Moroccan, but sugar's always good in a crisis."

She didn't need him to justify it. The sticky, nutty pastries were just what she needed.

She twirled the longest stalk of mint in her glass. Charles didn't know anyone there, as far as she was aware, but she'd had no idea about his friendship, or whatever it was, with Louie Steinman, so maybe scratch that from her musing.

He could have chosen the world, why Marrakech? The G20 summit was the only thing happening there and not elsewhere. The phone call he made in the middle of the night just before he went to meet Nancy Seymour, 'The White House Chief of Staff's office', how the woman had answered Eva's redial.

She watched the mint, letting her gaze soften, unfocus, as though she was trying to decipher one of those magic eye pictures. Charles had sounded like he knew the President, what if he did? He'd told her he'd interned in the US during his studies. The way he'd said his fake name, Maxwell Peyton, that's what had been odd about it, he'd said it in an American accent. And his being at the charm school, at least twice.

So he was American too, like the Professor, hiding as British. That could explain why she knew nothing about his family, why he didn't share stories from his childhood, nothing to do with the poor memory for such trivia that he claimed. Then why he was here. . .

No, he wouldn't, he wasn't a bad person. The Sherlock Holmes quote nudged at her again.

She knew exactly why Marrakech.

52

The building looked wrong, out of place and time. Not even the streetlights softened the square concrete block, a cuckoo amongst much finer architectural influences, to make it anything other than ugly. It was the sort of Lego building Charles had constructed as a kid.

In his favour, the streets around the building were almost deserted, the pious returned home from prayers, no reason for the summit delegates and their entourages milling around the Hotel Adina to leave their six star surroundings.

Still, he let his feet drift to a stop on a street corner, make a slow turn as if he were checking for non-existent traffic. Paranoid, sure, but better safe than not. After all, Jed Carson was in the same city, breathing the same air.

Charles had been a fool. How short-sighted to have been happy for Jed when the president died and he, as VP, succeeded him. How stupid to have felt a sense of pride that his friend was about to become a legitimate President in his own right, if the polls were the crystal ball they claimed.

Even more to not have realised they had sounded the death knell for everyone who'd helped Jed attain his ultimate power trip.

Charles pulled on the anger of his misplaced friendship and trust—at himself as much as at his now enemy—wrapping it around him. He tightened his backpack straps over his chest, drawing its contents closer to him. This was righteous, justified, this was the perfect karma. For Nancy.

He walked up to the building as though he belonged there. The card access panel looked curiously out of place, the twenty-first century reaching into an area of timelessness. Don't let me down, CJ. Tensing against the likelihood it would refuse him, Charles pushed the door.

CJ hadn't.

Charles closed it quietly behind him, waiting while his eyes adjusted to the gloomy interior. Low-level lighting showed him a boxy inside, a reflection of what he expected given the exterior view, and the perfect representation of the plans he'd found online. Maybe that meant he could trust all the information he'd found on this place.

He walked tiptoeing through a minefield carefully towards the danger area where the only person in the building should be.

Painted a godawful green, at his eyeline the door held a gift - a small square inset of wire toughened safety glass. Charles tensed against seeing someone looking out of it at him and peeped in.

A couple of TV screens to the right of the lone worker showed black and white images of the main corridor and the pump room. The guard wasn't paying attention to any of the systems he was supposed to be monitoring, his cap was half across his face, his body leaning backwards in the chair, a newspaper dropped into his lap where his arm drooped over it.

Charles fingertip-padded at the door. As immovable as he'd hoped. Doubly thank you, CJ, triple at the end of the corridor when the pump room door gave him access. CJ always charged too much, but today Charles was happy to pay it.

Machinery noise welcomed him in. He wouldn't need anything like the ten minutes CJ was giving him before he wiped the camera feeds and stopped jamming signals there.

Most of the underground infrastructure was just that, locked safely away from sabotage, interference and for the safety of the workers. But in each pumping station in the city a succession of hatches gave access to the water beneath his feet.

Charles snapped on the central overhead lights, plunging the machinery at the sides of the room into shadow. He pulled out a large container that could have passed as an odd thermos flask if there'd been anyone there to ask him.

Was he really going to do this?

What choice did he have? It came down to a simple equation, him or Jed Carson. The things they'd done had started innocently enough. Jed knew Charles never could resist an intellectual challenge, his casual 'I bet you can't' was all he'd needed to say and Charles was in. And it turned out better than he could ever have dreamt.

The cannister weighed heavier than its form, its contents. It was one thing, the piecing together of science to bend elements to his will. Playing God there, that was something else.

He checked his watch; the timing had to be perfect.

Jed wouldn't honour Charles' life, he'd find a way to

negate his insurance. And now there was Lily. All it would take would be for them to hold her hostage.

This was the only way.

And the innocents?

He placed the container beside him on the gangway. This would show the Nobel Committee just how urgent safe water was. How he deserved the damn prize, how his compound was a miracle worker. The money Stuart would siphon from Every Drop in safe payments would be enough to keep him and Lily hidden, running, but what kind of life was that for either of them? A better use of it was to live a good life, further his research, not waste his days hiding from the long reach of Jed Carson.

He was owed that.

It'd be just like a drug trial. There were always some casualties but, as they furthered the scientific knowledge, everyone overlooked that.

This was his stage, even though no one would know he was the player. Saviour, that's what they'd call him when he swept in to tell them how he could save their water source. It would become another stream of income, payment from a grateful city.

Charles gripped the edge of the main access hatch and pulled.

53

———

In the shadows of the tall banks of pump machinery Eva waited, breath held for Charles to prove he was the man she'd married, the man she knew, not the monster she was recording on Luke's phone. It was taking everything she had to not rush at him screaming for Lily.

This had been her worst case guess, she hadn't expected him to actually dream this up, let alone do it. But he was there. Trying to open the main access hatch, beside him a container that looked far too much like the one the saboteur had used in Tirupudur.

She stepped out from her cover. "Don't do it."

"Eva?"

"Stand up, away from the water."

"You don't understand—"

"I understand all too well."

He shook his head sharply, as if trying to reconcile her being here now, ahead of him.

"I think the Moroccan authorities, the Americans, every country who sent a leader here will be very interested in you attempting to poison the water supply."

"You think that's what I'm doing?"

"I know it is. Where's Lily?"

"She's safe and she'll continue to be so, you just need to let me do what I came here to do."

"You want me to look the other way while you kill thousands of people?"

"If you want to see her again, you will."

"You're trading Lily for everyone else?" The wave of shock, of outrage, swamped her. Her voice shook.

"If you want to look at it like that. I'll give you her address when I'm done." He gestured at the open hatch.

"You can't." She worked at Luke's phone, couldn't help flicking a glance at the door. Where was he? He was supposed to have her back. She pressed send on the email she'd prepared that would forward the video of Charles sabotaging the water supply to everyone she thought would be interested. The starburst rolled around in its little circle, buffering, buffering. Come on.

"You thought I'd just waltz in here unprepared? The signal's being jammed. You can't upload anything, your leverage is useless. Your back-up's locked in the security room. You're lucky."

"What do you mean?"

"He's The Society, Eva, the man you brought here. He's probably only waiting until we're in the same room to kill us both."

Luke would shoot his way out when he realised he was trapped. But what would he do then? Who would he aim at, who would he shoot? Hazel eyes looking at her then as his target? If that were true, why would he have let Eva take the real security guard's baton when their bundle of dirham and dollars persuaded him to take a long break?

"That's impossible."

"Why do you think I knocked him out at the airport? It was a trap. I heard him calling in our false passport names."

"It was a security check."

"Confirm, Eva Janssen travelling as Sara Peyton, Lily Janssen as Madeleine Peyton, does that sound like a security check to you?"

"That doesn't explain why you left me behind, Charles."

He looked at the canister. "I didn't appreciate you weren't on the plane until we'd begun taxi-ing and then it was too late."

"So you left me with a killer?"

"You were clearly safe, he's after me and you brought him right to me. You surpassed yourself." He looked at his watch.

Eva tried to not let his words hurt, she shrugged as though it was that simple to forget them. "It was that, wasn't it," she gestured at the flask, "in Africa and India? Whatever's in there?"

He considered, nodded. "It's genius, it's a shame it's come to this to convince the Committee."

"The Nobel Committee, this is about your nomination?"

He half-shrugged like it wasn't important at all. "Not entirely." He grasped the hatch's handle with both hands and pulled it. Hydraulics folded it neatly out of his way, the roar of the water surging beneath them, feeding the city, filled the room so Eva had to shout to pull his attention away from the tumbling dark mass.

"Tell me then so I understand."

She knew he couldn't resist the chance to show off.

"It's a two-stage process, the compound that I had added to your pipes, Eva, so Every Drop would be okay." The words cut deep. She was more sure than ever that Every Drop wouldn't be. "And an agent," he gestured at the container. "They're like a jigsaw, the compound creates a system at the molecular level that catches the molecules of the agent. When the agent was introduced into the water supply, the compound locked them away so they didn't harm anyone."

"But without the compound. . ." Eva couldn't say it.

He half-shrugged, not important in his scheme of things.

"Like I said, absolute genius. Every other agencies' pipes let the agent through, Every Drop's locked it away. The water they supplied stayed safe. That's why they should never have pulled the pipes down in Tirupudur. They were saving their lives."

"But why? Why would you do that, risk all those people?"

"It's obvious." He shook his head at her lack of intellect. "Stuart's been laying the foundations that everyone should pay for water, Every Drop's supply will become the gold standard and they'll pay handsomely for access to it. My royalties will give me financial freedom."

His calculation was perhaps the hardest thing to bear until he hammered a final nail into their relationship. "It's been a long time coming, to get to this point." He checked his watch again.

"If that's the agent in the flask," Eva tried to distract, "where's the compound here?" She could read him easily enough then. "So now you're committing genocide?"

"You're being overdramatic."

"What about Lily? What if she drinks it?"

"I'll tell you where she is and you can make sure she doesn't." He couldn't be bargaining with her life.

"Where is she? It's not safe for her to be here on her own."

He looked at the flask.

"Charles, please, don't."

"Carson has to pay."

"Jed Carson," Eva concentrated on looking confused, "what's he got to do with this?"

"It's his fault they're dead, Tony, Hunter, Nancy." The way he said her name hurt. "We helped him out a long time ago, did things we shouldn't have for him because he was our friend. He's overlooked that in his rush to clean house."

He checked the time again, half-nodded.

Eva placed Luke's phone on the polished concrete floor, the starburst still spinning, her video proof going nowhere.

Charles picked up the flask.

Eva retrieved the security guard's baton from beside the machinery where she'd been hiding from him, hoping he wouldn't arrive, hoping she'd completely misunderstood everything.

He unscrewed the top of the flask.

She hit the safety railing with the baton. The metallic clang rang loud in the space, even over the rushing water.

Charles jerked round to her. "What're you doing?"

She charged him, grabbing for the flask, aiming to knock him off balance. Smooth, slippery, he twisted up and away from her, steadying the container, keeping it upright.

"Careful, don't know what will happen if you get any on you."

"But you're prepared for a city to drink it!" She could hardly get the words out, her anger exploded in a red rage. She lunged at him, hitting out with the baton but an agony on her forehead made her drop it. Charles leaning close enough to kiss her in a mockery of the position they'd been in hundreds of times. But this time, his free hand pressed against her stitches, making her eyes stream.

She twisted away from him, her hands cupping around

the pain radiating out from her forehead. The baton clanged on the metallic gangway until Charles stamped on it, ending its chattering.

"Do it again and you'll never know where Lily is."

"You're not, you can't be abandoning her."

"That's your choice."

How could he have reconciled himself to leaving Lily alone in a strange place where she didn't speak the language, understand the culture? "She's eleven, you can't, you're her father, fathers don't do that."

"Her or Carson, Eva. Choose wisely."

He could have just tipped it in, far crueller to throw this non-choice at her. Worse, he handed it to her almost flippantly, the same decision her father had made. Her or a stranger, knowing his Evie was safe thousands of miles away, knowing the stranger in front of him would die if he saved himself.

Daddy, did it feel like this for you? Like your heart had shattered, like you couldn't breathe. Like there was no choice at all?

54

"Well?" Charles sounded almost triumphant. He thought he knew Eva, was at least bargaining on her doing what every mother would.

She pressed the twin of the bracelet her father had held on to when he made his choice against her wrist. Daddy, I understand.

"You don't need to tell me where Lily is so you can't put that in the water." Her voice was amazingly steady.

He did a double-take. "You're choosing Carson over Lily?"

"You underestimate me, Charles, you always have." And she'd let him. Her fingers worked the knots in her bracelet round and round. "I'm not choosing anyone over her, but I am choosing for you to not poison the water supply."

"But you'll never find her without my help, and there's a, a reason you need to, right now."

'You have resources,' Eva used Nora's reminder to quash the bolt of panicked dread that hammered through her. If the water wasn't poisoned, Lily would have longer.

"What reason, Charles?" She tried to keep her tone even, to not let him know what his decision was doing to her.

"You need to pick her, Eva, you need to choose Lily."

"You need my permission to do this? I don't give it. The water, I choose safe water." Always you, Lily, I always choose you. This way you won't be poisoned and I'll still find you. I promise, I'm coming, sweetheart.

"You don't get to take this away from me."

Eva was moving before he was. The knee brace he'd bought her, his last act of kindness to her, helping her limp towards him, a handful of steps, a mile in slow motion.

He turned away from her, lifting the flask, moving it over the opening.

Eva lunged.

She grabbed for him, reaching for his outstretched arm. In taking a jab at her, he was unbalanced. Charles dropped onto his side, holding the container upright, keeping its contents inside.

"Stop, you could get us both killed."

She leant over him, hands outstretched. "Give it to me, it's over."

He shook his head. "I didn't underestimate you, it was your choice to stay small. You could be so much more, but you're always too worried about everyone else."

She reached further, her fingertips a skin cell from grasping the container, from knocking it all over him. Could she do that, if that was her only choice?

But then he struck.

His foot slammed into her left knee, side on, pressure beyond the knee brace's design, and she tumbled to the metal platform. Her leg lit up from within, a popping explosion burning every nerve ending, radiating out in waves of sweat and nausea. He twisted away from her, stood the container on the gangway while he got back onto his knees.

He picked it up and tipped it over the water.

Lily, I'm coming. Eva dragged herself upright. She'd do this for her baby girl. Straining against the effort, the agony, a shuffling half step, another.

"You're going to do it, do it properly." Eva pushed the flask the opposite way to Charles' expectation, down through his gloved hands, down until the tumult beneath their feet that swallowed it.

"What did you do?" He looked horrified, as though he'd been trying to stop her from this madness.

"Where's my daughter?" she screamed.

"Half would have been enough." Charles stared at the rushing water that had devoured the flask.

"You got what you wanted now tell me where she is." He leapt up and ran out of the pump room. "Where is she?" The slamming door cut off Eva's scream.

She limped fast down the corridor, banging at the security room. Luke's words were lost between his space and hers, deadened to nothing by the locked door. She typed a note on his phone, maximised it and held it up to the window. 'Area jammed, water poisoned, look for an isolation switch, turn supply off, divert it.'

Luke moved to the control panels, scanning the calligraphied scrawls that meant nothing to her but thankfully something recognisable to him. Could he really be The Society?

She could still hear the rushing water as it made its way through the pipes below them in its steady swan dive beneath the city. Why wasn't it shutting down? Addison's bumpf had said it clearly enough, a sabotage-proof system.

The flask was definitely big enough to trigger the safeguard. Why hadn't it detected it and stopped the flow?

It was taking too long. How many thousands of litres had already sluiced through, picking up the agent and carrying it into the pipe tributaries that served a million people? And Charles, the only way she had to find Lily, was getting away.

Eva pocketed Luke's phone and limped out of the building, the door crashing closed behind her.

Charles was nowhere.

What could she do?

She turned a slow circle in the darkness, the buildings around her were no help. All she imagined was the men, women and children in them already dying. Lily. She half-dragged in a breath that was more sob. She wouldn't fall apart, she was the only warning, the only half-chance the people had.

Maybe half a chance might be enough.

They'd come from the south, her and Luke, when she'd believed he was on her side, but she didn't think there was anything there that would help her now. To the north then, out of the wider junction into narrow passageways, limp-running on though she wanted to lie down and scream.

The passageway led into a tiny square where she still couldn't see what she needed. Out of it on the opposite side, around the next corner, she barged into a moving obstacle.

He let loose a guttural stream that sounded like the swear words she might have muttered if someone had run into her.

"Sorry, pardon monsieur," she remembered the French for excuse me.

The smile on his too close face was nothing she wanted to see. She stepped away from him, turning carefully.

"Excuse me." She stepped to go past him, but he grabbed her.

"Why you running? We have lots of time."

She'd left her scarf in her hiding place in the pump room, stupid, stupid, her blonde hair a beacon, Westerner here.

"You need to go home, the water is mal. L'eau is mal," Eva mimed throwing up but he was only amused by her theatrics. She clutched her throat, mimed choking. Why wouldn't he understand? "You will die, mourir, everyone," she gestured around her. "Mourir. Vite. Family."

"Pretty." He stepped closer, a tightening noose.

"Get away from me."

He grabbed a handful of her hair, winding his fingers into it in an obscenely personal attack, pulling her closer to him.

"When I get what I want."

55

Walk away, Charles should just walk away, trust that his agent would do what he knew it would.

But Nancy deserved better. Hell, so did he. What he didn't deserve was to be looking over his shoulder for the rest of his life, always running, scrambling to stay one step ahead of an unknowable assassin who would come at him in the shape of a car, a slip in a wet shower, a tangy taste in his coffee to go.

Charles needed Jed to understand why he'd done it, how else could he avenge Nancy?

The Hotel Adina looked like a stock photo, an oasis of calm beyond the traffic and hubbub of surrounding crowds. A good message reinforcement holding a summit featuring advanced water technology where a desert city could display a run of fountains leading to the grand entrance.

He'd expected security to be tight inside the hotel, but they'd thrown a ring of muscle around it that stopped him before he got past the oasis frontage.

"Name." The man wasn't a Mr Universe but he was

somehow more intimidating for that. And the question was tricky, which name should Charles use?

"Dr Charles Buchanan." On his rush down there he'd practised, but he couldn't drop his royal family accent so easily, he'd been well-trained. "I'm the relief physician for President Jed Carson." Better.

"Dr Charles Buchanan on the list?" The guard said it as though he was addressing Charles, but his lapel mic, earpiece, whichever piece of hidden technology picked up his question, relayed the answer Charles expected. "You're not on the list, Sir."

"Yeah, I'm never on the list. Kind of a shitty protocol, I'm not important enough to be on the list, but I have clearance to save the President's life. I understand you're just doing your job. Is there somewhere I can wait in the shade, in case I'm needed."

The guard's eyes tightened.

"It's standard operating procedure. I'm always there in the shadows, but the other guy gets all the glory." Charles' childhood accent wasn't getting any easier to conjure up, his drawl just wouldn't.

"ID."

He pulled his driving licence out of his wallet, held his finger over the UK flag. "My hotel has my passport."

The guard gave it a cursory glance. "I'll ask them to let you in the hotel next door, they're broadcasting the summit on a live feed."

"Thanks, appreciate that."

Not as grand an entrance as the star hotel of the moment, but the cool embrace of its air conditioning in the lobby was very welcome. People in, people out, ringing phones, conversations, a muted relay from the summit showing on two large screens, one behind reception, one in the vast lounge.

Charles turned Lily's phone on to call the riad. Two rings, hang up, call right back. But the phone rang and rang on his redial, its shrilling siren muted from Charles' end. He'd told her to answer if he called. What was she doing? She had no phone to distract her, no internet because he was pretty sure she wouldn't know how to navigate the home screen on Terry's ancient PC now he'd set it to display in Arabic.

He switched off her phone, he'd try again in a minute.

But there, on the TV screen, was his karma. He watched the toast to begin the summit dinner. Per Larsson speaking in subtitles Charles couldn't read raising a glass and smiling at the assembled great and good. A water glass.

Larsson drank, the camera panned to the attendees in front of him doing the same.

He believed he'd timed it right, but had he? His agent would work fast, be strongest there before diluting downstream in a ripple effect. He'd been counting on the hotel having instructions to use the freshest water possible for the water jugs. It's what he would have done, had he been showcasing.

Where are you, Jed? There, just in shot, swallowing his water like a good leader.

When the cameras panned back to the top table, Charles sat in one of the chairs arranged in groups around low tables and tasteful flower displays and waited.

56

"I'm trying to save your lives." Eva ground out, her hand braceleting the wrist of the man who had hold of her. "Everyone's going to die."

He pulled harder at the knots in her hair.

"I really don't have time for this." Eva grabbed the man's football shirt and kneed him as hard as she could with her braced knee. It didn't protest at all at the up, down movement but he folded to the ground in a pain-pitched moan.

She ran back to a wider street where the city was more alive. She chose a woman dressed in a long tunic over trousers and a bright red hijab to ask, "Excuse me, do you speak English?"

The woman laughed. "I am English, from Peckham, 'ere on 'oliday."

"Where's the closest mosque?"

"You can't go in dressed like that."

But she could. "Do you speak Arabic?"

"Nah, just the Queen's English. Nearest mosque's that way," the woman pointed.

Eva saw the carved stone monument of the minaret

soaring over the buildings, probably only a couple of streets over.

But the entrance was closed, locked, when she tried the doors.

"You're a hard woman to keep up with." The English was welcome, the person speaking it wasn't.

"If you've come to kill me, can you just wait until I've warned them about the water?" Eva backed away from Luke.

"What're you talking about?" he followed.

"I showed you on your phone. Charles poisoned the water."

"Not that, why would I be here to kill you?"

"Orders. Charles told me, you're part of this group The Society."

He made a gesture brushing aside what she said, the space between them. "You want to know what my orders are?"

She took a step backwards. He copied, a step towards her. Hers backwards, his forwards. Eva jolted up against the corner of something.

Luke took another step, Eva couldn't move. "Gordon Stamford is the mutual friend between Addison and me. It's how I found you, Iago tracked my phone."

"You could just be saying that."

"Out of all the names to choose from, I went with Iago?" He put his hands on the wall behind Eva, either side of her head, and bent towards her. His breath tickled her ear. "Vincent doesn't know."

Eva felt her eyes snap open, heard her own gasp.

Luke pressed back off the wall. "Nora told me that'd mean something to you. Don't worry, she didn't tell me what, though now I'm intrigued." He took a half step away from her. "Believe I'm here to hurt you now? I tell a lot of lies in this job, but that isn't one."

Locks rattling on the inside of the building pushed her to decide. The doors to the mosque opened one at a time.

"You have to tell them to broadcast a warning about the water," she gestured at her hair. "I can't go in there."

"Me either, not armed. Stand closer." He held his right arm out and she did as instructed. "Holster's on my left." She slipped her arms into his warmth, understanding why he wore a jacket in the heat. He looked down at her, "I'm not giving you my weapon if I'm your enemy, am I?"

Eva shook her head. She unclipped the holster and pulled out his surprisingly heavy gun, under the cover of his closeness, tucking it into the waistband of her jeans beneath her t-shirt.

"Won't be long." He disappeared inside.

She stood stock still, hands hugging her stomach as though she was pregnant, holding the weapon tightly against her so it didn't fall onto the concrete and accidentally shoot one of the people now approaching the mosque. Or get her arrested.

So much time ticked by while she waited, so much water had rushed through the pumping station. How many people was it too late for?

Lily, don't drink the water. I'm coming.

57

The automatic doors of the hotel where Charles waited swished open to admit a man in Arab dress, two suited men behind him. Allahu Akbar wailed in with them, the call to prayer cut off when the doors closed.

Charles looked back at the footage on the TV screens and caught it.

The cameras showed the outward view of the delegates enjoying their formal dinner as if it was sited on the top VIP table. A trickle of tuxedo-ed men and glittery-dressed women were leaving their tables. It was working. He gave it a while longer, each minute a torture, longer than the previous one until he just couldn't sit there, passive, any more.

He power walked to the Hotel Adina, moping at his forehead with his handkerchief when he presented himself to the same guard he'd spoken to earlier.

"Hey, you remember I'm the relief physician for the President of the United States? Just got a call he needs me, can I go in? Just get me in the lobby, I still have to go through the

Secret Service to get anywhere near the President. Don't sweat it, I'm used to it."

"Sit rep?" The man asked his tech. "Status of US?. . .Roger that. Okay to send in the relief physician?. . .Sending in Dr Charles Buchanan."

Charles nodded thanks and walked past the fountains to the entrance. As easy as that.

The sumptuous foyer was certainly a couple of notches up from next door. A man with a weathered face and thick neatly styled grey hair in an expensive suit was holding a hushed but urgent conversation with the reception staff. They were good, Charles might not have noticed anything was wrong if he didn't know better.

"Please take a seat, Sir, I'll be with you in a moment." One of the man's underlings dismissed him.

"I have been, sitting. I got an emergency summons, I'm needed right away by the President of the United States, I'm his relief physician."

"Sir, I—"

"I get you're busy, but the guards outside cleared me, all I need's his room number. You all don't want him getting sicker here now, do ya?"

The man looked at his boss, who responded faster than Charles would have credited. "Suite Fifteen, Sir."

Security was heavy out of the lift, but Charles had expected that. "Dr Charles Buchanan," he announced, "the President's fallen sick, I'm one of his physicians." The guards hesitated, not briefed for this. "You won't let me through, fine, but you go tell him because I don't want his death on my conscience."

"ID."

Charles repeated the same charade. "They wouldn't put me up in these fancy digs." Inwardly he winced at the

Britishism but arguing over whether to let him through they missed it. "I know it's Suite Fifteen, I wouldn't know that otherwise, would I?"

"Where's your equipment, don't you need a doctor's bag?"

"We share medical equipment, too pricey for a kit each." He pulled his driving licence away from the guard and pressed the call lift button. "Why don't you just ask the President if I'm cleared to enter?"

Charles waited while his request was passed up the chain to their Commander in Chief, not sure which way his request would go.

"You can go in." The agent said after a few minutes.

"Dr Emmanuel Seaton." Charles heard the booming voice behind him when he was just a few steps away from the double doors with the number fifteen on them.

He turned around with a smile. "Emmanuel, didn't realise you were in on this gig too."

The round black man looked at Charles with the blank but not wanting to be rude look that Charles had seen so often at conferences. Charles held his hand out and withdrew it as Seaton went to grasp it.

"Sorry, force of habit, best not to, until we're sure of what we're dealing with. You up to date with your shots?"

"Naturally."

"Looks like this could be a mutation of the virus that swept through these parts two years ago. I was here then, had a mild case myself. You probably need to consider full PPE, it's pretty lethal. It showed up in Ethiopia last week. Look, I have some immunity, let me take this one. There's a lot of people falling sick, best advice? Go to your room and wait it out." Charles patted Seaton on the shoulder, "be good to see you again at the next conference."

He nodded. "Appreciate that."

"Not a problem, get the message out to the rest of the team. Stay safe." He watched Seaton until the elevator doors closed on him, taking him away from Jed.

And, just like that, Charles was in front of his old friend, his now adversary, arguably the most powerful man in the world.

"Jed, you don't look so good, buddy." Charles was over to him where he was sitting on the couch.

"Charles? What're you doing here?"

"Same as you, I came for the summit. Water, it's quite a hobby of mine. You must be aware my wife has a charity that dispenses safe drinking water in the Third World." Charles dropped his phony accent, curious, that he thought the one he grew up with was the false one and the one he'd affected, the British well-to-do, was now his natural choice. The brainwashing had really worked. "Would you like me to check you out, give you a once over. I've seen this before, this virus." He took hold of the President's wrist, counted his pulse rate, as rapid as he thought it might be.

"Couldn't get fresh water for the President, could you?" He looked around the room, huge arrangements of flowers and fruit on the table and desk. "No bottled water?"

The agent shook his head. "No Sir, water's safe here."

"Fresh from the kitchen's good then." Charles threw over his shoulder at the bodyguard.

Jed nodded his agreement with the instructions. Charles heard the issuing of the order to someone else. Of course, they wouldn't leave him alone. That simple, over-looked, truth meant he couldn't tell Jed the true nature of what he'd ingested. If he knew there was no coming back from it, Charles would spend the rest of his life in solitary and that was never happening.

"Where's my physician?"

"In isolation, all of them, this is a nasty virus."

"But I need something—"

The door opened and another suited, earphoned, Secret Service agent came in, had a quiet conversation with the first. Charles didn't have much time.

He dropped his voice. "How's Mack Hillard III these days?"

"We agreed never to speak of that." Jed shifted on the couch, his forehead beaded sweat as though the air conditioning wasn't on full blast.

Charles sat next to him.

 "You're not worried about catching it?"

"Not one bit. I just wanted to say a couple of words to you." He turned to watch Jed's reaction. "Nancy," her name sighed out of him, "Tony, Hunter, Duncan."

Jed waved a that's not important gesture.

"I don't understand." Charles said.

"Does it matter? That's all in the past."

Conscious of the two itchy trigger fingers standing near the door of the suite, Charles locked away what he really wanted, needed, to say.

"What about the rest of us who helped you? Rory, Ted, Aleksandr, me?"

"You were safe enough, I'm not stupid enough to harm my money tree. I wanted to shake you up a little, remind you who's calling the shots. We want more of what you just did, the poison thing, it's the flagstaff product in the arsenal of our special weapons unit."

Charles stared at Jed. He bought it? It was on him he hadn't looked too deeply at the shell corporation that CJ had sourced as the buyer. But it had been Jed behind it?

Jed looked at Charles, he was growing greyer by the

minute, his breathing becoming more laboured. But his eyes remained sharp, the knowing in them something Charles wanted to beat out of him.

"Ingenious by the way, we'd have paid more. Aleksandr," Jed shook his head, "his wife, as I understand it, were perfect test subjects. Your wife not so much, we dodged an international incident there, got the wrong target."

"You went after Eva?"

Jed pulled himself upright, not entirely succeeding. Another agent came into the room, right up to him.

"Are you okay, Sir?"

"Feeling a little rough, gotta admit, not bad enough to alert Owen though. Where's that water?"

Charles would have been surprised if the Vice President wasn't already aware.

"I'll chase it, Sir."

"You went after Eva?" Charles hissed again.

"I did think twice, innocent as she is in all of this. But, you were getting," Jed coughed. "You needed a tighter leash."

"You've overstepped." The rant, the rage, the gloating over what was happening to his former friend, Charles wanted to let it all loose. But scrutiny from the doorway and strategic points in the room, held him in check.

"I'm holding the cards, Charles. I wasn't going to tell you but hell, since we're being so honest, you should understand your position completely. Your Nobel nomination, why you lost it, I did that, I told them you'd plagiarised it, sent them the specs you drew up to cripple Hillard's product. All done under your birth name if you can remember, Maxwell Peyton, who had an unhappy meeting with the bottom of a cliff after you left the programme for the UK. A potentially brilliant man, life cut tragically short. So you see, your insurance, the one you were bleating about to Dennis, it's useless, it's already out there in the world. Any comeback over the Hillard thing can be explained away."

But I killed you, Charles screamed it in his mind. Him knowing he'd got the last shot in, the one that counted, wasn't enough. He wanted, needed, Jed to know it as he took his last breath. But if Charles gave into the white hot fury rampaging through him, his future would be worse than Jed's. He needed to leave before he couldn't hold it in check any longer. "I'll get you something."

"I'm just going to get some medication for the President, okay?" Charles told the agent. "I'll be back momentarily."

He walked towards the lifts. Over so quickly, after everything he'd expected to feel more.

58

"It was a clever idea." Luke handed Eva a glass of freshly squeezed orange. "You've probably saved thousands of lives."

But what about the ones who didn't hear the warning in the call to prayer before they drank? Before every mosque in Marrakech picked it up and broadcast it? What about Lily who wouldn't understand it?

She stared at the drink.

"I saw them make it, no water."

The juice was sweet, delicious. Maybe it would stem her rising nausea, tensing panic.

The restaurant was crowded, the laughter and chatter all at odds with what she imagined was happening behind closed doors in houses downstream from the pumping station.

"Why didn't you tell me we're on the same side?"

Luke leant in towards her. "Gordon wanted you to be unbalanced, to keep Charles off guard. He wasn't sure where his loyalties lay."

Neither was Eva.

Luke's mobile rang.

Please let it be something.

In the deepening chaos tearing through the city, a fan of banknotes was the best way to hail a ride. The man who stopped didn't have a taxi sign on his roof, nor a numbered sticker on the door. Eva didn't care.

Luke showed his phone, gestured with the notes, said something Eva had no hope of understanding. The man nodded and drove like the back of the car was on fire.

Dropped at the dead-end of a road, Luke rushed them on in the darkness where Google maps lit their path through a maze of pedestrian only walkways.

He stopped in front of a riad set below the pavement level. "This is it. But it could be nothing to do with Lily."

Eva nodded, yes, yes, but it might.

The tile set into the wall beside a substantially padlocked wooden door read 'Riad Lucky Eight'. How did this fit into Charles' life? Who lived here?

She pulled at the padlock. Charles had locked Lily in? A six-digit combination code, she had no idea where to begin guessing. She tried his date of birth, then Lily's, even hers. They were all wrong.

"Eva," Luke's voice was all reason, his hand in his jacket. "Out of the way, behind me."

He fired into the hinge that held the hasp on the door. Once was enough to tear it away from its housing though the echo suggested he'd shot his whole magazine into it. "That'll bring the authorities. They already have a report of a suspicious smell, that's how Nora found this place, so they'll come quicker now. Wait there until I call you."

"Not a chance."

"Stay behind me then."

She nodded. Come on, come on.

Following his broad shoulders, his surefooted steps, they walked into the cooler air of the unknown, one silent step, two careful strides.

"Lock the door," he whispered.

The bolts slid across as though they'd just been oiled.

Luke peered out of the short hallway, his gun held in front of him. Cautious movements across a small courtyard, his gun pointing ahead, at the upper levels where bright lights blazed against the full darkness of night, to the opposite side of a plunge pool. A door ahead on their left from which leaked the suspicious smell.

"Wait there." Luke hissed, nodding at the tiny room ahead of them that housed the staircase that led to the upper levels.

She shook her head.

"We're easy targets here, I can't check and protect you. If it's—you don't want to see that. Go."

Eva stepped into the shelter of the room, turned to watch him.

Not Lily, it couldn't be Lily, Eva would know wouldn't she?

Luke steeled himself, took a breath, and opened the door. A buzzing confirmed Eva's worst fears, even before the gut-heavingly awful odour reached for her. Not Lily, not Lily. Eva grasped the newel post. It couldn't be. Please.

Luke was back in the courtyard, closing the door quietly, gulping in the fresher air. He shook his head. "Not Lily."

He pointed up the uneven staircase, and she followed him around its 180° turn onto the galleried balcony on the first floor, off which were several rooms.

"Wait there." He motioned for her to move up against the whitewashed wall that leached its coolness into her through her clothes. The stench from downstairs wafted towards her, making her gag. Was that why Charles had said she needed to get to Lily quickly? She swallowed hard, breathed through her mouth. This must be the right place?

Luke went into each room on their right, gun at the ready, arms sweeping cautious arcs, coming out again in seconds. A clatter from the room furthest away from them on the left tensed them both.

Luke was there, tiptoeing towards the door. Eva felt as if she might snap into tiny pieces.

A groan reached her from that far corner.

She wasn't waiting.

It was a kitchen, the room into which she charged, but she saw only one thing.

"Lily!"

"Mum?"

"Are you okay?" Eva rushed to her, hugging her tightly. Thank God, thank God. Her baby girl, safe again with her.

"Do you have any painkillers?" Lily wriggled out of Eva's arms, gripping her stomach. In the harsh overhead light she looked grey.

"What's the matter?" More than Mum-mode, Eva snapped the question out. "You didn't drink the water?"

"Of course I did. You know about single use plastic." Her face screwed up against the pain. "The President of Morocco's all over the news telling everyone it's safe, that's what the summit Dad was going on about is all about. What is it with you and him and the water, it's not like I've been drinking all the vodka."

A big plastic bottle of water sat beside the sink, the seal

of its top still intact. "Didn't he tell you to drink the bottled water?"

Lily winced, holding her hand against her stomach. "He didn't tell me anything, he hasn't been here most of the day. I've been so bored, this holiday hasn't been any fun."

She wobbled a little. Eva only just caught her before she passed out.

Too late, she was too late. The words hammered at her beyond anything, beyond the argument she'd have with Charles—argument? She'd kill him.

As Luke carried Lily to the nearest bedroom, Eva saw it. A flash of neon yellow half under the mismatched run of kitchen units. The note he'd left their daughter. 'Don't drink the tap water, drink this instead.' She imagined the Post-it losing its stick against the damp plastic, fluttering to the floor where Lily wouldn't read, heed its warning. He hadn't even bothered to make sure she understood.

Lily came round before Eva had arranged her face into her mum's everything'll be all right mask.

"Sweetheart, you need to drink this." Eva gestured for her to sit up, holding out the glass of salt water Luke had made. "Quickly, come on, it'll make you feel better."

"Painkillers will make me feel better. Don't you have any?"

"They won't work, you need to be sick. The water is poisoned."

"Mum—"

"Just do it," Eva snapped. "You need to drink now."

"What's the matter with you?" Lily groaned around a wave of pain that almost bent her in two. "I have a bad period pain, the worst ever. I need a painkiller. The water's fine, there's a well in the cellar. This place isn't on the main supply. You'd think Dad would know, it's his brother who lived here."

"His brother?"

"My Uncle Terry, except he was dead when we got here."

Eva pulled Lily into her arms and hugged her like she would never let her go. Anything else would wait.

"It's going to be some debrief." Luke said.

59

I t was an unlikely battleground.

Eva watched the TV in the minimalist office while she waited. The voiceover sounded strange, familiar but not familiar, a knowledge she should have had but one denied her by her father's absences from her childhood. The language might not have spoken to her, but the images on the screen did. Weeping, wailing adults, bewildered crying children, a row of flagpoles with the flags of the countries of every nation who'd attended the summit flying at half mast, a flashback to that awful night in Marrakech three weeks ago. It didn't ease her guilt that the authorities still praised the warning rung out over the city through the mosques. She couldn't help but feel responsible, even though the sabotage-proof system had kicked in as she'd gambled and diverted the supply when it detected the flask. She should have stopped Charles tipping any of his agent in.

Eva stared at her left hand, her rings nothing more than a subterfuge, an augmented reality, just for the next few minutes.

She flicked off the TV; it was time.

The knock at the neighbouring office door reached into her space, a short sharp one rap of the knuckles. The phone on Eva's desk rang.

"Ready?" Kristina Ekstrom asked.

"Ready, I'm on mute." Eva muted her phone.

"I'm putting me on speaker," the quality of Kristina's voice changed, more echoey but the system was a good one. Her 'come in' was clear.

Eva had replayed this moment, planning how it might go. But none of it had prepared her for the wave of fury that tore through her when Charles' cut-glass accent came down the phone. She needed to calm herself, this was no good if she couldn't hear anything through the rushing of blood in her ears, the demand for justice her heart rapped out, the 'how could you' she wanted to scream at him.

She relaxed her grip on the handset, slowed her breathing. This was now what she felt for the man who'd been her husband for seven years and her first proper relationship before that when she'd been just eighteen?

When had love turned to hate? Was it in the pumping station or when she stood on the wrong side of a padlocked door in Marrakech?

Had it been an incremental thing, the eroding of what she thought they'd had, as she learned his secrets, or when he'd pulled her in harm's way? When she'd seen him with Nancy? Or had it been from their second beginning? She could be honest enough to admit she'd always found being a single parent a struggle, too much a mirroring of her own childhood, that she hadn't looked too hard, just gratefully assumed the Charles that came back to her was the one who'd walked away.

She should have been more wary, she should have been stronger. Ensam är stark. You were right, Daddy.

"Please, call me Kristina." Kristina's confidence down the phone handset grounded Eva. "Take a seat. I'm glad you responded to our reaching out. With a new Chairperson we thought it an opportune time to enhance the process by which we consider work for the Nobel. Coffee?"

"Can I meet the new Chairman while I'm here?" Charles asked.

"That's not how the process will go."

Eva had to admire Kristina's coolness. She would have thrown the pot over him, but that wouldn't avenge Per.

"So, Charles, obviously after what happened in Marrakech and at the water sites in Africa and India, it's clear that keeping water supplies safe is one of the world's most urgent needs. I understand that you've invented a compound that can do that. Can you explain it to me in layman's terms?"

"It's my pleasure." A cup chinked onto a saucer. "The compound sanitises water from the deadliest of bugs, it uses a lock and key mechanism. If you think of a contaminant as a key, the compound acts as a magnet, if you will, attracting the microbes to it and enclosing them, locking them safely away."

"But it's not a biological agent. Please correct me if I'm wrong."

"No, you're quite right, it's more of a chemical agent."

"Can this system collect any contaminant?" Kristina asked.

"I am confident it will sanitise water regardless of the contaminant involved."

Eva let his self-congratulatory waffle wash past her, but she knew how important it was for him to spell it out.

If they just kept him away from any water supply, everything would be fine. No agent, no need for the compound.

"The Committee received intelligence that this wasn't your original—"

"I invented my work while I was still using my birth name. I've brought my original birth certificate, together with my legal change of name to Charles Buchanan. I didn't plagiarise my own work." And still he surprised her.

"This will need verification."

"Naturally. In the meantime, I've patented it under my current name for any application of my two-part process."

Kristina probed gently, expertly, trying to tie Charles up, but he was clever. If she got a little too close to his truth, he wielded his scientific armour, long and important sounding words used to bedazzle the blonde he thought was his only audience.

Then Kristina must have believed he'd relaxed, become cocksure enough. "Your statements given in here will go before the Committee to complement your application. Are you happy to give your consent to that?"

"Of course."

A chair moved over the wooden floor. "Thank you for your time, Charles. Just wait there, someone will be along shortly."

The door to the room in which Eva waited opened just a few seconds later and Kristina came in. Eva lay the phone handset on the desk for Kristina to listen to now and stood up, smoothing her skirt.

"You were amazing." She hugged Kristina.

"Lycka till! But you don't need luck, you're your father's daughter after all."

Eva smiled her thanks at Kristina's confidence and picked up the bottle of Scotch and two carefully wrapped glasses, one in pink bubble wrap, one in white, from the desk.

She blew out a breath. This wasn't going to be easy.Her turn now.

Her battle.

60

———

Eva paused on the outside of Kristina's office door. It should be fury surging through her, but she just felt an overwhelming urge to cry. She could conjure up one of the many news images she'd seen over the last couple of weeks to arm herself to get through this. Deaths in Morocco, many nations mourning their leaders. The terrible sight of soldiers in Seitu and Tirupudur keeping the people calmer while the agencies tried to deliver on their promise of safe water.

Her father, she should channel him. She would have, if she could have remembered much beyond the canonised version her eight-year-old mind and experience gave her. Beyond doubt, from all his stories that she'd read, reread, played, replayed, she could use his tenacity, his need to get to the heart of the matter, to lay bare lies and dissembling until he revealed the truth. She was his daughter, after all.

She pulled up a smile—easy, breezy, isn't that what the Americans said?—and let herself into the mirror image of the office she'd just left.

"Eva?" Charles looked like she'd hit him with the bottle.

"What are you doing here? I mean, it's good to see you, I didn't realise. . ."

Her heart contracted. "You've forgotten I'm half-Swedish? Everything is gone from my life now, so why not make a new start here?" She held his gaze, giving him the chance to do the most important thing and ask about Lily, to do the right thing and apologise.

"That's great, that you're moving on."

"You're not going to ask me about Lily? About what you did to her?"

He did a double-take. "I went back for her but there were police everywhere so I—"

"Left her again. She drank the tap water, Charles, your note fell off the bottle so she drank the tap water."

He had the grace to look appalled. Eva hardened her heart. She didn't want him to know Lily was healthy, spending time with Per's widow while Eva did this. A sharp break was the kindest thing in the circumstances.

"I never meant—"

"For someone who never meant so much, you've caused enough destruction." She softened her tone. "So the Nobel Committee will reconsider your work, I understand."

"After this year, I'm not holding my breath. I was convinced Per would make it a done deal."

Eva broke the seal on the Scotch bottle with more force than it needed. Not a thought for her loss? He had been her godfather, her mentor, her family. She'd spent sleepless nights wishing he'd followed Addison's lead and just opted for a neat whisky.

She unwound the pink bubble-wrap and placed the glass on her right. Folding the packaging, she laid it on Kristina's desk.

"You drink Scotch now?" Surprise hitched Charles' voice up.

"There's lots about me now that's different. Still no water, ice?"

He shook his head. The irony.

She unwrapped the white bubble-wrap, her wedding and engagement ring clinked against the sturdy glass as she placed it on her left. Undoing the lid of the scotch, she waited for him to talk to her. He watched her pouring a measure into one glass.

"You know where the tradition came from, the clinking of glasses?" She filled the silence. He shook his head. "It came from right here, when the Vikings would go to each other's halls and drink to peace or co-operation or the formation of raiding parties. They'd smash their tankards into each other so that the liquid slopped from one to the other. If the drinks were poisoned, both would die. Now we all use glasses, it's become a gentler touch."

The scotch glugged into the other glass.

"Why are you here?" Charles asked.

"As our marriage is over, one of us has to start divorce proceedings. Kristina mentioned she would be seeing you, so I realised it could be me."

He nodded. Not even trying to save it? Had their life together been such a farce? How had she never noticed? Even looking at him now, she still couldn't see a different man from the one she thought she knew.

She pushed the glass on the left-hand side towards him, the left, the link to her heart. The room was drowning in irony now.

He lifted it, inclined it towards her. "Skol."

"I don't feel like toasting you, Charles, There's nothing for me to celebrate here."

"You brought the scotch." He sipped it. "Not bad."

"Per bought it for you, he wanted us all to spend Christmas together."

Charles tried it again. If he apologised, she wasn't sure she wouldn't smash the bottle over his head. "Very good, in fact."

"Who was she, Charles, Nancy Seymour? To you, I mean. Was she your mistress?"

He looked at the amber liquid in his glass instead of her. "She was who I left you for the first time but things didn't—"

"Don't insult me with lies, not now, not after everything. You took so much from me, at least I deserve your truth, don't I?"

He nodded. A sip more of Dutch courage. "I left her to be with you when I realised what you were doing with Every Drop. I'd discovered the agent before then, but I knew I could make an antidote to it. It was my agent that helped Jed Carson become a senator by contaminating the oil of one of his big rivals. Running for office in America is impossible without mega money. Thanks to my tech, Jed cleaned up, wiped out his competitor, took over his assets, his company. Turned it around, cashed in big time. Then he invested in my research to show he was legitimate."

The politics didn't interest Eva, though the listening audience wouldn't feel that way. She allowed herself one final personal question. "You were always intending to go back to her, weren't you?"

He nodded.

Eva gripped the edge of the desk. "Every Drop's being dissolved. Did Stuart tell you?"

"No, I, it wasn't like that, it wasn't meant to be—"

"Wasn't meant to be?" Eva almost shouted.

"It was an insurance policy. The monies paid by people

for safe water would reimburse Stuart and myself for our time invested in the company, and provide ongoing income, enough that I could disappear. Jed Carson was working his way down his hit list, he had a long reach."

Eva reined in her outrage, her anger at him, her grief at who he really was. She needed him to give her everything. "Your emergency fund, that was from the sale of your two-part process, wasn't it?" He nodded, but she needed verbal agreement. "So who you sold it to had the knowledge and intelligence to manipulate your formula to work as a poison? They should work in your lab."

"Well, no, obviously I had to help." He tossed the rest of his Scotch back. "But it's ironic that a US weapons unit bought it. I gave Jed the weapon he used against us—"

"I'm sure you didn't give it, I'm sure he must have paid handsomely for it."

"Not handsomely enough."

She placed a pen in front of him. "Is all of this why The Society was after us?"

"No."

"Explain it to me." It was too hard to look at him. She fussed with picking up the A4 envelope from Kristina's desk and drawing out the contents.

"My former colleagues, Tony Banks, Aleksandr Oblov and myself, we instructed them to kill Jed Carson when Duncan disappeared."

"Duncan?"

"Someone else I trained with. He vanished about a month ago, his body still hasn't turned up. We took out a contract on Jed Carson in self-defence. But the money I was counting on to pay my share of their fee, well, CJ kept more of the broker's fee for arranging the sale of my process than he should have, so I came up short. You don't mess with them, we short-changed them, so they came after us in retaliation. We're very fortunate to be alive—"

"You're alive, Charles, because I got the contract on you cancelled." Eva snapped. "Though I expect Jed's team is still after you. Isn't killing the President treason?"

He moved in his chair in something resembling a shrug. So cold-hearted?

Eva distracted herself by pouring him another drink. "What about the other leaders you murdered, almost forty at last count, their partners, aides, half the hotel guests? What about the Moroccans you killed? How do you live with that?"

He leant forward to take the glass, "it was just like a drug trial. There are always casualties in those, but the knowledge gained and the leap ahead is worth the price. The greater good wins."

"It was too high a price."

He took a mouthful of scotch, drank it slowly before replying. "Scientific advancements cost."

The effort of holding herself so tightly in check so she said nothing tensed her back, shoulders, jaw to breaking point.

She laid the document on the desk in front of her. "One last question, why the charm school? Why pretend to be British? The Americans are our allies, aren't they?"

He half-laughed. "You think so. There's a distrust even between allies, we all feel more comfortable dealing with one of our own. Suspicion never falls on them, only on the outsiders, and you Brits are the worst for that."

She pushed the divorce papers across the desk to him and he signed by the pencilled crosses reading none of the text. "You always wanted to be like your father," he laid the pen down parallel with the top edge of the document. "My parting gift to you is to say if you'd known the first thing about who he was as a person, you wouldn't chase your starry-eyed version of him. He was egotistical, he'd stoop as low as he needed to get the jump on someone for his exclusive."

Eva looked an icy warning at him. "Maybe I'm exactly like him. I know there's enough evidence that was how he could be. But he would never knowingly have done harm to anyone. I knew the real him better than anyone, so did my mother. Why do you think she practically abandoned me when he died, let me raise myself? Because although she'd always looked elsewhere, she knew what she'd lost, that she'd never find it again, that mix that delighted, magnetised people to him, a heart that was pure."

"You can twist any evidence to say what you want it to."

"That's not very scientific."

He downed the rest of his drink and made to stand up but she held up one finger, who knew it was such a powerful gesture. "One thing you might like to know, for scientific purposes."

"What's that?" He leant forward in his chair.

"Did you ever test your agent in anything other than water?" She held back all her emotions, channelling nothing other than innocent curiosity.

"I told you it can be adapted to be used in anything."

"How do you feel, Charles?"

His gaze snapped to the bottle on Kristina's desk. Eva tossed the lid to him, the tiny puncture hole in its centre made by a syringe clearly visible.

"But, you wouldn't." He slumped as the realisation hit him.

"I think you'll find I did." She moved the bottle to the side. "It works well in alcohol, in case you were wondering."

He stared at her untouched drink, sweat breaking out on his forehead.

"It was so helpful of you to leave your holdall behind at the riad. The compound and agent are being reverse engineered by British Intelligence. But I took a bit, for a road test. The agent's in the Scotch. Our scientists weren't sure it would work, thought alcohol might kill it but I can tell them the test has been a success. Or not, depending on who you are right now."

"But you, you," he conjured up a shout from somewhere.

"You can come in now." Eva didn't need to raise her voice, her quiet statement was heard by her audience on the other end of the muted phone and down the camera feed watching the scene from behind her.

Charles whipped round at the door opening but he wouldn't recognise the tall brown-haired man in a black leather jacket and jeans who came in.

"This gentleman is going to escort you to where you're going." Eva told him.

"What, take me where?"

"That's the question, isn't it? Who hates you the most, Charles?" Eva asked. "You have your whole journey to figure it out. Is it the Moroccans? Maybe the Russians, could be any one of the countries whose leaders you killed. What about Britain? In all your learning how to be English, did you forget we don't like being embarrassed? What about your countrymen? They don't like their President being assassinated. Thinking it over should keep you occupied. And you were right, by the way."

"What? What're you talking about?"

"I do always think too much about other people. You see that as a weakness, I think it's a strength. Right now you should be grateful. The glass I gave you had been coated in your compound, if the alcohol didn't burn it away." She looked at the untouched one, "I chose not to give you that one with no compound in it, not because you didn't deserve it but because I don't want to live with the knowledge I killed you."

"Let's go." the man crossed the room to Charles.

"Don't send me with him." Charles said. "That's on your conscience."

Eva shrugged. "What they choose to do with you is nothing to do with me. I've done the right thing in handing you over to justice."

"I'm not going anywhere. You can't do this."

The man withdrew his service weapon. "It's already done."

61

Eva studied Owen Benfleet's face on the secure video call while he watched the recording of her last meeting with Charles. Gordon stopped it at his admission that the US had been training sleeper agents to pretend to be British.

"Mr President, you understand now why this was for your eyes only."

Benfleet looked sincere. "I appreciate you being so circumspect."

"I realise you're very busy with the change of administration." Gordon went on, "so just two more minutes of your time, if you will."

Benfleet smiled and nodded, Mr Benevolence.

"Just so we're absolutely clear from the outset of our working relationship,' Gordon went on, "I'm spelling it out. We are more than allies, we have our special relationship to consider. Obviously we won't stoop to blackmail with this dynamite. However, as insurance, we'll be keeping it safe."

"I think we can both agree is not in the best interests of either of our countries for this to enter the public arena."

"I think you'll find the United Kingdom is the wronged party here and that's the message the evidence reinforces. I should also tell you that we have evidence that your predecessor instructed the assassination of several of his former colleagues. Something else we'll be keeping safe."

Benfleet inclined his head. Would he curse or thank Jed Carson's untimely demise, giving him the top spot when he hadn't even spent a day in office as a VP?

"Well, if there's nothing more, Gordon."

"Just the one thing, Mr President, decommission the British village mock-ups. That kind of hackneyed tradecraft crap belongs in the Cold War, where it was born. From the Russians, I'd understand it, from you?" Gordon shook his head. "I know that wasn't on your watch, but this is day one of a better relationship, isn't it?"

The president nodded. "It is."

"If a satellite were to fly over any of the co-ordinates of these places on, say Monday, it'd see nothing other than rubble?"

"It would not."

"Thank you for your understanding."

Gordon cut the link and pulled a bottle of whisky out of his desk drawer. "I think we've earned this."

Eva looked at the drink in horror.

Luke laughed. "Don't tell me you're not a whisky girl anymore?"

"I never was."

"In this line of work, you usually have to take what's on offer." Gordon poured three measures and handed them out. "Job well done." They chinked and drank. Eva shuddered. "Forgiven me yet for not telling you about Luke?"

She nodded.

"Your takedown of Charles, that was masterful." Luke raised his glass at her.

"It was hardly a do or die chase across the rooftops or any of the other things you spies get up to."

"The greatest misconception, that." Luke said. "It's our biggest asset. Mostly we're making use of what we have around us, of anything in the environment we can turn to our advantage, of anything we know about our enemy that can be used against them. You did all of that."

Gordon leant back in his chair. "If I ask you to come back and work for us again, will you say yes this time?"

"There is one thing you should know though, before you decide," Luke said. "Your husband was right when he said I'm The Society."

Eva nearly dropped her glass.

"They came onto the scene about five years ago completing a number of high-profile assassinations, causing havoc with no agenda." Gordon gestured at Luke, "You tell her, it was your idea."

"After they killed my partner, I caught one of their assassins in a sting operation and we got what we could from him to take them down. The group had a die or disappear policy so we mopped it up, but their name was known, their reputation feared. We agreed it was something we could use, so we took it over, not really convinced it would work but we've managed to save a lot of people who would have been killed otherwise and make sure those ordering the assassinations got the justice they deserved."

"That's what this unit is." Gordon said. "We're an extension to MI6 to anyone who doesn't know the truth, licence to operate globally. And, of course, there's cross-pollination and co-operation between us. The Society is what we're asking you to join, Eva."

Eva closed her mouth. "It might have saved me a few sleepless nights, few heart palpitations if you'd told me earlier."

"Need to know, hence the strict security here, our closed door policy—anyone not part of our unit in the building and we lock it down further. We achieve a lot of good if that secret is kept."

With Every Drop under investigation its reputation, and Eva's, was shot and it would have to be wound up. If the charity couldn't be her father's legacy, maybe this could. It would be nice to be back amongst people she liked and respected, doing something that still made a difference.

But putting herself in needless danger wasn't the way to parent Lily, especially as Eva was a single mum again.

"What?" She looked from Luke to Gordon, having their own conversation. "Trainee what?"

"First lesson." Luke said. "Every field agent, spy as you so lovingly call them, starts as a trainee. How about it, trainee Agent Janssen, has a ring to it, don't you think?"

62

"Lily!" Eva waved as she saw her coming out of the school gates in a huddle of girls.

Lily looked as though Eva had turned up naked. She said something to her friends, and they hugged each other as though they wouldn't be seeing each other ever again. Certainly not as though they hadn't spent all day together, would be tomorrow, and would probably be online to each other all evening.

Eva gave them their space.

"Mum, what're you doing here? It's not cool, meeting me from school. I'm nearly twelve, I can get home by myself."

Eva laughed. "When you're thirty-five, you'll still be my baby."

Lily rolled her eyes. "What's up?"

"Thought we might go for dinner."

"Why?"

"Well, we have to eat. Where d'you fancy going, anywhere you like."

"Anywhere?"

"Apart from a champagne and caviar bar, obviously, not

until you at least look eighteen." Lily rolled her eyes again. "What about a Mad Hatter tea party?"

Lily grinned in a very unlike-an-eleven-year-old way. "That sounds great."

The lemonade came in little bottles with 'drink me' labels tied around the necks. The Battenberg cake had a skewer through the middle on which a tiny flag demanded 'eat me'.

"We should toast." Eva picked up one of the bottles. "You go first."

"To being twelve, skol."

Eva laughed and toasted her daughter. "Skol, to being twelve, that's a special birthday."

"Your turn." Lily held up her bottle ready.

"I had an offer today, to go back to my old job."

"Are you taking it? You do need one."

Eva smiled at Lily telling her how it was. "I do. The thing is though, it will probably mean I have to go away from time to time. What would you think about that?"

"I can stay with Anya, her mum won't mind. Anya's stayed with us lots of times." Lily looked excited at the thought.

Single mums helping each other out, that could maybe work.

Lily waggled her lemonade bottle and Eva gasped.

"Mum, you all right?"

"Yes, of course, everything's good." She'd never noticed it before in Lily but it had been right there in her expression, a glimpse of Eva's father in his granddaughter's smile, as though he approved.

Working in intelligence would be a more fitting legacy for him, for Eva to truly follow in his footsteps, doing what she could to keep her loved one safe, to shine a light on the truth he paid such a heavy price to find. Proof every day, if she needed it, that she hadn't chosen to stay small.

"So are we toasting it, or what?" Lily asked.

Eva clinked her bottle to Lily's. "To running towards the bullets."

DID YOU ENJOY THIS BOOK?

Did you enjoy this book? You can make a big difference to my career

Reviews are the most powerful tools in my arsenal when it comes to getting attention for my books. Much as I'd like to, I don't have the financial muscle of a London or New York publisher. I can't take out full page ads in the newspaper or put posters on the tube or subway (yet!).

But I do have something much more powerful and effective than that ...

...a committed and loyal group of readers.

Honest reviews of my books help bring them to the attention of other readers and that allows me to keep writing.

If you've enjoyed this book (and want more!) I would be very grateful if you could spend just a couple of minutes leaving a review on the book's amazon page. You can go straight there by clicking this link:

UK

   US

Thank you so much

Coffee and movie soundtracks fuel my writing so if you've really enjoyed it, you can buy me a coffee!

https://ko-fi.com/karenguyler

Let me know and I'll send you a short story as a thank you :-)

FREE STARTER LIBRARY

GET A FREE BOOK AND SHORT STORY SET IN THE SOCIETY'S WORLD

Building a relationship with my readers is the very best thing about writing. I occasionally send newsletters with details on new releases, special offers and other news on my books.

If you sign up to the mailing list I'll send you :

Dare You? an introductory novella

There Can Be Only One a short story

both set in The Society's world

You can get the novella and short story for free by signing up at http://karenguyler.com

Being part of my readers' club also gets you access to free bonus epilogues and short stories and book offers, what's not to love?!

ACKNOWLEDGMENTS

Writing is mostly a solitary thing but the bringing together of a book takes a team and I'm very blessed to have the best people around me. You know who you are! But, in case, you need reminding, my heartfelt thanks to each and every one of you:

To my wonderful husband, Dave Guyler, for making my beautiful office a reality, I'm grateful every day for such a lovely workspace (and you probably are too when I'm pacing around plotting and reading the book out loud....) To my fabulous daughter, Makenna, thank you for your invaluable input and encouragement, for fitting reading and rereading The Society into your crazy busy schedule, and for making so many coffees, merci mille fois. To my lovely son, Connor, you visual techy wizard you, for creating this gorgeous cover, you know you have that job going forward, right? To my other lovely boy, Kade, thanks for all the interruptions of videos I just had to see right then and for now understanding that the best way to come up to my office is bearing a cup of tea. To my 'gained' children, Adam Wilson, for being patient every time I say, 'Adam, why has this tech done that?' and Natalie Wickenden for spreading the word.

To my street team – you are all awesome! Thanks for your input, for helping me shape this story into the best it can be and for being the best cheerleaders and telling everyone about it: Beverley Bishop, Daniela Cole, Nick Cook, Katie Cooper, Deb Day, Makenna Guyler, Helen Hanna, Nikki Klein, Jon Mayhew, Mark Robinson, Richard Stone and Clare Wakelin, thank you.

To the Collective, you crazy, funny, wise lot. Thanks for the wisdom, the advice, the laughs, the camaraderie and the encouragement – my mad plan for this year is all your fault.

To Mariëlle Smith, wordsmith extraordinaire, (https://mswordsmith.nl) for helping me find the hidden nuggets in the blurb and for that 'bitch-slap from the universe' card back in Edinburgh. Here it is, 'my own fucking magic'.

To 20BooksEdinburgh, where I found my tribe, you all rock, and can't we dance?! With special thanks to Jasmine Walt and Craig Martelle for your generosity in helping me to be part of it.

To Redouan Sadak for clarifying the things in Marrakech that I didn't notice when I was there. And, thanks, too, for the honey

To everyone else making their way up the mountain, we've got this.

ALSO BY KAREN GUYLER

Have you read them all?

In the 'The Society' Series

Dare You, book 0

When he approached The Society to take care of his embezzling, cheating business partner, Trevor Young thought they were just a gun for hire. But he broke the one important rule that he thought didn't matter. Never break the contract. Now, The Society are in control. And Trevor's life is the one on the line. How can he turn things around?

Free to download: **https://books2read.com/u/baZzoP**

The Society, book 1

When a former colleague of Eva Janssen's is poisoned instead of her, her usually quiet world spins out of control. Who is targeting her? And why? Separated from her husband and daughter while on the run, Eva realises they've become pawns in a deadly power game. But she has no idea who the players are, and how can she fight back when danger's coming at her from where she least expects it?

Buy it **https://books2read.com/u/bpzp8l**

The Lynx Assassin, book 2

Eva Janssen's trial mission should be easy but she hasn't learnt that a plan never survives contact with the enemy, even if you know who you're fighting. And she hasn't understood what it means to be part of The Society. When she finds herself on the wrong end of the Lynx Assassin, a weapon smarter and more deadly than the best human, first she has to survive.

Buy it here: **https://books2read.com/u/b6O2zx**

In the 'Dateline Zero' series

The Only, book 1

The Government stepped up after a devastating flu pandemic to save what remained of the British people. And if they are told where they live, what to eat, what job to do, the Government can keep their promise they'll be safe. Maya Flint wouldn't dream of breaking the rules, until her brother's life is on the line.

Buy it here: **https://books2read.com/u/mBZPvO**

The Disappeareds, book 2

Moved to London to work at Science Academy just like she bargained, Maya Flint has everything she wanted. Except her best friend, except her family, except her safety. And now something big is coming, something that has a dictator running scared. And a man scared is capable of anything. Stop him, Maya must, but what if the price is her soul and what if he gets to her first?

Buy it here: **https://books2read.com/u/mYZo8p**

The Reckoning, book 3

Set adrift in a stranger's life, remembering nothing before this summer, can Maya Flint find her way back to those she cares about? Will she learn that some things, some people, are not to be trusted before it's too late? And what happens if she does?

Buy it here: **https://books2read.com/u/bQJ9jd**

Standalone

Celebrations, but not as we know them

Ten teeny tiny stories of things we celebrate, only sideways.

Buy it here: **https://books2read.com/u/3k5rYL**

ABOUT THE AUTHOR

Always being the new girl at nine schools on two continents was no fun at all so books became the only constant in Karen Guyler's life, even if they didn't help her get out of sports days. Now settled in Milton Keynes, England, Britain's best kept secret, she juggles reading with writing, her children husband and dog – a much nicer mix! On mostly sunny days she'll be trying to cajole her gorgeous dog out for a walk though has had to abandon the idea of dictating while walking because all the 'sit', 'stay', 'don't do that', 'leave', 'come back' played havoc with the characters' lives.

She also teaches Creative Writing for Adult Education with lots of laughter in amongst the word wrangling and discovery.

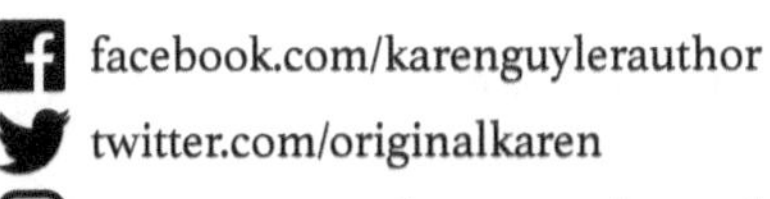

facebook.com/karenguylerauthor

twitter.com/originalkaren

instagram.com/karen_guyler_author

An Unexpected Books ebook

First published in Great Britain in 2021 by Unexpected Books Limited

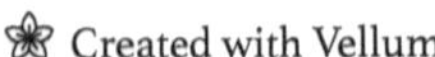 Created with Vellum